Everyday
Madness

First published 2021 by
FREMANTLE PRESS

Fremantle Press Inc. trading as Fremantle Press
25 Quarry Street, Fremantle WA 6160
(PO Box 158, North Fremantle WA 6159)
www.fremantlepress.com.au

Cover image: Vincent van Zalinge, unsplash.com
Design: Nada Backovic, nadabackovic.com
Printed by McPherson's Printing, Victoria, Australia.

 A catalogue record for this
book is available from the
National Library of Australia

ISBN 9781760990091 (paperback)
ISBN 9781760990107 (ebook)

Fremantle Press is supported by the State Government through
the Department of Local Government, Sport and Cultural Industries.

Publication of this title was assisted by the Commonwealth Government through
the Australia Council, its arts funding and advisory body.

Susan Midalia

Everyday Madness

 FREMANTLE PRESS

Susan Midalia is the author of three short story collections, all shortlisted for major Australian literary awards: *A History of the Beanbag, An Unknown Sky* and *Feet to the Stars*. Her debut novel *The Art of Persuasion* was published in 2018. She also works as a freelance editor, mentor and workshop facilitator, and has had articles published on contemporary Australian women's fiction in national and international journals.

To my book club friends
Pam, Vic, Lucy, Lekkie, Carmel and Sherry
and to Gail

Bernard

'Did I tell you the news?' Gloria said. 'Wendy has a brand new grandchild.'

Bernard stared at the toast on his plate. Another piece wouldn't hurt, would it, if he sacrificed the jam?

'You'll never guess her name, Bernie. It's something to do with the weather.'

He sighed. 'Is it Heatwave?'

'Don't be silly.'

'Cyclone, then. Or Hurricane.'

'Of course not!' Gloria shook her head. 'Well, if you must know, it's Raine, with an *e* at the end.'

'Better than Hailstone, I suppose.'

Any sensible person would have given up by now, but Gloria was undeterred, carrying on about this miraculous grandchild's hair and ears and those beautiful eyes that looked straight into yours as if the baby already knew you.

'Do you remember that feeling, Bernie? When Karl was a baby?'

'I remember him screaming round the clock.'

That didn't stop her either, veering off like she always did, about someone else's son now, taking his parents on a holiday to a country starting with M and how kind because he was always busy, wasn't he a doctor, a doctor for kidneys or maybe the liver ... pausing for breath ... starting up again about some woman's knees, arthritis, poor thing, trying a new kind of ointment or cream ...

Bernard looked through the window at yellowing lawns, wilting roses, a dog pissing on a letterbox. The footpath would be baking hot in the middle of the day, so that one, two, three barefoot steps would make you howl like a mad thing with the burn. He'd done that once, as a child, to see how much pain he could endure. But now he was a man who'd put childish things away, sitting at a table, trying not to watch his wife spooning gallons of creamy yoghurt into a bowl, spreading jam as thick as a brick on her toast. He used to love her hearty appetite, they called it, before the days of clogged arteries and late-onset diabetes. But now, sitting across the table, all he could see was her wobbling double chin, the meaty flesh of her arm as she reached across the table for the milk. Not that he could talk, with those sloppy rolls of fat around his middle. But at least he was making an effort, a month now at the gym, bristling with legions of muscular young men and bouncing young women with bud-like breasts and taut, silky legs. All the beautiful people working out on the machines, that glowing, heave-ho chorus of the modern, managerial self: I work out, therefore I am. All *he* could manage was trudging on the treadmill, an incline of seven on a really good day. Like a moaning Sisyphus he was, walking up, sliding back, over and over again.

'Bernie. Are you listening? I asked if you had any plans for your holiday? I thought we could go to the zoo, or maybe to Yanchep, they have those cute koalas and I haven't seen a koala in years and it's lovely there, remember the time we rowed on the lake ...'

What would he do on his holiday? He would read another book about a crafty detective; another magazine in which the same old *experts* frothed at the mouth about the appalling state of the nation. He would try not to picture being summonsed to an office and told that his services were no longer required.

He might catch up on some sleep, he said.

He saw Gloria frown, then sigh, then start up again about a new puppy down the road, very cute but such a yapper, and what about Christmas, she said, was there enough white wine, Donna always loved her wine, and should they have turkey, a few years since they'd had turkey ...

It had been years since he'd taken her to bed. Years since he'd looked at her with love.

ΔΔΔ

For the sake of their guests at the table, Bernard smiled, nodded and made small talk, although Christmas, quite frankly, gave him the shits. Frenzied shoppers buying electronic gadgets at obscenely inflated prices, planting herds of plastic reindeer to light up their yuletide gardens. Reindeer, for crying out loud, in thirty-five degree heat. If there was any kind of god, he'd stop this heat right now, but the Maker didn't seem to be listening to anyone's prayers for relief. Or maybe he was the maker of Fujitsu air conditioners.

Bernard watched Gloria dishing out the turkey as she dished out the news of their son's second marriage. *Imposing,* she called it, when she'd clearly meant *impending,* although Bernard would bet his bottom dollar that the nuptials would be grand. Their son liked to boast about the money he made from conquering difficult teeth: filling, straightening and whitening, capping and implanting, while his patients paid through the nose, as it were.

'Is that a new hairstyle, Gloria? It's ever so flattering.'

Donna Stone and her *ever so: our new curtains are ever so elegant ... this turkey is ever so succulent ...* But no, Gloria said, *not a new hairstyle, left it too late ... a bit forgetful these days, what with my nerves and all.* But then she perked up again, rattled on about singing in church last night ... only at Christmas ... lifted her spirits ...

'But no grandchild this year,' she said. 'So sweet, young Ella, so clever ... but we hardly ever see her these days.'

She sighed heavily, as if to add weight to her lament, but it made no difference to Bernard whether the grandchild was there or not. What did he know about little girls? What did he know about his son, for that matter? He'd never been a *hands-on* father: isn't that what they were called these days? His own father had been the fists-on kind, until Bernard grew too big to pummel into submission.

'What about Ella's mother?' Donna said. 'Is there a new man on the scene?'

'Not as far as I know,' Gloria said. 'Not even a man *behind* the scenes. Waiting in the wings.'

Well. That was a surprise: a *bon mot* from his wife. But there was nothing surprising about Lionel Stone, with his lip-smacking taste for money, launching into the same lecture he'd given them last year: *huge drop in revenue ... rising taxes ... always happens under Labor, they'd tax the air if you didn't watch out*. But Donna objected, trumpeting the virtues of the prime minister, *ever so articulate and smart, speaks fluent Mandarin as well*.

Bernard ground his teeth. Why had Gloria invited these people? Lionel with his money talk, a wife who thought life was a knees-up in a tavern. Because they were neighbours: people who lived in close proximity. Because they'd invited them for Christmas last year, along with some irritating woman whose only topic of conversation had been her ailing dog.

Lionel smiled across the table. 'And how's business, Bernie?'

Bernie. Why did people always reduce him to the chummy diminutive? Or *mate*. Or *old son*. He told Lionel that business was *just fine, encouraging figures*. He didn't let on that the last vacuum cleaner he'd sold was three weeks before Christmas, a robovac for a young couple living in a one-room apartment. One room was pretty much all those robovacs were good for, going for a song at one thousand, nine hundred and ninety-nine dollars.

'And how's the gym going, mate?' Lionel said.

The gym was also going fine, thanks.

'Good for you, old son. You'll get those kilos off in no time.'

Lionel had already announced his exercise regime: four mornings a week at the gym, jogging in the park after work. He was working on a woman as well, according to a story he'd offered Bernard on the sly, the two of them queueing at the ATM. Lionel's woman was *hot to trot,* apparently, *with an arse a man can really get his hands on.* Bernard had flinched at both the crudeness of the man and his presumption of matey approval.

Did Donna know about the other woman? Or did she look away? Because we can always choose not to see, Bernard thought, trying not to sink in his chair. We can always choose not to suffer.

'Are you watching the new series of that renovation show?' Donna said to no-one in particular.

Bernard had seen it just the once, dismayed by the six-bedroom extravaganzas with their sculleries and entertainment rooms, gardens with jungles of hanging baskets and meandering pathways, plashing waterfalls and statues of naked women. In renovation shows as in life, it seemed: a man could never have enough.

Donna leaned across the table, asked Gloria if she was finally getting some sleep.

Gloria frowned. 'It's not good, Donna,' she said. 'I lie awake at night for hours on end.'

Lionel laughed. 'The older you get, the less sleep you need,' he said. 'Old people don't use as much—'

'Gloria's not old,' Donna snapped. 'And insomnia's the work of the devil.'

She made more sympathetic noises to Gloria, dispensed advice and offered her *ever so effective* pills.

Bernard always looked forward to sleep, that nightly drift into oblivion. Waking up was a problem, though: that moment when he stumbled out of bed and tried not to think about work and sex and love. Especially love. A man could go mad with thinking and you had to keep moving forward, *put one foot under the other*, according to his German mother. *You must be psycho*, she'd say, when she and her only child had the same thought at the same time. She'd made him smile, with her mangled English. He loved her, and she'd loved him, and then she died.

Ella

Her mum didn't want her to die! That was her lame excuse for saying *fuck* when some dude cut in front of them and she had to slam on the brakes. Then a bit later, another *fuck* when some old lady rode up their bum, tooting her horn like crazy. But now there was a lot less traffic and no more *idiots* and *morons* on the road, so her mum was starting to relax, humming along to Jason Mraz's dumb song about chilling out but melting cos he's madly in love. What a douchebag! Ella wished something loud and crashing would come on the radio instead, like the Black Eyed Peas, and she wished she could look like the lead singer with her curvy boobs and legs that went on forever.

She took a bite of her Cherry Ripe. Her mum always bought her a Cherry Ripe when they stopped at Settlers' Roadhouse on their way to Dunsborough, and every year the place was full of women checking out dumb women's magazines and fat guys pigging out on pies. This time some old guy had smiled at her and asked if she liked swimming. Duh! Why else would she be wearing a T-shirt that said *Vitamin Sea* on the front? And even worse, every single kid in the place was checking out their mobiles and it was so not fair that her mum wouldn't let her have one until she started high school. One whole year and three whole months to go! Her friends all had mobiles, they'd had them forever, and she must be the only person in the whole universe who didn't. It was majorly embarrassing, and every time she argued with her mum, she'd get a lecture about *cyberbullying … distraction from schoolwork … destroying conversation*. Like, you couldn't have a conversation on the phone??? Then she'd say more stuff about boys wanting you to send pictures of yourself with no clothes on. Seriously! As if she'd do a dumb thing like that! And when Nana offered to buy Ella a phone for Christmas, her mum only said *Thank you, Gloria, but no*. Which was her nice way of saying *Thanks a million, now I won't hear the end of it*.

Ella looked through the window but all she could see was dry grass, sagging fences and sheep looking stupid in a sheepy kind of way.

She glanced across at her mum, who was concentrating on the road so that Ella didn't die. She didn't want her swimming out too far, either, once they got to Dunsborough, even though their usual spot had miniscule waves that weren't much fun at all. Why couldn't she go to a real beach with real waves, like Lola and Fern did? They could stay home by themselves as well, and they hadn't been abducted by aliens, had they, or kidnapped by some crazy bikie gang. And then just last week, when Ella went for a sleepover, her mum told her to *keep safe*. She was so OTT.

Her mum turned down the radio and cleared her throat.

'So how's your father these days?' she said.

'OK, I guess.'

'Well, you spent a long time on the phone last night. I was just wondering if—'

'I was telling him about school and going to Dunsborough and what I got for Christmas.'

Not a mobile phone. Still, she *did* like her mum's present: bookends in the shape of two cute flamingos. Their feathers were bright pink and their heads were tucked into their necks and both of them were standing on one leg. Her mum thought the birds might encourage her to read, and Hanna had given her a book, though you could read books on a phone, couldn't you?

'So did he say anything about ...' Her mum stopped. 'What's her name? Imogen?'

' 'She comes from somewhere in England that sounds like snot.'

'*Snot?* Are you sure?'

'Upton Snottyville. Something like that.'

Her mum laughed, then turned up the radio to listen to the weather, which basically came down to ridiculously hot and hotter. Then she turned down the volume again.

'Did your father say when he's getting married?' she said.

'No.'

'And I guess the wedding will be in Sydney.'

'Sydney's dumb. Luna Park's just a bunch of stupid rides with kids screaming like they're going to die, and Bondi must be the dumpiest beach in the entire universe.'

She didn't tell her mum about her father at the beach. How he'd kept staring at all the girls in bikinis. It was gross. It made her feel sick.

'But you liked the zoo, didn't you?' her mum said. 'You love zoos.'

'It was just a whole heap of animals scratching themselves and looking bored out of their brains.'

'Ella! You've never told me this before.'

'Told you what?'

'That you didn't enjoy yourself.'

Ella heard that flutter in her mum's voice, meaning she was getting uptight. But why did she keep making her go to Sydney and have *a relationship* with her father, when there was nothing between them except a whole heap of desert. Still, she didn't want to make her mum more fluttery, especially while she was driving.

'The zoo wasn't all bad,' she said. 'There was this black hairy spider with pink toes that made it look kind of crazy.'

'Pink toes?'

'Yeah, like it went to one of those nail salons, just for fun.'

'You'll have to show me a picture sometime.'

Well, I could do that right now, Ella thought, if I had my own mobile.

She took the last bite of her Cherry Ripe, let the chocolate melt in her mouth. She stretched her legs and looked out the window again, but it was just more dry grass and straggly trees, with a whole bunch of cows all facing the same way. Did they even know they were doing that?

'Look, a Christmas tree,' her mum said. 'See the orange blossoms? I wish I could grow them but they don't do well in the suburbs.'

'It's a bit of a dumb name,' Ella said. 'Like, the flowers come out at Christmas, so what shall we call this tree, guys? I know, I know: a Christmas tree.'

Her mum pulled back her shoulders, which meant she was trying not to be cross or was gearing up to give another lecture.

'I'm really looking forward to a break,' she said. 'No assignments, no tests, just sleeping in and reading rubbish.'

Her *lying-down novels*, she called them, because they helped her to relax. Hanna was always telling her mum to relax, and she had a really cool name, Hanna Kiss, like the lead singer in a band. She did interior design and looked like a model and she didn't have any kids, she said they were messy and rude and lied to you and then ended up marrying someone you hated and asking for a million dollars to buy a house and they never paid it back. Ella didn't know if she wanted kids either. Lola's little sister was a pain and Fern's little brother was a bigger pain. He'd once pulled down his pants, waved his willy all around, and said that Fern was stupid because she didn't have one. Fern said he was stupid because he didn't have a brain.

'Let's have breakfast on the balcony,' her mum said. 'We can get croissants and listen to the birds. Remember last year? How that crow stole a piece of apple from your hand?'

Ella remembered the crow was black and bold, with beady eyes. But it wasn't being a thief, was it? It was just being a crow.

'We can go for a swim after breakfast,' her mum said. 'And maybe a bushwalk after that?'

'And Scrabble,' Ella said.

Hanging out in Dunsborough, even without her friends, was much better than going to Sydney or visiting Grandma and Grandpa in Melbourne. Grandma kept telling *Eleanor* not to put her elbows on the table and to say *napkin* instead of *serviette*. Plus she sniffed all the time, like everything was getting up her nose. Grandpa was always grouchy when he came home from work, telling *Eleanor* to get her fringe out of her eyes and work hard at school if she wanted to make something of her life blah blah blah. How come they were such pains and her mum wasn't? Well, most of the time she wasn't, and she still looked pretty when she wasn't all stressed out, with big green eyes and golden hair that didn't come out of a bottle. Not like Fern's mum, who dyed her hair a brassy yellow, and her eyebrows were dark tattoos that made her look surprised all the time. And maybe she'd had a boob job too because—it was the Black Eyed Peas on the radio!

'Turn it up, Mum. Please. It's my favourite song!'

Her mum turned it up and the music was pounding and the words were about to kick in. So it didn't really matter that her friends weren't here and she didn't have a phone and her father kept perving, when she could just bounce in her seat and open her mouth and sing at the top of her voice.

'We're on holidays!' she shouted, then cranked up the volume even more.

In the afternoon they drove into town to buy fruit and fresh fish, plus a big bag of Smarties and bottles of lemonade for Ella, and three bottles of wine for her mum. Because Dunsborough meant breaking the rules. The place was packed, not a parking spot anywhere, so her mum kept circling round while Ella tried not to watch three girls walking past in their super-short denim shorts. They looked like they owned the world, or lived in a big house, with their very own TV and computer in their bedroom. Her mum had given her *the talk* about using the internet, and she made Ella use her laptop in the kitchen or the living room where she could see what was going on. But it meant there wasn't much to do in her own room except listen to music and sleep. And do homework. Her mum wouldn't let her paint her room black, either, it was *much too grim*, she said. At least I have the stars, Ella thought, stuck on the ceiling and on one of the walls, but they weren't nearly as cool as Lola's purple beaded curtain and her feather boas scattered everywhere, which kind of made up for all the stuffed animals heaped on her bed. Fern had a cool hanging chair in *her* bedroom, and this new girl at school, Naomi from Canada, which might as well have been the moon, had movie posters stuck all over her bedroom walls: terrified people with blood spurting out of their mouths and *monsters with demonic eyes*. That's how she'd described it, anyway, because Ella had never been to her house and maybe she never would because Naomi was the coolest girl in the class, maybe even the whole school. She said *monsters* like *marn-sters* and *demonic* like *demar-nic*, and she was going to write a horror movie so she could walk the red carpet at the *Arse-cars*. And you must never call her American, she said, because Americans loved war and Canadians loved peace.

'Praise the lord,' her mum said. She ducked into a parking spot between two massive cars.

Ella saw a girl in a bikini top walk past. She had really big boobs. Ella wondered if she'd ever get any kind of boobs. She hadn't even started her periods. Lola and Fern had, they said it was a pain, and they hated the way boys kept staring at their boobs instead of their faces. Like people staring at my nose, Ella thought, only it was one lump instead of two, and when that awful Tyson Miller told her she looked like SquarePants Big Nose, her heart had plummeted to the ground. She made herself not think about it as she got out of the car. She made herself think about the pet shop in the mall, with all the crazy clothes for dogs in the window. Last year she'd seen plastic puppies dressed in tuxedos and tutus, and one in a Darth Vader outfit, and some kind of Scottish dog in a tartan coat and beret. Her mum called it *an obscene waste of money* but Ella thought they were cool, just a whole lot of fun to look at. *Look on the bright side*, that's what Nana liked to say, *Every cloud has a silver lining*, and a whole lot of other stuff as well, and after they'd left Nana's one time, Ella's mum had let out a ginormous sigh and said *Yak yak yak, it's enough to drive you crazy*, and then she'd gone all red and said *Don't ever tell anyone I said that*.

Ella shuffled into the mall behind her mum and: surprise! Hundreds of kids staring into their phones! If *she* had a mobile she could message her friends right now, or google to find out stuff, like the name of the first woman to go into outer space. She'd tried that on her mum when they were setting off down south, but her mum only said *Did you remember to pack your toothbrush?* It hadn't worked, either, when Ella showed her Fern's photos on her mobile: poetic ones of flowers and the ocean, and arty ones of people's ears and toes, but her mum only said that Fern was *very talented*. Lola was very talented too, she'd won heaps of medals for swimming. Naomi was top in maths and science and her mum was a lawyer who kept people out of prison and she'd even been on the news. Naomi was thinking of being a lawyer, too, if she couldn't make it in the movies, she said, but she'd never once bragged about her mum. That's why Ella liked her, and why she liked Lola and Fern: they were impressive but they didn't show off. *She* didn't show off, either, at least she didn't think so, but she wouldn't have minded being more impressive.

Maybe they'd like her flamingos. They weren't obvious, like the stuffed toys on Lola's bed, or the messages on Fern's T-shirts, like *Keep Calm and Hug a Panda*. The flamingos were ... what were they? *Zany*. How did she know that word? Where had it come from? It was like putting a gleaming pebble in your pocket but forgetting it was there, until one day you reached in and felt something pebbly and took it out and there it was! A shiny kind of word for flamingos!

Gloria

She stared through the window at the flamingos, hoping to cheer herself up. All those bright pink birds across the street, so many you could hardly see the lawn. What a treat for Wendy's birthday, and how sweet of Max to surprise her like that. He'd always been one for flowers and chocolates, even when it wasn't Wendy's birthday, and last month they'd gone all around Australia in a caravan and had a wonderful time, judging by the photos and the smiles. Should I pop in for a visit? Gloria thought. But Max was home all the time now, ever since he retired from the police force. Not that she didn't like him, he was a big, burly man who always wrapped her up in a great big hug, but now she and Wendy had to go out for a coffee if they wanted some time alone. Not that they gossiped about Max, Wendy never gossiped about anyone, and anyway, she was happy. Not like poor Trudy, who'd never had a man in her life, and now her nasty sister had come to stay for a bit. Gloria wouldn't pop in there, either, because the sister was a pinched kind of woman who kept complaining about Trudy's cooking and the hard bed and the sagging pillow. Trudy was a saint not to scream in her sister's face, and she hardly ever mentioned her arthritis, even though she hobbled with the pain.

Gloria looked back at the flamingos. Why were they all standing on one leg? No one knew why they did that, not even the people on that nature program. Bernie didn't know either, when she'd asked him, but even if he had he wouldn't have bothered telling her. Clipping off his words, or pouring sticky words all over her, wishing she'd go away. Wishing she was dead, probably. He thought she didn't notice. He thought she was too dumb to feel hurt. Just because he'd been to university and she'd left school at fifteen. She'd had a decent job at the Morley Post Office, sorting out parcels and stamps, handling money and all the grumpy customers. Couldn't he remember how good she'd been at all that? But she had to stop thinking all the bad things, she mustn't even start, because then she'd toss and turn all night and she just couldn't stand feeling stretched out and empty in the dark, forever and ever, staring at the ceiling, then dragging herself to the kitchen for a glass of water. Donna's pills hadn't helped, but Donna was always kind and why couldn't Bernie be kind? She'd tried to make him happy, she'd really truly tried, but— she snapped herself out of it. She needed to get a move on and clean the oven, but she was feeling so tired and weighed down, like she was lugging a huge bag of washing on her back. If only she could sleep. She would feel so much better if she could just drift off to sleep.

She made herself turn from the window, walk towards the kitchen and the dishes. A clean house for a new year, that's what her mum used to say. Not that it made any difference, one year the same as the next, Bernie snoring away at night and sleeping in the daytime now because he was on holidays. Holidays. Holy days. Gloria didn't believe in God anymore, even though singing the hymns had been lovely, good for the soul, they called it. Did she have a soul? Did anyone? Did it live inside us somewhere, or was it something that floated around us over our heads and why was she even thinking those things when her body was making her so heavy? Fat Gloria. Fat old Gloria, that's what she'd become. She'd see it on Bernie's face. Not that he was an oil painting, either, and wasn't she the one who kept their life going, when all was said and done? She did the shopping and cleaning and washing and cooking, she even paid the bills, while he just sat around reading things that made him mutter and go red in the face. She thought there'd be Christmas to look forward to, but Meg had taken Ella down south again, saying no to an offer of a mobile phone, her voice like a stone in your shoe. Sounding more and more stony since the divorce. Not that she came round much anymore, or brought Ella round. It used to be fun when Ella was little and she and her Nana made pancakes and cupcakes and Ella would make up stories and read them out loud and once she'd said *Listen Nana, I can skip along the lines*. So clever, she was, only not the rude clever of her father.

But what if she turned out to be like Karl? What if she grew so full of herself there was no room for other people?

Was that why he and Meg split up? And what did it take to leave?

Gloria rubbed her eyes and the tiredness hit her in the head like an axe. She'd told Dr Marr about not sleeping and feeling all knotted up and he'd asked her what she did with her time, drumming his fingers on the desk, not looking her in the eye. So she'd told him she did the housework and shopping and watched TV and sometimes she got to see her grandchild, the sweetest girl, although not very often, not nearly as much as she'd like. And yes, she had friends, so kind and caring, she was very lucky. And how are things in your marriage, he'd said, still drumming his fingers on the desk, but how could she say she was lonely and sad when she had a lot more than other women did, with a man to provide for her, a roof over her head, and he hadn't ever laid a hand on her. Well, he hadn't touched her in years in any kind of way. But how could she say that to the doctor? To anyone? And how could she tell him about her son getting married to a woman she'd never even met, someone called Imogen from somewhere in England like a lady with long white gloves. Karl hadn't sent a photo or said much about her at all, except that she was beautiful and worked with reflexes or something like that. He hadn't invited them to the wedding either, he said Sydney was too far away, *You'll find it too much, Mum*. Too much of *her*, that's what he meant. He didn't need to say it. So in the end she hadn't told the doctor what was really on her mind or in her heart, she just said she'd go mad if she didn't get some sleep, her friend's sleeping pills hadn't done a thing. Then he'd folded his hands and looked her in the eye at last and told her not to take other people's pills and he thought she was depressed. Then he'd written a prescription, torn off the page like a snap, told her not to worry because so many people these days took pills for depression, then he'd more or less shooed her out the door. He always called her Gloria and she always called him Dr Marr because he'd never said to call him Patrick. The name was written on his door, but he'd never once said.

She flopped down on the kitchen chair and fanned her face with the hem of her dress. The air con was on but she was still feeling hot and maybe it was the anger that made her feel like that, with Bernie not talking to her, not wanting her, not wanting her for years. Oh he'd wanted her the first time he'd laid eyes on her, it was all over his face, blushing and stammering when he asked her on a date. A play at the university, where he was studying, he wanted to be an architect and plan houses in his head. She'd never been to a play before and she thought there'd be marble stairs and a red velvet curtain and people dressed up to the nines. She'd worn her best dress, a blue Empire line, but when Bernie met her at the theatre he was wearing old jeans, like he was taking her to the Rosemount Bowls. And then that play: there was nothing on the stage except a chair and a bucket and three men walking in and out of a room without any walls.

In and out, ganging up, with lots of places where they didn't speak for ages, then suddenly a really horrible fight at the end. But everyone kept laughing, even though the men were nasty and cruel, and it bothered her, the laughing. She knew there was something that she didn't understand, about the play and the people in the audience, their jumpers hanging down to their knees. It made her feel small, even though she was tall, and she'd grown into a beauty like her mum always said she would. Bernie used to tell her she was beautiful. He'd buried his face in her hair and said he was sorry, he'd never been with a girl before, and she'd stroked him and said it was fine, just fine, because she didn't want to hurt his feelings. And then it got better, she showed him how to please her, and he'd even said he loved her, lying in one another's arms. Did she love him back? Well, he was shy and sweet and when they had sex he'd always ask if she was OK and no boy had ever asked her that before. Not once. And when she got pregnant he didn't get angry or tell her to get rid of the baby. He never said she'd tricked him into getting married, either. She would rather have died than do a thing like that. That's when she knew he was decent, that he'd stand by her through thick and thin and that's what mattered most in the world. That's what she'd thought, at the time.

But why was she going backwards like this, all the time backwards, when it didn't change a thing and there was washing to be done. Bernie's shirts, his socks and undies. Her summer dresses, the ones she could still squeeze into. She made her way to the laundry, one heavy foot after another. She lifted a shirt from the basket, saw a stain on the collar. She needed to spray it, then wait for the liquid to sink in. One minute, it said on the label, but she always waited longer just to be sure, standing by the sink and wondering what to do after that and after that.

ΔΔΔ

'You're not hungry, Gloria?'

What did he care? What did he care if she shoved meat into her mouth or not?

'I can't eat,' she said.

'What do you mean? *Can't*?'

He used to say that to Karl when Karl was a tiny boy. What do you mean, *You can't eat your peas, you can't eat your carrots? What's the matter with you?*

'I can't swallow,' she said. 'The food gets stuck in my throat.'

'Maybe you should see the doctor,' Bernie said. Offhand, like saying she should open the curtains.

But she didn't want to see the doctor again. She just wanted to drift away, fall into the longest sleep. And now she couldn't eat, either, when she'd always loved food, all the time, to fill up the emptiness inside her. She found herself standing and walking to Karl's old room, lying on the bed again, staring at the ceiling again. She tried to make her mind go blank, let go of the tightness and let sleep come in and—what was that? It was flitting past the window in a black pointy hat, someone with a sharp ugly face. Who was it? Was it outside or inside? Where had it gone? She hauled herself up to look, her heart beginning to thump, thump, but it was gone. The face. She slumped down on the bed and kept really still, her heart still thumping with the pointy hat, the ugly face. She looked across at the window again but there was only the fence and a dried-up shrub, so it must have been a dream, that *thing* flitting past the window. A dream when she was wide awake, already knowing that she wouldn't sleep, already dreading the blank white ceiling and the dark all around her and inside her too, the darkness she'd never felt before and how could she make it stop? How?

Bernard

He'd woken from a dream—caressing a curvy woman with long dark hair—to find himself in darkness. What time was it? His mouth was as dry as a desert. As his eyes adjusted to the gloom, he slowly made out the blinking clock on the bedside table, the tatty wardrobe, a half-open door. And then he sensed it: the empty space beside him. Gloria was missing again. Last night, stumbling to the kitchen for a glass of water, he'd glimpsed her through the doorway of Karl's old room, lying in Karl's old bed and staring at the ceiling. How long had she been there, lying as stiff as a mummy? She'd been behaving oddly in the daytime too, hunched up on the sofa when she watched TV, not saying a word, picking at her food, pushing it round the plate with a weary fork. *So tired*, she'd said, *so tired*. He'd almost shouted at her then. How could she be tired, doing a bit of cleaning, gossiping with the neighbours, when he was the one who had to slog at work all day. She hadn't even made dinner last night, didn't have the energy, apparently, so he'd been forced to heat a can of tomato soup, washed down with the last of Lionel's cheap and nasty red, the same red he'd given them last Christmas.

He needed a glass of water, every night the same in this heat. He lumbered out of bed, fumbled down the hallway into the dark living room. He groped for the light switch, made his way towards the—it was Gloria. Lying on the sofa, curled up tight, her face turned to the wall, her pink nightie flowing like a tide.

'Gloria?'

Nothing.

'What's the matter?'

Nothing.

'Are you feeling sick?'

No word, no movement. Was she even breathing? But then, slowly, slowly, like a creaky machine, she turned to look at him. A long, unblinking stare, as if he were a stranger. It was odd. *She* was odd. Unnerving. Was she in pain? She didn't answer. Should he prod her into speaking? Command her to speak? But then it hit him: a stroke. Was it a stroke? Should he call an ambulance? But a stroke made your mouth droop, didn't it, made your face lopsided? He'd googled what might happen if he didn't get his blood pressure down.

'Do you feel numb, Gloria? Speak to me.'

'No.' In barely a whisper.

'Are you in pain?'

'No.'

Well, at least she was speaking now. But how could that be right, with her body curled up like that, her voice so faint? Should he call that ambulance? Or one of the neighbours? But he didn't really know them, didn't want them poking and prying. He bent closer to her face, her pale, blank face, asked her what was wrong.

'I feel nothing,' she said.

'*Nothing*?'

'I just ... can't go on.'

His chest tightened.

'Call Meg,' she said.

'Meg?'

What did she mean? Meg wasn't a doctor, was she? Hadn't she gone back to study, something to do with speech? What would she know about this ... whatever was happening? But what else could he do, hurrying now to the bedroom, grabbing Gloria's phone from the table.

He saw that his hands were shaking as he scrolled for a name, pressed a button.

The ringing stopped … a drowsy voice and … 'It's Bernie.'

Silence. 'It's three am. What's wrong?'

Gloria asked him to call … talking strangely … said she couldn't go on. He was breathless now, remembering the pale face, the faint voice … No, no pain … no, doesn't look like a stroke …

'Does she take any medication?'

'Medication?'

'Pills. Does Gloria take any pills?'

At least he knew about that. 'Cholesterol and blood pressure, like me. And she's got these new ones. I remember her saying they were for her nerves.'

He remembered not asking why she needed them.

'Do you know what they are, Bernie?'

'What do you mean?'

'What type? The brand?'

'No.'

'Well go and check. Now.'

As if she were talking to a misbehaving child.

He hurried to the bathroom … he'd never thought … she wouldn't, would she … his wife … He saw packets, blood pressure and cholesterol pills, and a new packet with pink writing. He hurried back, read out the medical name.

'I don't think Gloria's been sleeping,' he said, in a rush now, trying to make sense of it all. 'She's not eating much, either. I thought she was trying to lose weight again, but she seems … I don't know … far away. I've never seen her like this before. I … I don't know what to do.'

'It sounds like Gloria's depressed,' Meg said. 'The pink pills she's taking, they're anti-depressants.'

'But ... I thought she had nerves.'

'That's another name for anxiety, and some anti-depressants have a high anti-anxiety component. It's ... look, I don't want to give you a lecture. It's just that Gloria's new pills might not be working for her. Sometimes they can make a person's depression feel worse.'

Depressed? Worse?

'But what should I do?' he said.

'Just keep an eye on her. In case.'

'Of what?'

'If her breathing becomes laboured, or she says she's feeling ill. That's the time to call an ambulance. But try not to worry. I don't think Gloria's about to die.'

Was that meant to make him feel better?

'Look, I can't come over right now,' Meg said. 'I can't drag Ella out at this hour.' He heard her long sigh. 'I'll come around in the morning, OK? We'll take Gloria to my doctor for a second opinion. We'll get her medication checked, for one thing.'

'*We*? But I'm ... I'm not good with ...'

He heard himself sounding as feeble as his wife. And he'd heard it in Meg's sigh as well.

'I'll see you in the morning,' she said. 'Goodnight.'

He closed his phone slowly, turned to look at Gloria. Should he try lifting her from the sofa, make her more comfortable in bed? But her back was like a wall looming against him, and still she didn't answer his questions. Anything to eat ... drink ... turn up the aircon? But he had to keep an eye on her, in case ... He could not, must not, fall asleep until help arrived in the morning. He would have to pass the time somehow ... picking up his magazine, sitting in his armchair, reading a few pages, taking nothing in. He looked up and listened, but there was nothing to hear: no snoring, no snuffles, not a peep. She still wasn't moving, either. How long could a person stay like that? *I feel nothing ... I can't go on.* He'd never heard Gloria say such words, so halting, so barely there, with her nightie draped around her like a shroud. That's how he saw it now: a terrible pink shroud. Who was she, this silent creature lying on the sofa? When she'd been a babbler for so many years? His father had called her simple, had told his son he was throwing his life away by marrying such a stupid girl. But she'd been kind to a clumsy young man, so patient. She'd taught him how to please her, had made him feel like a man, had made him feel ... what had he felt? Wanted. So how could he have abandoned her, or told her to get rid of the baby? When he'd seen the fear in her eyes, heard the trembling in her voice.

He'd been a young, eager fool in that year of sexual pleasure. He'd been the best man he could be when the pleasure came with a cost.

ΔΔΔ

When Meg phoned in the morning, he told her that Gloria had finally roused herself, then slouched to the bathroom, slouched back to Karl's old room. Her breathing seemed fine, she didn't seem to be in pain, that was good, wasn't it? But Meg simply issued a staccato of facts: called her GP, booked an appointment, needed Bernie to babysit three hours max. She'd bring snacks and he must phone her if there were any problems. Was that clear? Bernard felt stung. It was true that he hardly knew the child, but he could manage, couldn't he? It was only three hours, and she wouldn't smash every plate in the house, surely, or charge out the door, run away. Besides, he needed to do something useful, while Gloria sat in some stranger's office with Meg as her translator. What did he know about her condition, after all? About depression that needed a doctor, special kinds of pills to ease the troubled mind?

He'd read some articles at uni, way back in the '70s, about the dethroning of Sigmund Freud. He'd seen psychiatrists on TV who were chillingly deranged. He'd seen *One Flew Over the Cuckoo's Nest*, which made him shudder to recall it.

But for now he must wait for the child. Shield her from the sight of Gloria looking so unwell. Would Gloria understand this, tell him it was the right thing to do?

If she could find her voice.

If she cared to speak to him at all.

ΔΔΔ

As he watched Meg walking up the driveway—a brisk-looking woman with bright gold hair—he realised that he hadn't even thanked her. She must have thought him rude, but the truth was, he'd been upended. Afraid. So as she stood before him, upright, tight-lipped, he told her he was grateful for her help. That he couldn't have managed without her.

She gave him a wry smile. 'Well, someone has to do it,' she said. And then, turning to the child: 'Why don't you go inside, I'll just have a quick word with your grandpa.' She turned back to look at Bernard. 'I've explained to her that Gloria can't sleep or eat,' she said. 'That something might have gone wrong with her brain, but the doctors should know how to fix it.' She shot him a warning look, as if he might object. 'It's nothing to be ashamed of, Bernie. I want Ella to understand that.'

The woman was so reasonable, he thought.

'I'll go and get Gloria now,' she said. She passed him two plastic containers. 'Snacks. Sunscreen.'

She was organised as well. She'd pulled a few strings, while he was a useless puppet dangling in the air. He followed her into the house, smiled awkwardly at the child, strained for something to ask her, could think of nothing. She looked alarmingly thin, but he couldn't say that, could he? My, you're so skinny, doesn't your mother feed you? He turned to see Meg leading Gloria into the room. His wife's face was pale, her body drooping, and he wondered if he should offer his hand, his shoulder, say something, anything. But she didn't look at him, didn't speak to him. As if he wasn't there.

He heard the sound of the car starting up. Stood in silence.

'Nana's going to see a doctor,' the child said. 'Her brain's not working properly and the doctor will make it right again.' She looked at Bernard intently. 'Have you ever seen a picture of the brain?'

'I have, actually.' Relieved to have an answer. 'It looked like a whole lot of sausages curled around each other.'

'It looks more like a whole lot of worms,' she said.

'Maybe the brains *I* saw belonged to a butcher.'

He was making a joke but she didn't laugh. OK. It wasn't funny.

'What did you bring to play with?' he asked.

'I don't play with toys anymore.'

'Would you like to watch TV, then?'

She pulled a face. 'There's only kids' shows in the morning.'

What now, he thought.

'I didn't bring my book, either,' she said. 'It's about a boy called Tom who goes back in time and meets a girl called Hatty. Do you have any books? On an iPad, maybe?'

'I only have detective novels,' he said. 'Sorry. And I don't have an iPad either.'

He didn't say: I threw out all the other books when I dropped out of uni. All the classics with their bucolic landscapes, moral dilemmas, witty repartee.

'This girl at my school, Naomi, her mum likes detective novels,' Ella said. 'She always reads the ending first so she knows who the murderer is. Then she doesn't have to worry that she might be wrong.'

'Well, that's one way to look at it.'

'What's the other way?' she said.

'You can try to pick up clues along the way. Pretend you're the detective. You know ... be clever.'

'But Naomi's mum's already clever. She's a famous lawyer and she keeps people out of prison.'

Fair enough, Bernard thought, even though the law was inclined to be an ass. Besides, his novels were much too racy for a young girl. So. No games or books to give her. She had no interest in morning TV. He was beginning to feel a bit rattled, and there were three more hours to go.

Then an idea popped into his head.

'Would you like to learn some new words?' he said. 'They belong to my other language.'

She gave him a puzzled look. 'Did you make it up yourself?'

'No. It's the language I spoke as a child.'

'Like a secret code?'

'No, nothing like that. It's the language of my birthplace. Germany. I can still understand quite a lot of it.'

Ella nodded. 'Mum told me that if you learn a language when you're little, it always stays with you.'

'I believe that's right.'

'Oh, it's definitely right,' she said, emphatically. 'And if you learn a new language when you're older, you use a different part of your brain because you have to memorise all the new words and that makes it harder to remember them.' She sighed. 'That's a lot of remembering,' she said.

Bernard hid a smile.

'Mum's studying to be a speech pathologist,' she said. 'You have to know a lot about the brain so you can help people learn to speak better.'

'That's good of your mother, isn't it?'

Ella considered this. 'She's OK,' she said. 'Only she won't let me have my own mobile phone.'

'Well, I'm sure she has reasons.'

'Oh, Mum's full of reasons. Only sometimes they're not very reasonable.'

He couldn't hide his smile this time.

'Shall we have a look at my language?' he said, then waved her towards the kitchen table. They sat down, side by side, and he opened his laptop, googled the link.

'I'll read the words aloud,' he told her.

'I *can* read, you know,' she said. Indignant. How old was this child? Eleven? Twelve? Had she started high school?

'Just listen to this,' he said. '*Freundschaftsbeziehung.*'

She looked up at him, perplexed.

'It's German for an act of friendship.'

'Well.' She sat back. 'German people must take a long time to make friends.'

Bernard had to laugh. She *was* a funny child. He scrolled down to find another word.

'Look at this one. *Dummkopf.* A *kopf* is a head, so *Dummkopf* means you have a dumb head, you're a stupid person.'

She pulled a face. 'But I'm not a stupid person. I'm not a genius or anything, but I'm not stupid.'

'Of course not, I didn't mean you. But maybe you're one of these.' He pointed at the screen. '*Morgenmuffel*. It's a person who feels ruffled up and sleepy in the morning.'

'I am, I am,' she squealed, suddenly delighted. 'I'm a *Morgenmuffel.*'

She'd pronounced it perfectly, too. Then he remembered the longest German word he knew, learned off by heart to use as a party trick at uni. Once or twice, because he'd rarely gone to parties.

'*Donaudampfschiffahrtsgesellschaftskapitän*,' he said. 'What do you think of that?'

She gasped. He translated: the captain in charge of the steamboat that sails up and down the Danube River.

'That's amazing!' she said. 'That person must be super important to belong to a word so big.'

This was better, Bernard thought. This was going quite well. No-one could say that he, Bernard Newman, useless in marriage and fatherhood, disappointed with life, no-one could say he wasn't trying. He was amazed, too, at how easily the German words rolled out of his mouth. He hadn't spoken German since he was a boy, with his mother trying hard to learn English, his father refusing to speak their native tongue, even changing their name from *Neumann* to *Newman* for the sake of his plumbing business. Best to fit in, he'd said, not stick your neck out on some Aussie chopping block.

The child was getting fidgety now, squirming on the sofa, so Bernard asked if she'd like to do some drawing. Wasn't that what children liked to do?

'I can't draw,' she said.

'But anyone can draw.'

'Oh, I can put marks on a page with a pencil. It's just that the marks aren't any good.'

Well, the child clearly wasn't boastful.

'Once, at school, we had to draw a horse,' she said. 'So I just drew a tail and told my teacher the horse was galloping into the distance.'

Ingenious.

'Did your teacher get mad at you?' he asked.

'No, she just laughed. A lot.'

'Lucky you had a teacher with a sense of humour. When I was a child, many years ago, my teachers were ...'

He made himself stop. Why bore the poor girl with his tales of schoolboy woe? The teacher pulling your ears when you couldn't answer a question. The dusters thrown at frightened little heads.

'You didn't have TV back then, did you?' Ella said. 'Or mobiles or video games. So what did you do for fun?'

'I read a lot of books. Listened to the radio. But my weekly highlight was a trip to buy lollies.'

Ella looked stunned. 'Really? You mean, just going to the supermarket was a big deal?'

'We didn't have supermarkets either,' he told her. 'It was a lolly shop in the main street of a country town. I went there every Saturday morning, with money from my mother. She put a coin in my hanky and tied it up in the corner with a knot. To keep it safe, you see.'

'But didn't you have a pocket? Or a wallet or something?'

'I did have pockets, yes, but there was something special about that coin tied up in my hanky. It was ... well, my mother taking care of me.'

He could see her watching him with dubious eyes. Trying to work him out.

'So how old were you?' she said.

'Oh, seven or eight, I think.'

'And your mum let you walk to the shops on your own?'

'Well, the world was ...' How could he explain 1950s Australia: a small country town where people knew their neighbours, kept an eye out for others. *Too many eyes*, his father used to say, but not to the neighbours, because his eyes were always on his plumbing business.

'The lolly shop was just a few doors from my house,' he said. 'And so I'd walk there quickly, then stand in the doorway and just look.'

'At what?'

'At all the lollies packed in huge glass jars standing in a row on the counter. They looked like jewels, purple, pink, red and blue, shining in the sun. I just liked to watch, take it all in.'

'I did that, too. In Dunsborough, me and Mum looked for ages at a bobtail goanna waddling across the path. It was all scaly and it should have been ugly but it was kind of beautiful in a slow and scaly way.'

It was Bernard's turn to be delighted.

'Guess how much money I had,' he said.

Ella screwed up her nose. 'Two dollars?'

'Threepence.'

'What's that?'

'A tiny silver coin. So tiny you wouldn't even see it lying in the street. People don't make them anymore.'

'Because people want big money?'

'Something like that, yes.'

'So which lollies did you like best? I like Freckles and Strawberry Creams.'

'And so did I. Loved them. But my favourite were Cobbers.'

'What are cobbers?'

'They're a hard caramel toffee coated with chocolate, so hard that when you chewed it, your jaw would ache for days. And here's an interesting fact, Ella. *Cobber* is also a word for a friend, an Australian word, but you don't hear it much anymore.'

'Why not?'

He didn't know this either. But now that he'd started reminiscing, heading down a gravelly road in a distant country town, he began to paint a picture of the annual fancy dress ball held in the local hall. Children dressed up as animals, kings and queens, sailors in natty jackets. He saw his mother sitting upright at her sewing machine, smiling to herself, proud of her creations. She'd made him an astronaut, he said, and a pirate, a penguin. Robin Hood, with a bow and arrow, a jaunty peaked cap.

'I know about Robin Hood,' Ella said. 'He robbed money from the rich and gave it to the poor.'

'Correct.'

'No-one should be rich. It isn't fair.'

'Is that right? How rich is rich, then?'

She screwed up her face, as if thinking hard.

'No one should have more than a million dollars,' she said.

'And why is that?'

'Because why would you need any more? You'd have a house and food and clothes, and still have heaps left over to have fun. Any more would just be greedy.'

'Ah. But what would happen if people had more than a million? You know, if they won Lotto, or worked hard to earn their money.'

She looked at him as though he was a *dummkopf*.

'They'd give it to people who had less than a million.'

'And what if they didn't want to?'

'You'd make them.'

'How?'

She frowned. 'I'll have to think about that,' she said.

Then she asked him for a drink. *Please.* She had good manners, but she didn't seem like Miss Goody-two-shoes, either, as far as he could tell. He poured her a glass of apple juice, and as he watched her taking small, dainty sips, saw the darkness of her eyes above the glass, recalled her eager questions and her earnest remarks, he had a glimpse of why Gloria loved her. He'd seen his wife from afar, making pancakes with the child and not minding the mess. He'd seen her painting Ella's face. He'd seen her teaching some kind of knitting. Maybe she would have made a good teacher of young children. He'd never told her that. Should he tell her when she came home? Would it make her feel proud, or disappointed? Angry? They'd never talked about such matters. They'd never talked about their son either, except for surface things like skinned knees or the runs he'd made in cricket. Karl's marriage and fatherhood, too, had been confined to the visible: flowers for the wedding, baby photos, the fancy pram they'd bought for Ella. They'd never once discussed the divorce. Gloria had been puzzled and Bernard had switched off. Why hear about another failure? And what had Meg been to him then? He hardly knew her now. She'd gone back to university; she could be rather frosty; she was helpful, even kind. She was Ella's mother.

Ella put down her glass, asked for something to eat.

'Your mother left you some snacks,' he said. He couldn't remember where he'd put them.

'I wonder if she gave me chocolate biscuits.'

'I don't know.'

'Do *you* have chocolate biscuits?'

Bernard was wise to that old trick: that much he remembered about his son. He didn't want to cross Ella's mother, either, who at this moment would be helping solve the problem that his wife seemed to have become.

He heard his mobile, rushed to pick it up. Thank goodness it was Meg. The doctor had been *reassuring*, she said. Gloria was *fragile, but willing to talk*.

Bernard waited. Was there something coming that he wouldn't want to hear?

'The doctor wants to try a different medication,' Meg said. 'And he'd like Gloria to stay in a clinic until there's an improvement.'

'A clinic?'

A long silence. And then: 'Gloria's been hallucinating. Seeing things that aren't there. Hearing voices. They're called psychotic episodes.'

He felt his stomach lurch.

'But there's no need to panic, Bernie. She's not ... you know ... permanently afflicted. My doctor told her the episodes might never happen again if the new medication works. And the clinic can make a big difference. The doctor's made enquiries and we can get her in today.' She cleared her throat. 'You don't mind all this, do you?'

'Mind?'

'Me making all these arrangements. I don't want you to —'

'No, no, not at all. I'm ... it's good of you.'

He wanted to say that he knew nothing about those voices and sleepless nights and food that got stuck in your throat.

He asked how long Gloria would have to stay in the clinic.

'She won't *have* to stay,' Meg said. 'She hasn't been committed. But it could be weeks.'

Bernard swallowed hard. How much would *weeks* cost?

'It sounds like the right place,' Meg said. 'The doctors will monitor her progress, and she'll have individual therapy, group work if she wants. Even art classes, singing, a whole range of activities.'

Bernard felt himself sinking. The place sounded like a fancy resort, and he was a salesman, not the owner of the company. And when could he talk to Gloria, now that she was getting some help? Should he wish her a speedy recovery? Say something, anything, to let her know he was thinking of her. Even if he wasn't sure what to think, what to do, paralysed by doubt and the loss of everything he'd hoped for, that *she* must have hoped for, when they were both very young.

He felt a tug on his sleeve, looked down to see Ella staring up at him.

'Is that Mum?' she said. 'Can I tell her something?'

He handed her the phone.

'Pop showed me some amazing words in German,' she said. 'And guess what else? His mum turned him into a penguin!'

Worse things could happen, he supposed. And he was pleased that Ella had enjoyed herself. That was something, at least, to hold onto.

Meg

At least *Ella* had enjoyed herself. After all her scowling and sulking, wanting to stay with one of her friends instead of being *dumped* at Bernie's, she'd actually had some fun. A lot more than her exhausted mother, staring at a cafe, longing for a jolt of caffeine, trying to make sense of it all. Gloria had looked so pale on the drive to the clinic, her knees trembling, and not saying a word, until—unexpectedly, bizarrely—she'd blurted out that she didn't want Bernie to visit her. Spat it out, in fact. What on earth was that about? The man wasn't a monster, and he must be paying for the clinic: a salesman would hardly be rolling in the dollars. Oh, you could tell they weren't madly in love, but how many couples professed undying devotion after decades of married life? Continued to worship each other with their bodies?

She could still hear the venom in Gloria's voice: *I don't want to see him at all.*

Who knew the truth of other people's marriages, when you hardly knew the truth of your own?

And just now, in the clinic. Gloria staring at the wall for long, blank minutes, or speaking in tiny, breathless stutters, like a stroke victim suffering from dyspraxia. No, stroke survivor, the lecturer had insisted, because pity didn't help people to recover and self-pity could make them regress. Meg knew she had to toughen up if she wanted to last the distance: one more year to have *M.R. Flynn, Speech Pathologist*, printed on a card. She'd already done bridging courses in statistics and anatomy, stumbling across that bridge sometimes, even wanting to throw herself off when she couldn't remember vital facts. She'd also studied a cadaver, to learn about the vocal folds and their surrounding muscles; she'd kept telling herself it mattered and had managed not to faint. She'd loved the practicums, though, working with stroke survivors, children who stuttered, children on the autism spectrum; people struggling to recover the self they used to be, or the self they were hoping to become.

She remembered Gloria's final, whimpering plea in the clinic: *Please come back and see me.*

Didn't she have friends to help her out?

Meg sat back in her seat, remembering. The hours that Gloria had babysat when Meg was ill or needing a break. More hours once Ella started kindy. Always happy to oblige if Meg had to stay back at work. Happy to do drop-offs and pick-ups, *No trouble, Meg, anytime at all.*

But then things change, Meg told herself. A child wants to play with other children. A child needs more stimulation.

Still, Meg knew what depression could feel like. She knew about pills that helped her to sleep after she'd left her marriage. Pills to soothe the anger and the bruise of her heart.

She checked her phone. She had an hour before picking up Ella from Fern's. Fern had a new puppy, and *No, Ella, a puppy is too much work right now, walking it, feeding it, picking up its poo.* Their two goldfish had been easier, although Flippy and Floppy had eventually gone belly-up, and the three hermit crabs had died of stress. Tell me about it, Meg thought. She carefully opened the door to avoid scraping the red Volvo parked perilously close to her second-hand Toyota. The last thing she needed was a massive panelbeating bill. Money was tight since she'd gone back to study. Not that Karl had ever minded paying his share, both during their marriage and since the divorce, insisting on paying for Ella's flights to Sydney, and half the cost of her physical needs. He'd always been generous with money, as well as with women. There'd been *affairs*. Meaning: he'd fucked two other women—two that she knew of, at least—in the first few years of their marriage.

So what if he was acquiring a brand new wife? Or hadn't had the courtesy to phone her with the news? They hardly ever talked these days, even on his occasional trips back to Perth, taking Ella to the local pool, the movies, ice-skating, the Royal Show, a constant round of activities. Being the good father, so he didn't have to talk with his daughter. Rushing back to Sydney and his lucrative business.

She shrugged him off, focused on the task at hand: coffee. In a hip-looking place with black walls and scratched leather chairs, a few people standing at the counter. They looked hip as well, the kind of people who'd take forever to order soy decaf or almond milk something, short or long, milk on the side. She always ordered *milky and very hot*, even if the barista gave her a flicker of contempt. She edged forward slowly and a guy in front of her turned around and—fuck! Black coffee splashed on her shirt. Her favourite white shirt.

'Oh, hell, I'm so sorry. I'm ... are you alright?'

She could see the black stuff plastered to her bra. She looked up to see the man looking red-faced, still rushing out apologies ... *did I burn you ... oh hell ... so sorry*.

'I'm fine,' she said, curtly.

'Let me—'

'Forget it. I said I'm OK.'

But she wasn't. She was angry with herself, as if she was somehow to blame for the ugly stain, for the clumsy man's distress. Why was she feeling so naked, disgraced, heading into the heat and glare, feeling useless and stained? And now she couldn't find her fucking car keys. Then she sensed someone behind her, heard that man again, bleating more apologies, offering to pay for the damage. She turned to face him and shouted, shouted, to leave her alone.

He looked like she'd punched him in the face.

She willed him to go away, but he kept standing right in front of her, and looking, just looking, with his dark blue eyes.

She felt the spark.

'It was an accident,' she said. 'It's OK.'

'But I've ruined your shirt.'

She shrugged, tried to look casual.

'You really *do* look a mess,' he said, and rushed in with another offer to pay. She thought he might whip out his wallet, but instead he held out his hand.

'Hal,' he said. 'I'm a clumsy idiot.'

He had a firm handshake. She felt the charge.

'Meg. And ... well ... I was going to throw this shirt out, anyway.'

'Do you have to go ... I mean ... are you on your way to something? Where coffee on your shirt will be a problem?'

He was sweet. He looked around forty and was easy on the eye. Undeniably.

'It's fine, really,' she said. 'I'm on my way home. It's where I've just been that's the problem.'

He raised an eyebrow. Why had she just told him that?

'I've just taken someone to a clinic,' she said. 'The psychiatric clinic around the corner.'

Hadn't she seen him somewhere before? Those sharp cheekbones; a rather haunted face.

'She's ...'

What should she call Gloria? The mother of a man I used to love? The mother of a man who'd agreed to impregnate me? *If it will make you happy, Meg.*

'A friend,' she said. 'She's normally so cheerful and ... well, I've never seen her like this before. So deeply sad.'

He was watching her closely. Taking her in, it seemed.

Ah. Now she had him. She'd seen him in Dunsborough, in a cafe. He'd been sitting alone, his hands curled around a cup, and she'd found herself staring, felt desire prickling her skin. Ella had been with her, of course.

She heard her own mother's voice in her head: *You've made your bed, Margaret, now you have to lie in it.*

'I think I've seen you before,' she said. 'In Dunsborough. A couple of weeks ago.'

'Maybe. I was there a couple of weeks ago.'

'Were you doing anything special?'

Why had she asked him that? To find out if he was taken? Wasn't that how things started? Unless you were the kind of person who didn't care about *taken*.

'I was catching up with some friends,' he said.

She wanted to say: you looked beautiful. You looked alone.

'I saw you in a cafe,' she said, as if that made a difference to whatever it was she was doing. 'The cafe with ...' She laughed. 'It doesn't matter.'

'Well, your shirt matters,' he said, and gave her a rueful grin. 'Why don't we ... I mean ... we could find a shop and—'

'That's kind of you, but there's no need, honestly. And I don't have time. I have to pick up my daughter.'

'Oh. Sure. Of course.'

He sounded disappointed. As though he should have known she'd be *taken*.

'Well, it was nice to meet you, Meg,' he said. 'I'm sorry it—'

'Wasn't under better circumstances,' she said, and laughed.

It really was time to go, before she was undone even more.

She walked calmly to her car, opened the door, slid inside, put on her seat belt, turned on the ignition: five routine actions to keep herself steady as she watched him walk into the distance. A tall, lean man. Dark-haired. When was the last time she'd felt like this? Karl. And then nothing since except a date with a man who'd given himself a pep talk in bed; she hadn't answered his calls. A few dates with a former colleague who'd done nothing but complain about his wayward daughter, his idle son, the government, his gout and the heat. She hadn't answered *his* calls, either. And then, two years ago, Dean, a speechie she'd met through a friend. He'd listened to her moaning about her boring office job, had enthused her about his work. Then he'd teased her that she wouldn't meet men: ninety-seven percent of speechies were female, he'd said, making a joke to come on to her. He was intelligent, courteous, but without that bullshit masculine gallantry that made her want to laugh. But after a few months it had more or less petered out; that unmistakable spark simply wasn't there.

Had she been disappointed? Not really. Did she want to try again? Probably not. All that effort it took to ask the right questions, always look your best, make a good impression with your sparkling repartee. And besides, she had a child to care for, who she would always care for. It was as simple, and as wonderful, as that.

ΔΔΔ

Meg knew that other mothers found her anxious. They never said it, but it wasn't hard to tell. It had happened just now, dropping Ella off at Lola's. *You have a new swimming pool?* Meg had said, and Audrey had laughed, insisted that she knew how to do mouth-to-mouth. It had happened last week, when Ella had a sleepover at Fern's: *Stay safe,* she'd said, and Judy had raised a tattooed eyebrow and smirked. Still, Meg thought, she wasn't as bad as she used to be—sobbing when she left Ella at childcare, imagining all kinds of perils at kindy and school. A rusted nail in the sandpit, venomous snakes on an excursion, even a severe allergic reaction to peanuts (Ella wasn't allergic to peanuts). But over the years she'd trained herself to be calmer, had gradually conquered her more irrational fears. And besides, other mothers were sensible. No computers in bedrooms, and age-appropriate dress, although some of Fern's T-shirts, like *Bowling Sucks,* were just a touch too *out there* for an eleven-year-old girl. In Meg's opinion. Still, *Bowling Sucks* was absolutely nothing compared to the T-shirt she'd once seen on a teenage girl: *I Fuck on a First Date*. Had her mother, father, any responsible adult, given her a talking to? Tried to rip the shirt off her foolish body? And what about the other girl, ten or eleven at most, strutting in the mall last week: a tight skirt barely covering her bum, a halter top over a flat chest; heavy eyeliner, bright red lipstick. With no idea that trying to look *sexy* could turn out to be a trap. When even being modestly dressed and make-up free was dangerous enough.

She'd seen a man in Settlers' Roadhouse staring at Ella's T-shirt. Staring at Ella while he smiled.

She snapped herself out of it. He was just being friendly.

Have a good time, Audrey had said as she waved Meg goodbye. *Have some adult conversation for a change*. Another single mother, Audrey, like Judy: members of the tribe of the terminally knackered. Dropping off their kids, rushing from work to pick up their kids, looking after other people's kids, arranging weekends for their kids. Even mothers with husbands who pushed the pram or taxied their kids to outings still did most of the childcare because they earned less money than the fathers who worked, who stayed back for drinks so they could climb the greasy pole of promotion. Who'd called feminism irrelevant? All those young women who'd bought the myth of equal pay, that's who, and who'd never heard the stats on domestic violence. Who thought an unknown man patting your bum was flattery, and an overweight girl meant letting down the side. And don't get her started on the plight of women in the third world: the honour killings, female genital mutilation, the banning of education, contracep—fuck! She swerved to avoid a car cutting right in front of her, saw a man give her the finger. She watched him hooning into the distance, doing a hundred k's in a fifty zone. Fucking Perth drivers. And where were the cops when you needed them?

She pulled into Hanna's driveway, her car undented, her body intact. She took in the newly painted purple door, part of Hanna's renovations in the gentrified suburb of Maylands. As much as Meg loved her friend, had shared years of confessions, gossip and laments, she was relieved that the makeover was finally complete. She'd been bored witless by Hanna's complaints about unreliable or incompetent tradies, by her breathless admiration for imported bathroom tiles and ornate door handles for imported doors. But Meg had held her tongue: Hanna was her oldest, dearest friend, and obsessing about your renos was hardly a mortal sin.

She stepped out of the car and phew! The heat! Slamming into her face.

But there was Hanna: smiling at the door, her arms open wide. Her warm, welcoming hug, then a dramatic ushering inside.

'Like the paint job?' she said. 'Ivory. Much subtler than China White or Polar.'

It struck Meg again: Hanna's lustrous dark hair and piercing blue eyes, those chorus-girl legs. Her friend was a knockout at forty, while Meg was feeling knocked right down, out for the count.

'You look terrible,' Hanna said.

There were two things Meg could always count on from her friend: a shocking lack of tact, and kindness.

'I've found a remedy for *terrible*,' Meg said, and plumped down on a chair (new, in a funky patchwork fabric).

Hanna clapped her hands. 'You've had some great sex.'

'Honestly, Hanna.' *This* was adult conversation? 'I meant the uni break.'

Hanna plumped herself down on a red leather sofa (also new). 'Well, the break had better kick in fast,' she said. 'You look ... really, Meg, what's wrong?'

Hanna had always been a great face-reader. Mind reader. It was often a comfort, and sometimes a confrontation.

'There's a problem,' Meg told her. 'One I could really do without.'

So she tried to unravel the story of Gloria, in so far as she could tell it. The chain of events, the symptoms, because the causes remained unclear. The latest she knew was via a phone call to the clinic. Gloria still wasn't sleeping or eating, but at least the voices hadn't come back.

'Poor thing,' Hanna said. 'I can't imagine Gloria—'

'Being clinically depressed? I know. But she seems angry too, angry with Bernie, at least. She won't let him visit her.'

Hanna took this in. 'Well, maybe he'd be glad of a bit of peace,' she said. 'I mean, I don't want to sound cruel, but ... remember that picnic in King's Park? I timed Gloria talking, and it was twenty minutes before she paused for breath.'

Meg shrugged. It was true enough.

'And so full of clichés,' Hanna said. 'You could see why they wouldn't get on. Bernie seems like a smart kind of guy.'

'But it's Gloria who's shutting him out,' Meg said. 'And maybe Karl getting married again has made her feel worse. I suspect he won't invite his parents to the wedding. I know they've never been close, but a milestone like a wedding can—'

'More like a millstone.'

'That's an old joke, Hanna. And it wasn't funny the first time.'

'So did Karl phone you? To boast about his latest squeeze?'

'Ella told me. And Gloria told me as well, just before we took off for our holiday.' Meg sighed. 'That probably didn't help her either, not being round for Christmas.'

'Meggie.' Hanna sat up. 'You're not blaming yourself, are you?'

She wished Hanna would offer her some wine.

'Let me pour you some wine,' Hanna said.

'Just one glass. I have to—'

'Pick up Ella. I know.'

Hanna offered a full glass of red, and Meg had to smile. Hanna's *one glass* was always more like two.

'So Karl's getting married again,' Hanna said, sitting down. 'Shall we give his bride-to-be his sexual history, Meggie?'

Meggie didn't find this funny.

'My only concern is for Ella,' she said.

'Well, she's always been your concern.'

Hanna had a way of saying it without saying it: loosen the reins on your daughter. Lighten up, have some fun. Like the fun Hanna had with her lawyer friend James. No promises, no commitments, and definitely no wearing of pyjamas. A woman could do a lot worse, she said. Take her ex, for example: a man who'd berated and bullied her but had known how to please her in bed. But if Meg ever found herself missing those moments of pleasure—it was years ago now, but some things you couldn't quite forget—she would remind herself that Karl was a dentist: a slightly less erotic profession than a sewerage engineer.

She didn't tell Hanna about the coffee incident. About the man she'd taken a liking to. Lusted after. Because she knew precisely what Hanna would say. Why didn't you make the first move? Where's your feminist fire?

Hanna leaned forward in her chair. 'If you want to hear something else depressing in a funny kind of way ...'

Meg knew she was in for a long, dramatic story.

'Yesterday, I ran into someone from my old bogan school,' Hanna said, waving her hands about. 'Straightaway she tells me all about her four kids and *the most gorgeous hubby in the world*. And what are you doing these days, Hanna? So I tell her I work in interior design, and how it's all about art that we live in. But you wouldn't be interested, Cherie, I said. She wasn't.'

'You're being a snob, Hanna.'

'And *I'm* telling the story, Meg. So. Cherie asks if I'm married, and no, I said, tried it once, but he wasn't gorgeous, like Cherie's husband clearly was in the photos she shoved under my nose. And no, no kids, I told her, and well! The look she gave me! As if I was dying of some terrible disease. Then she showed me hundreds of photos of her daughters, Pixie and Trixie, Scamper and Fluffy. *My darling angels*, she called them. And then: here's the climax. Cherie puts her hand on her heart and says she *really truly hopes* I'll find a man to make me happy. Because everyone deserves to be happy, she said, even you, Hanna. Even me! As if I'm an alien species.'

She was glowering now, remembering.

'It was like meeting a woman from the fifties,' she said. 'Or those women in America right now who think being happy is more important than having choices. I mean, give me a break. The Surrendered Women, they call themselves. In capital letters.'

'So what are they surrendering?'

'Their minds. Apparently a woman's life is much *easier* if you let your husband tell you what to think, where to live, what to do, what to wear, whether to have kids, when to have sex.'

'It sounds religious.'

'It sounds insane. Which is pretty much the same thing.'

Meg swirled the wine in her glass. 'Still, that doesn't mean that your old friend from school—'

'Not a *friend*, Meg.'

'It doesn't mean she's deluded. Or that you have the right to judge her.'

'I know, I know,' Hanna said, rolling her eyes. 'But it was the way she looked at me, pitying me. Who cares about art that we live in when you don't have a hubby or kids?' She looked around the room, waved her hands about. 'I could use a rich hubby right now,' she said. 'It will take me forever to pay for this lot and I haven't had a pay rise in years. I might have to take in the ironing.' She slapped on a grin. 'So how's my best girl?' she said.

'Growing taller by the week.'

Ella's school skirt needed letting down, and her school shoes were pinching her toes.

'And growing away?' said Hanna.

'Of course. But at least she came with me to Dunsborough. And she's eased off hounding me for a mobile phone.'

She registered the stiffness of Hanna's smile.

'There's so much for a kid to deal with, Hanna. Boys asking for nude photos. Girls sending bitchy messages.'

'You've told me all this before.'

'And you're not a mother.'

'Well, you're right about one thing, Meg.'

ΔΔΔ

As she folded the last of the washing, Meg remembered last night's TV show, *The Art of Folding Clothes*. The presenter had graceful hands and a soothing voice, but why was she considered an artist? Wasn't she merely cashing in on the relentless search for novelty? Meg looked across at Ella, who was lolling on the sofa, reading the final pages of *Tom's Midnight Garden*. Actually finishing a novel, in these days of celebrity magazines, Facebook and Twitter. She'd had her ears pierced last year and wore tiny silver studs, but she'd never asked for a stud in the nose, or even worse, the tongue, which every speechie knew gave you a lisp and endless infections. No hankering after make-up, either. Ella's only stab at rebellion so far? Wanting her bedroom painted black. Her thin, knock-kneed child, but healthy, too, brimming with energy, and it took Meg back, as it sometimes did, to when Ella was barely three weeks old. A listless, floppy baby refusing the breast hour after hour and her mother knew that something was wrong, terribly wrong. Yelling at Karl to drive faster, faster, making him run a red light, just get to the fucking hospital, just go, go. But it was alright in the end, blessedly alright. It wasn't meningitis. It wasn't anything sinister. An unspecified virus. Four days in hospital, with Meg refusing to leave her baby's side, the nurses telling her to have a break, for goodness' sake. Karl dragging her away for some fresh air, good coffee.

She had known it then, as she knew it now: she would die to keep her child alive.

Karl had never felt that intensity, not as far as she could tell, for his only child. He'd had his moments of delight, splashing with Ella in the local pool, or laughing at her staggering in Meg's knee-high boots, with his sunglasses perched on her nose. But he'd never thrilled, as his wife had, to the first step, the first words, the wet kisses, the fierce hugs. Ella had been an obstacle, a source of deep resentment, *the perfect contraceptive*, he'd once sardonically remarked. So how could Meg possibly say that to her child? When Ella had first asked her, years ago now, why her father lived so far away, Meg had resorted to a cliché. *We drifted apart, Ella. It's what sometimes happens to a couple.* Her daughter had never pressed her. And why would she, after all, when her two best friends had single mothers, when TV shows were full of single mothers. Yesterday's scandal, today's breezy normal.

She could still see Karl's face when he'd eventually confessed: puzzled, even slightly amused, that she should take his affairs so much to heart. She'd kicked him out when Ella was three.

'Are you OK, Mum?'

'Sure. Why do you ask?'

'You've been folding that dress for hours.'

Meg laughed. 'It's the latest art form,' she said. 'I'm practising.'

Because it was better to laugh and fold and lie than admit she was falling into sadness. Her marriage had failed. She was the one who'd ended it, but it was a failure nonetheless. And before she knew it, her only child, too, would be out of the picture. Her daughter in a ball gown standing next to some gawky young man, while her mother was left holding the camera, saying smile, again please, just one more shot to give me something to remember.

Something happened to your sense of time after you had a child. Rocking your baby in your arms, steadying her to sleep, you seemed to dwell inside time itself: enfolded, blissfully calm. Holding your toddler's hand as you walked together in the park, time moved slowly, patiently, lovingly. And when her daughter stopped to watch an ant carrying a leaf, time was lit up with her wonder, like a bright silver star on the map of a mother's life. Then time began to blur on the first day of childcare, the first day of school, when you stood at the door feeling stressed and bereft. But now, over the last few months, time was beginning to move more rapidly, with a daughter's coltish leaps and eager bounds, leaving her mother behind. Which was just as it should be. Which sometimes, not very often, just every now and then, made her mother feel wretchedly sad.

Gloria

Time must be passing, with people coming into the room and leaving, then other people coming in. A lady holding a cup who didn't clank the spoon and *Here you go,* she said, *everyone loves Orange Creams.* But Gloria couldn't even nibble, or swallow the soup, even though the doctor kept telling her to try. The doctor wore big black glasses and his face was like a boy's and he looked her straight in the eye. Even sipping the tea was hard, with her throat so tight, the tea staring up at her. There was a different lady with a jug of water and another one to make the bed. All these people, trying to help, with the nights so hard and long and dark. The doctor said the new pills might take time to help her sleep but when would that be? All the tossing and turning and sometimes crying, slow trickles down her cheeks. Even worse was the night a man shone a horrible bright light in her face and said *Take these pills* and she knew they were the wrong pills they were pink and the new ones were purple. He was trying to poison her and *No, no*, she screamed, and pushed the tray away. Then the nice doctor came in the middle of the night and said *There, there, Gloria, you're right, there's been a mistake and here are the right pills*. It made her feel better that she wasn't going mad. That was something to hold onto.

Would Meg come to see her again? What had they talked about? Had they talked at all? About sadness. And the voice. The voice inside her head that was dark and growling and sounded like the devil, telling her she was a bad person, a very bad person who deserved to die. It made her put her hands over her ears and shake so badly but it hadn't come back. Maybe the tree outside her window was keeping it away, and being cared for, even if the people were strangers. Cups of tea and not clanking the spoon and the girl with the bright red hair who made the bed and said *There you go, Mrs Newman, all nice and cosy again.*

Ella

She usually felt cosy in bed, like she could stay there forever and doze like a cat, but tonight she kept turning over and over, thinking about Nana. Her mum said she was in a place that was quiet and pleasant, but how could it feel like that if you couldn't eat or sleep because something had gone wrong with your brain. How come a brain could do that? Why would it *want* to do that? Something else was bugging her, too, in the darkness. How Pop hadn't talked about Nana, he hadn't seemed worried at all. If anything went wrong with Mum, Ella thought, I'd be a complete mess. Like the time her mum slammed her hand in the door and Hanna rushed her to emergency, full of moaning people and sad-eyed people and people with scars on their faces. It had all been a bit scary.

Ella turned over in bed again and something else came into her head. Maisie from down the road. She'd seen her in front of the rows of chocolate and she looked really different, with boobs and lots of make-up and complaining about *so much fucking homework in high school, no time for fun anymore*. Ella was glad her mum was far away in the canned vegetable aisle so she didn't hear *so much fucking homework*, but she wasn't glad about no time for fun, when school would be harder and there'd be heaps of kids she didn't know and she'd have to start thinking about what to do with her life and *life* was too big a thought to get her head around. She only knew what she *didn't* want to be, or couldn't be. She couldn't be a speechie like her mum because you had to know a lot about the brain. She couldn't be a doctor, either, like Lola's mum, because you had to know the science of the body, and you'd have to prod and poke in weird places. She wasn't sure about doing Hanna's work either, because Hanna said people ignored her advice and ended up blaming her for their *disasters*. Like putting glossy wall tiles on the floor, she said, and slipping over all the time, or putting carpet on the stairs and feeling like an animal was crawling through their house. And *no way* would Ella be a dentist like her father. You'd have to stare into people's mouths all day and smell their stinky breath. Her father had told her a dentist joke the last time she went to Sydney, how he had to fix the rotten teeth of a man who'd invented something special that changed the world. Her father said he'd shown the man *the latest in dental technology: a toothbrush*. Ella didn't think that was funny, and even if she had she wouldn't have laughed because of those girls in bikinis. She was ready to come home after that and she didn't need her father, anyway. It was the same for her two best friends. Lola's dad had taken off to America and Fern's mum had kicked out Fern's dad, only she'd found a new man straight away. Fern said it was like her mum had found him on eBay and had him delivered to the door. Only now he was gone and Fern was glad because he kept asking her about school and he burped all the time. It was like that guy Ella's mum had dated for a while. Not the burping, but he'd asked her *every single time* how school was going and he was SO boring. But he didn't come round anymore and her mum was too busy with study, she said, and anyway, she would always put Ella first. Ella liked that her mum cared for her and didn't carry on about what she was going to do for the rest of her life, but she wasn't too sure about always coming first. Coming second or third was fine, unless you got a lame certificate with *Good effort* in big gold letters plastered on the top.

Ella turned over in bed again. How could she get to sleep with all this thinking? She'd be even more rumpled up in the morning if she didn't get to sleep, even more of a *moofle* than usual.

She saw her door slowly opening. She knew her mum hadn't knocked in case Ella was asleep but she always knocked in the daytime. Fern's mum didn't and last week Fern got mad at her and said all she wanted was her very own space, away from her mum and her revolting little brother. But all her mum said was *Don't call your brother revolting*.

'You're still awake, Ella? Are you OK?'

Ella saw something in her mum's hand, asked her what it was. Her mum turned on the bedside lamp, sat down on the bed.

'Check this out,' she said.

Ella sat up to look. It was a photo of her mum and Hanna, grinning like a couple of idiots, their arms around each other. They both had ridiculously fluffy hair.

'It was taken at university,' her mum said. 'I was rummaging through some old photos and ... I mean, just look at us.'

Ella laughed. 'You look like a couple of poodles.'

'It's called a perm. Short for a permanent wave.'

'Short for a permanent mistake, you mean.'

Ella peered at the building in the photo. It looked old, with green plants growing all over it.

'I might go to university one day,' she said. 'But I'd have to get really good marks, wouldn't I?'

'You've got years to go, Ella. Just try to enjoy your studies.' Her mum gave her a soft kind of smile. 'Try to get some sleep now.'

'Can I ask you something?'

'Of course.'

'Pop doesn't seem worried about Nana. He didn't talk about her once.'

'Well ... he probably didn't want to worry *you*. But Nana's going to be fine. Like I told you, she's been given new pills that will act on her brain to help her sleep and eat again. She won't have to suffer much longer.'

Ella thought of that quiet, pleasant place, and Nana's brain going wrong. 'What does her suffering feel like?' she said.

'Depression? I've heard people call it a long, deep sadness that feels like it will never end. Sometimes ... well, they can't see the point of living.'

Ella couldn't imagine wanting to be dead. When Tyson made fun of her nose, she wished she were dead, but she knew she hadn't really meant it.

Her mum took Ella's hand. 'Everyone gets sad now and then,' she said. 'And that's OK. It makes you treasure the good feelings, not take them for granted. But Nana's sadness is much worse than that. It needs to be treated by a doctor.'

'So how did she get like that? She's always so ... you know, she talks all the time about good stuff.'

'I don't know, Ella, that's the truth. We don't always know about people's inner lives.'

'What's that?'

'Their thoughts and feelings.'

Inner lives. So there was a name for the stuff that swirled in your head or sometimes banged about.

Her mum let go of Ella's hand, gave it a gentle pat. 'There's no need to worry about Nana,' she said. 'The medication will help her feel better. We have a lot to thank science for.'

Ella nodded. 'Ms Evans said science is amazing, and girls can be scientists, too, we're just as clever as boys. But Callum said that girls can't pee standing up and Naomi said that boys can't have babies and that was way more important.'

Her mum smiled. 'Great comeback,' she said. 'And you know, Ella, what you said about Pop before? Sometimes people don't speak because they're too full of emotion. They get choked up with feeling.'

'Like the time you went to Emergency? I was too scared to say anything.'

'Like that, yes.' Her mum stood up and her face looked a bit creased now, with all the thinking and talking. 'I hope I haven't stopped you from getting to sleep,' she said.

'No. I like it when you tell me things.'

'And you know you can ask me anything you like. I'll always try to make sense.'

Ella was glad to have a mother who made sense, who answered her questions properly. Except when it came to a mobile phone and not letting Ella stay home by herself. Not letting her paint her bedroom black. Still, at least she didn't make her go to bed at eight o'clock, like Fern's mum. Fern said she'd let *her* kids stay up past midnight and have really loud parties on the roof.

ΔΔΔ

It was a really fun day, hanging out with Lola and Fern. Lola's blonde hair was tied up in a knot, which showed her long graceful neck. Fern was wearing a T-shirt that said *I'm famous but no-one knows it*. They tried teaching Ella to rollerskate, picked her up when she fell over, then tried again. She spent most of her time with her bum on the ground, but her friends didn't laugh, and they didn't bring their iPhones, either. Ella's mum let them make their own lunch, and she didn't pull a face when they made massive peanut paste, banana and jam sandwiches. Then Ella took her friends to her room and they thought her flamingos were cool. Lola said that flamingos had nothing to do with books, so that made them even cooler. Then they all talked about this girl from another school, she was only eleven and she had a big party and some kids ended up drunk and spewed all over the lawn. Gross! Then they talked about Nathan because just about every girl in the class was in love with him but Fern said he was *full of himself*. Ella didn't have a crush on him but she liked the way his hair flicked around his face. She had a bit of a crush on Billy, though, with his shy kind of smile and the longest eyelashes in the world and he wasn't loud and rough like a lot of the other boys. But she would never tell anyone that, not even Lola or Fern, because Billy was way too good-looking for her. Anyway, Fern thought he might be gay.

Then they painted each other's toenails in a cool purple nail polish that Lola had nicked from the chemist. But she'd never do it again, she said, her hands went all sweaty and her heart was banging so loud she was *terrified* the chemist would hear it.

Fern looked kind of wise, and her eyes always went darker when she did that.

'There's some preacher guy in England,' she said, 'who reckons it's OK for starving people to steal food from shops. He said Jesus would approve.'

'But that's not the same as stealing nail polish,' Lola said.

They looked at their toenails and no-one said a word and Ella could tell they felt guilty. But the colour looked cool, just the same. Then they played a game of Scrabble and Lola won easily because she kept picking up the high-scoring letters. Only Ella didn't say that, it would make her look like a bad loser. Well, she was a bit, when it came to Scrabble. Still, she managed to make the word *ai* three times. It meant a three-toed sloth, she'd checked it on the net. She was glad to have friends who liked playing Scrabble, when other kids at school thought it was lame. And she was glad that that her mum didn't pop her head into the room to ask how they were doing. Not once.

In the afternoon, they all sat down to watch *The Bold and the Beautiful*. It was full of women with big hair and big boobs who slapped each other a lot because they were cheating with other women's husbands. The acting was SO bad, like this woman turning her face just before she got slapped and then screaming like she'd actually been hit. The whole thing made them laugh like crazy. There was a guy called Thorn with teeth like piano keys who grew up thinking that his sister was dead. You just knew he was going to find her one day, and she'd have gleaming white teeth like him, even though she'd been kept a prisoner in a basement for years and had never once used a toothbrush. In one scene the characters had no clothes on, but you only saw boobs. For some weird reason they didn't show a willy. Not that Ella wanted to see one, but it was still pretty weird that you couldn't. Her mum said the show made women look stupid and Lola said that's why it was funny. Ella's mum said she didn't think that was funny but she laughed along with them anyway, when some woman squealed in a hysterical voice *You've never really loved me, Ridge*.

∆∆∆

Ella's mum always said sorry for her cooking, but it wasn't as bad as she made out. It wasn't all that good, either. Tonight's macaroni cheese was a bit lumpy and tasted more like milk than cheese, but Ella ate it because she wanted her mum to stop saying sorry all the time. Hanna ate it too, between mouthfuls of moaning about her job. How her boss wouldn't take the hint about a pay rise and it wasn't fair, she was the one who brought in all the clients, *the bags-of-money-but-no-taste clients who want indoor wicker furniture and salmon-coloured spas and kitchens with enough wood to give environmentalists a heart attack.*

She laughed. 'I sound like a grumpy old woman,' she said.

'Well, you don't *look* grumpy,' Ella said. 'You look amazing in that dress.'

A white, tight-fitting dress with lace all over it, and long, floaty sleeves.

'Bless you, my child,' Hanna said, and smiled. 'I'll leave it for you in my will.' She raised her glass of wine. 'So, have you finished the book I gave you?'

Ella said she was confused about the ending. She couldn't tell if Tom's adventures had really happened or if they'd only happened in the mind of the old lady who lived in the same house. Her mum explained how there were different kinds of real: the outside real that everyone could see, and the one in your head that was real for you but might not be real for other people.

'Like me when I was little,' she said. 'I thought there was a giant friendly toad living in our garden but my parents told me it didn't exist. In fact, my father told me I was mad.'

Hanna shook her head. 'They had no idea about a child's imagination,' she said. 'They had no idea about anything, really.' She looked across the table at Ella. 'Do you know my favourite character in your book?' she said. 'It's the old lady, who was wise and kind, like the mother I would have liked for myself. But she was also a bit withdrawn. She didn't get out much, did she? Maybe she needed a bit of a shove.'

Her mum sprang from the table. 'Ice-cream, anyone?' she said. 'There's Grand Marnier or English Toffee.'

'Always good to have a choice,' Hanna said, and gave Ella a twisted kind of smile.

'Some people should mind their own business,' her mum snapped.

Ella stared at her mum. Did she need a shove to get out, like Hanna had kind of said? Did this mean that her mum was lonely? Unhappy? Not Nana's never-ending unhappy, or the hunched-over-your-lunch-at-school unhappy, when a boy called you SquarePants Big Nose. Maybe it was the kind of unhappy when you listened to a sad song and felt a bit weepy, but you didn't know you'd been feeling weepy before.

Bernard

Gloria was *clinically depressed.* The official, clinical diagnosis over the phone. Mrs Newman still wasn't sleeping or eating, apparently, but she wasn't hearing voices anymore. That was good news, wasn't it? But it was four days of reports at one remove because Gloria kept refusing to see him. The man she'd been married to, for better or worse, for nearly forty years. Every time he phoned the clinic he was given a variation on a theme: *Your wife is in the shower, Mr Newman; Your wife is resting; Your wife is too tired for visitors.* But she must have had enough energy to make up excuses, even if she spoke in a whisper, because a whisper could travel miles across the suburbs and strike at Mr Newman's angry heart. He was forking out for the clinic, wasn't he? A thousand dollars a week! He'd nearly passed out on the spot. How long was she going to stay in that place, anyway? He wasn't made of money. Karl was made of money. Bernard had phoned him to tell him the news, half hoping he'd offer to contribute to the cost, half hoping that he wouldn't. He didn't. All he gave his father was *That's a shame,* as though the dish he'd ordered in a restaurant had just been taken off the menu.

Bernard pictured his son wrenching out a stubborn molar, his face grim with satisfaction.

He hauled himself up from the sofa, went to make a coffee. He hadn't eaten his usual breakfast of bacon and eggs because there was no bacon and no eggs. He made himself a coffee, then realised he'd run out of milk. Three of his work shirts had turned pink in the wash, and the toaster had decided to expire. Even everyday machines were conspiring against him. He should drive to the shops and buy food, buy a new toaster, come home and scream at the wall. And what would he do for the rest of the day? The same thing he'd done on Wednesday, Thursday and Friday: have an early dinner, read a bit, go to bed. Try to sleep. He hadn't been sleeping well. The night filled his head with things he wanted to forget, that he didn't want to think about now. Even restful music on the radio didn't stop him rumpling about in bed, right side, left side, right side again.

Was that how it felt for Gloria? Staring at the ceiling, world without end, in the darkness?

He walked to the window, looked out. He saw verges. Houses. Lawns. Flowers. Shrubs. Trees. Letterboxes. Cars. A bicycle. That made nine groups of things. One more would make ten. You couldn't really count windows because they were attached to houses. Ah, driveways. That made ten things. But he couldn't stand at the window all day. Maybe he could play a game of bridge, if he knew three other people to play with. He could vaguely remember using ruffs and dummies, dead hands, with three boys from uni. There was Mal, Mal Wilson. Malodorous, people called him, because ... well, it was obvious as soon as he walked into a room. He'd gone on to run a business; Bernard had seen it in the local paper, tiles or ceramics, so Mal must have discovered deodorant. There was Fred Felon, too, another name to joke with, along with Pete somebody or other. Bernard could still picture him: a big gut, a full beard, a jolly grin, like Father Christmas at the age of nineteen. And then there was Bernard Newman, who'd come in for some blokey teasing: *Newman? I'd hate to see the old one.* He wondered what had become of Fred Felon and Pete what's-his-name. Would they still be friends? Would they get together for a beer, a game of bridge with a new addition to the crew? Would they ask: whatever happened to their old mate Bernie, and that sexy-looking bird he'd managed to snare? They'd seen her once in the distance but he'd kept her all to himself. He dropped his studies, didn't he? Wasn't he planning to be an architect?

He'd kept her all to himself because she'd left school at fifteen. He'd dropped his studies because he couldn't keep his trousers zipped up.

And now? He no longer looked at buildings, not properly, anyway. Not with eyes that took in the shimmer of a glass high-rise or a noble turret gracing a church. As a child he'd been entranced by the Hay Street entrance to London Court. Seven years old and goggle-eyed, he was, gazing at the tower, at four mechanical knights magically appearing from behind a castle door, jerkily advancing, jousting with their lances. Later, he'd discovered the treasures inside the arcade—the gargoyles and masks, shields and crests. He would touch his mother's arm and say *Look, Mutti, look*. But now he'd become one of those people who saw buildings as things on top of other things. He'd never been serious anyway, and whatever studious itch he might have felt had been well and truly scratched by the need to earn a living, with a wife and baby to support. He'd started off in hardware, went on to auto parts, then furniture, before landing in what he hoped would be his final resting place: vacuum cleaners. But business had been slow, and getting slower. Most days not a single pair of legs walked into the store.

And the magic of London Court? He'd learned that it was all mock-Tudor. Mock-history imposed onto a mock-English city, where men in heavy suits and women in hats and gloves sweltered in Australian heat. His mother always made him wear a tie on an outing to the city; she must have understood that a migrant child must be fitted out in order to fit in.

Evening came and he turned on the TV. He could watch a mindless show about dancing or a mindless show about cooking. Some legal show in its third series, but he'd missed the first and second. He settled on the news, which began with a parade of local catastrophes: a truck overturned on a highway, a congested freeway, a burst water main. Then a glimpse of the Queen wearing some lime green outfit, a capacious handbag strapped over a regal arm. What on earth did the woman keep in those handbags? Hundreds of personally monogrammed handkerchiefs? A gun? Then a flash of images, people marching in the street, holding banners marked with foreign words. He saw *Algeria* spooling on the bottom of the screen. So the protestors were probably pumping their fists about corruption, poverty or the abuse of human rights—the important, terrible catastrophes. People's faces were blazing with anger and conviction, and in that single moment Bernard was taken back to Perth, 1971. *One, two, three four, we don't want your bloody war*. His father had spied his protesting son on TV, had stood waiting at the door, enraged, calling Bernard *a Communist dog*, threatening to throw him out if he ever marched again. And then that sickening night over dinner, his father ranting again about those *dirty Commies*, thumping his adopted patriotic chest, proud of all the Aussie boys fighting for freedom in Vietnam. But Bernard had no intention of fighting and had worked up the courage—voice trembling, hands shaking—to say what was on his mind: *I'll go to jail if my number comes up*. It was an unjust war, he'd staunchly declared, and conscription compounded the injustice.

His father had raised his fist and bellowed: *What kind of man have you become?*

But Bernard's number hadn't come up, and his father died three months later. It was some kind of freedom, he supposed. At least his mother had enjoyed a few months without her tyrannical husband. Some peaceful time in which to sing without being mocked, to eat what she liked and when she liked, to sit in her garden for restful hours. When her coffin was lowered into the ground, Bernard had sobbed as if he'd never stop.

Gloria had been standing by his side. She'd taken his hand and hadn't said a word. Had she known there was nothing to say?

Not that she'd ever spoken much, in the days when they were young. She'd barely managed a sentence when he'd brought her home for dinner, four months pregnant and starting to show. His mother had smiled shyly, chatted nervously, but his father had kept his head down, gobbled his food, didn't speak, then rushed off to watch soccer on TV. Bernard had been mortified, angry, and sorry for the shy, pale girl sitting by his side. But *he* hadn't said a word, either, to protest or console, or place a friendly hand on her shoulder. When she must have been feeling mortified herself. Lost.

And what might she be feeling right now? Angry? Confused? Alone? Or would she have company to cheer her up, because she'd always been one for company. Even at that ghastly Christmas dinner, when she must have been feeling churned up inside, she'd chattered away to the guests and occasionally to him: the husband who taunted with indifference or flattened with sarcastic remarks. Like a pair of un-matching bookends, they were: a hard-hearted husband and a soft-headed wife. Mr Too-Big-for-his-Boots and Mrs Pink Fluffy Slippers. He'd told her once that those slippers were ridiculous. Had she taken them to the clinic? Should he look to see if she'd left them behind, offer to bring them to her? Was it his fault? The breakdown. Isn't that what people called it? As if you were a machine whose parts had suddenly failed. Had the loss of their son added to her pain? Had the impending, imposing marriage, the wedding to which they weren't invited, been the final, humiliating blow? And what would happen when Gloria came home? Would they continue to live as they'd lived for years: a wife endlessly talking, a husband trying his best to ignore her.

He'd read somewhere that by the age of thirty, the chances of people changing were highly remote. That your character was set in plaster and would probably never soften again. Where had he read that? Somewhere online? Something vaguely scientific, anyway, about the hardwiring of the brain in one's formative years. Nothing like a scientific study to prove that you were doomed.

He must stop brooding. He should head off to the gym and pound out his turmoil on the treadmill. But he had to throw some shirts in the washing machine, and he had to shop for food; last night he'd finished the last can of tomato soup. But somehow eating had begun to feel rather pointless, as he stared through the window at tired shrubs and grey, corrugated fences. Here he was, in Dianella: named after the Roman goddess Diana, the virgin who loved the moon. Or was it hunting? Either way, it was a ludicrous name for row after row of drab houses, a letterbox shaped like a swan, another in the form of an Aborigine standing on one leg. In this city called Perth, to honour the birthplace of some Scottish military type, re-named the City of Lights by an American astronaut buzzing round the earth. City of Lights? When it was one bland suburb drifting into the next, sprawling outwards to countless miles of sand and rock and messy scrub. Would his life have been better in Germany? In his picturesque village of gentle snow, medieval buildings, a church with pale pink walls. He might have married a pretty fraulein if he'd stayed in that picture-book town. He might have eaten rollmops for breakfast, worn lederhosen, had two strapping sons and one winsome daughter to care for him in his dotage. He might even have moved to Berlin and become a notable architect, or a venerated professor of law.

He remembered amazing Ella with some ingenious German words. He remembered her wanting to take from the rich, and the childhood stories he'd told her. He remembered her big brown, enquiring eyes, and the way she'd called him a penguin.

Had he laughed when she'd said that? He hoped so.

ΔΔΔ

Vacuum cleaners had once been a cumbersome necessity, but now they were marketed as must-have accessories in sparkling metallic green or glossy purple, bold red or electric blue. The upright, the stick, the canister, the barrel, complete with turbo heads, ducting brushes, crevice tools, supa gulpers. He knew all their names and functions, could show you how to balance price and serviceability, although a clever salesman always leaned towards price. No, not *salesman*: these days you were called a *salesperson*. Of vacuum cleaners for carpets, hardwood floors, furniture, vehicles, corners, stairs, whirring and sucking and whirring again.

Not one customer all morning.

He thought of the neighbours who'd called him last night on the landline, to ask about Gloria, of course. Donna. Wendy. Trudy, was it, so quiet he could barely hear her. Three concerned maidens all in a row. They hadn't seen Gloria around for ages, they said, and she wasn't answering her phone. Each woman had asked him: *Whatever is the matter?* Hospital, he'd said, nothing major, mumbling something about her gall bladder, and yes of course he would pass on their best wishes, and yes of course he would let them know when she was up to having visitors. When the truth was he didn't want them gossiping, passing judgment, taking pity on his wife. He owed her that much, at least.

He looked towards the door of the shop. No one.

At least the boss wouldn't suddenly turn up to see the lurid wasteland; he rarely put his foot inside the door. Bernard's last boss had written him a reference for the current boss: Mr Newman was *keen to learn,* apparently. Indeed, all his references attested to this virtue, before the shops either shut up shop or found younger, cheaper slaves to do their bidding. Nearly forty years ago he'd had to learn about hardware, to pay back Gloria's father for the first and only house they'd ever owned. Gloria's father, a man who'd railed against Gough Whitlam as a threat to national security, house prices and the amount of daily sunshine. And what came next, Bernard thought. Eight years at auto parts, until the big companies put on the squeeze. Then a stint in furniture, tape measure and smile at the ready. He'd sold a lot of expensive leather lounge suites and hideous vinyl pouffés, thanks to his *excellent people skills*: another virtue listed on his references. So helpful, according to the customers, couldn't have asked for better service. Until the downturn in the housing market, when his virtues were no longer required.

And now? He'd once sold a vacuum cleaner designed to suck up the hair of a dog or cat. These days he'd be grateful if a dog or cat padded through the door.

He saw his colleague giving him a wave. Not that *colleague* was the right word for a nineteen-year-old boy with gel-encrusted hair, metal in one eyebrow and attitude all over his face. Three months he'd been here, spending his time checking his phone or checking the latest sex toys online; his girlfriend was, apparently, *into games.* What was the boy on about now, making odd shapes with his hands? Bernard shrugged, made a show of checking his computer. He saw one new email. From the company head. The invisible boss. Bernard had a feeling and the feeling wasn't good.

Dear Mr Newman

He took in the few brutal lines in a flash: *professional service, difficult economic circumstances*. Wishing him *all the best for your future endeavours*.

He'd been fired. Given the sack. Not even offered a face-to-face, vaguely human encounter. *Dear Mr Newman*. He might as well be *Dead Mr Newman*, according to the boss in his handmade suit and shiny Volvo. If only the email had been a letter: Mr Newman could have torn it up and chucked it in the bin. But then what? Who was going to employ a fifty-nine-year-old salesman? Who knew virtually nothing that would make him employable. He'd had a hard enough time learning to navigate computers, and now he'd have to navigate the dole queue, face robotic bureaucrats who reduced you to a number, made you register for so many jobs a week. Was it four? Six? More?

He'd never been on welfare in his life. He'd hated selling vacuum cleaners, but work was work, and he wasn't selling heroin or poker machines.

How could he manage now? And how could he keep paying for that clinic? He felt the bile rising in his throat at *professional service*, at *difficult economic circumstances*, and at Gloria, too, for being depressed, for shutting him out. He walked to the door of the shop, stepped outside, took in deep draughts of air, was given a wave from the owner of the food shop next door. One of those health food joints flogging fifty-dollar bottles of stuff that promised stronger muscles or spiritual salvation, for all he knew or cared. The owner drove a brand new, sleek black Holden. But how long before *they* lost their jobs, those workers at the Holden factory, everyone buying Japanese cars these days because Australian cars were shit. That's what the boss at auto parts had told him, umpteen years ago. Macka, Macka McBride. He'd also told Bernard that he watched porn because his wife had stopped *giving out*. Porn was better than the real thing, he'd said, because you only had to please yourself, *one hand on the tiller*. Bernard had felt a stab of disgust and he felt it now, at this shitty place called Australia: bosses chucking people in the bin, people watching porn and buying sex toys, men masturbating themselves into a stupor while some anonymous woman sold them sex on the phone. It was sickening. Deplorable. His own car was shit. A white Datsun, parked in its usual spot, baking in the sun. It had rust on the fenders. The brakes needed to be checked. There was a dent in the front passenger side that Gloria claimed she knew nothing about. He knew nothing, either. He'd lost his job, been clumsy with condoms, with his hands, with his words. Would his life have been better if he'd been more careful? If Gloria had been less kind? And what would he say to her now: a husband who'd been given the boot, the arse, the gold medal in redundancy? And what would he tell Karl, when he phoned with the latest report? Should he say: I've suffered the death of a salesman? Or: why don't you come and visit your mother? You're marrying a woman your parents have never laid eyes on, you have a daughter you hardly ever see, you don't have a smudge of gratitude in your cold, hard heart for all that your parents have given you.

He heard himself laughing out loud. Right there, in front of the shop.

He wondered if that's how it felt: madness.

Gloria

She couldn't be mad, could she? Because she'd had some sleep
and the nice doctor had said that sleep would help her brain
feel more clear, more calm. That things might make more sense.
He hadn't said what those *things* might be and she didn't want
to think about that now. All she knew, all she felt, was a kind of
peace settling around her, inside her, a feeling she remembered
from a long time ago, before sadness and regret and not knowing
what to say took all the sense away. She turned her face to the
window, saw a light drifting through. Sunshine. Soft sunshine,
making her feel quiet in her head and all over her body.

'Hello, Gloria. May I come in?'

A strange woman was standing at the door.

'I'm Dr Gray.' She stepped into the room. 'Please call me
Connie.'

A short, stumpy woman with a cross-looking face.

'I'd like to talk with you, if that's alright.'

The doctor sat down on a chair and looked even shorter, her
legs dangling in the air like a child.

'You look rested, Gloria.'

Rested. Is that how she'd look in a mirror?

'I must have had some sleep,' she said. 'I feel … not so tight
inside.'

'That's marvellous.'

'So … so how long have I been here?'

'Ten days. It can be quite dramatic sometimes.'

'What can?'

'Getting some sleep. Getting those neurotransmitters fixed.'

Gloria startled. 'What does that mean?'

'It means that the new medication has started working. It usually takes weeks, sometimes months, for people to start feeling better.' The doctor leaned forward in the chair. 'We're delighted you've had a good night's sleep. We think you're making progress.'

'Who's *we*?'

The doctor leaned back. 'Dr Kapoor has briefed me about you. He can't see you for a while because his wife's just had a baby.'

'A baby. A boy or a girl?'

'A girl. Hena. It's an Indian name, meaning *flower.*'

'What a lovely name.' Gloria let out a great big sigh. 'My son was such a sweet baby.' She fumbled at the quilt. She didn't know what else to say, except that her son was *very clever*.

'What does that mean, Gloria?

'He's a dentist. He studied very hard. But his marriage fell apart and he went to live in Sydney. I ... well, I hardly ever see him.'

'And how does that make you feel?'

Gloria took this in. No one had ever asked her that before, not even Bernie. Especially not Bernie. So how *did* she feel, really? Sad, angry, hurt, all mixed up together. But how could she say that out loud?

'I don't feel much of anything,' she said.

The doctor gave her a sad kind of look. Or maybe doctors just looked that way when they talked to sad people.

'Does your son make the effort to keep in touch?' she said.

'Well, we talk on the phone sometimes.'

'So you're saying you don't feel close to him?'

'I'm saying we talk on the phone sometimes.'

Should she come right out and tell the truth? I don't love my son. I don't even like the man he's become. Was that what the doctor wanted her to say?

The doctor frowned. 'Perhaps you can tell me about your husband,' she said. 'Bernard, is it?'

'Bernie.' Gloria shrugged.

'So how does he ... how do you feel about your marriage?'

'My marriage?'

'I mean ... well, how does your husband treat you?'

Gloria felt her mouth go tight. 'Well, he doesn't beat me up, if that's what you mean.'

The doctor nodded, slowly. 'So ... was there violence in your own family? Was your father—'

'No! Dad was a really gentle man.'

'That's good to hear, Gloria.' The doctor looked down at a clipboard on her lap. 'Is your husband gentle, too?'

What could she say about Bernie, after all these years?

'He's clever, like my son,' she said. '*Our* son. But ... well ... we made Karl together, but it doesn't feel like ...' What was she saying? What did she mean? 'My husband thinks I'm stupid.'

'You know that's not true, Gloria. Don't you?' The doctor's voice was all quiet now. Soothing.

'Sometimes ...' Gloria stopped. Started again. 'I know I'm not stupid, but ... well, that's how he makes me feel.'

'And how does he do that to you?'

Gloria pictured Bernie sitting in his armchair. She pictured bringing him a cuppa, then him looking down nose at her when she tried to speak.

'He doesn't want to talk to me,' she said. 'He ignores me a lot of the time.' She took a deep breath. 'He makes fun of me. The things I say.'

'And how does that make you feel?'

'Like I'm not worth anything.'

The doctor nodded. 'Which is a terrible way to feel, isn't it?'

Gloria fumbled at the quilt again. 'I don't understand how it happened,' she said. 'He wasn't like that to begin with. He was kind to me. The first boy who was kind to me.'

'How was he kind, Gloria? Can you remember?'

Gloria felt her face go red. 'In bed, I mean.'

Because they'd hardly spoken at all.

'And then ... I got pregnant. Before we were married, I mean.'

'Well, that wasn't your fault, was it?'

Gloria considered this. All those years ago. 'It wasn't anyone's fault,' she said. 'Bernie didn't make me feel it was, anyway. And I wanted to make him happy. But ... well, I didn't. And now ... I don't love him anymore. Maybe I never loved him.'

'That's OK, you know.' The doctor gave her that sad smile again. 'You don't have to love him.'

But she was meant to, wasn't she? Wasn't she meant to make her husband happy? Didn't Wendy make Max happy? They were always laughing and still holding hands after all these years and he'd planted all those flamingos for her birthday. But I don't hold my husband's hand, she thought. I never know what to buy him for his birthday and one time I bought him a watch with a black leather band but I never saw him wear it and a long time ago he gave up his studies to look after me. I never thanked him for that and I know he's unhappy but I don't know how to change that and I don't want that voice coming back into my head saying you're a bad person, Gloria, a terrible person who doesn't know how to love and who has to take pills and who deserves to die.

'Are you interested in music, Gloria?'

The doctor's voice, returning her.

'People in here get together to sing. It can be very therapeutic.'

Therapeutic?

'Or art classes or ...'

But Gloria wasn't listening anymore. She said she was tired. She heard the doctor asking about giving Bernie a message, but what would be the point? The words would only be weeds stuck in the wrong place and she didn't know how to find a better place and live there for the first time. The doctor was leaving now, telling her to get some more sleep if she liked, sleep was good, she'd come back and see her tomorrow.

The door closed.

Sleep was good. But then what if she couldn't stop sleeping? What if she never woke up? Karl had felt like that, a tiny boy too frightened to go to sleep and it had frightened her too, the way he'd cried and said *No, no, I won't go to sleep, I won't*. She didn't know what to do. And then one night he told her, his chubby face all crumpled up and tears on his cheeks, how a boy at school said his grandpa had died in his sleep and would that happen to him? He didn't want to die in his sleep, he didn't want to die at all. So she'd held him and rocked him and told him it only happened to old people and he would wake up in the morning so big and strong. That must have been enough because he went to sleep that night and every night after that, knowing he wouldn't die. And now they talked on the phone sometimes and it was over in a flash because he was always *busy, got to go, Mum, sorry*.

ΔΔΔ

She saw a shimmer in the doorway, a kind of shimmery shape. But it wasn't a person, it was more like a feeling, a soft blue feeling, spreading over the room. She wondered for a moment if it was Jesus coming to see her, telling her that all would be well. But she didn't believe in Jesus anymore, or the wafer and the wine, the priest in his long white robe. Even Mary with her soft blue dress and the baby in her arms.

She heard a faint tapping at the door. Who was it now? The door opened. Meg.

'May I come in, Gloria?'

'Oh yes. Please.'

Meg was real in a bright blue dress like a summer sky. Gloria remembered those skies, from a place that felt a long way away but she knew she would have to go back there, to Bernie's hard face and his cutting words and she didn't know how she could bear it.

Meg placed a small bag on the bed. 'A new nightie for you,' she said.

Gloria felt a bit choked up. She opened the bag and saw purple fabric and sprigs of flowers and *Oh, how pretty,* she said, *how good of you.*

Meg sat down on a chair, smiled.

'The nurse told me you've had some sleep,' she said.

Gloria nodded.

'You certainly looked rested,' Meg said. 'Are you feeling better?'

'I am, yes. My head ... it's more clear.'

Meg brushed back her hair. She had lovely gold hair, like the sun.

'I've been to see you before,' she said. 'But you were tired and didn't feel like talking. I'm so pleased you're feeling better.'

It was good of Meg to visit. But wasn't she busy with studying, even though she'd studied before? All kinds of things Gloria had never heard of, things with *ologies* in their names.

'How are your studies going?' she asked. 'With people who can't speak, isn't it?'

Meg looked surprised, then smiled.

'That's right,' she said. 'Or sometimes it's people who use the wrong words, or words that don't make any sense. Not to others, anyway.'

'So why does that happen?'

Meg folded her hands in her lap. 'Their brains have been damaged in some way,' she said. 'They've had a stroke or been in an accident or ... you don't want to hear about that, Gloria, let's—'

'But it's about helping people, isn't it?'

'Yes. When they find the words ... well, it helps them to feel less alone.'

It made Gloria think of her friends. Donna and Wendy and Trudy. Who hadn't come to visit. But she mustn't go down that road. She mustn't.

'So what do you do to help?' she asked.

'Well, we give them different kinds of exercises. For their speech, I mean. And I have to remember two important rules: never pretend to understand people if you don't, otherwise they won't make any progress. And you mustn't pity them, either, because they need to keep believing they can get better.'

Gloria liked hearing about these things, and it was good to be outside herself, not all locked up inside.

'My favourite time was working with a child,' Meg said. 'A three-year-old boy who stuttered quite badly. I don't find stuttering very interesting, to be honest, it's not all that challenging, but the boy was so cute. He told me he wanted to be a firefighter and become *the savoury of the world*. I had to stop myself from laughing.'

Gloria didn't laugh either. She was thinking of something else.

'Did you ever want another child?' she said.

Meg's eyes went wide. But then she settled into a smile again. 'I have Ella,' she said. 'She's all I could ask for.'

'She *is* a special girl, Meg. My only grandchild.' And then Gloria remembered. 'Unless Karl ... I mean ... you wouldn't mind, would you? If he had another—'

'No, no, not at all. But ... well, it's kind of you to ask.'

Then they both went quiet. It was a hovering kind of quiet. And now that she'd asked about Karl, Gloria wanted to know more.

'Were you very unhappy, Meg?'

Meg looked down, then up into Gloria's face. 'We were both unhappy,' she said. 'No-one was to blame.'

Gloria wanted to ask her even more. But she didn't want to pry and snoop and be told to mind her own business. Not that Meg would say that, but how could you know what people were thinking, even when they told you?

'And you, Gloria? Are you ... I mean ... has Bernie been to see you?'

In this quiet room, just the two of them, Gloria wished she could tell Meg the truth. But she didn't want to weigh her down, either, didn't want to weigh anyone down. No-one likes a moaner, her mum used to say. Moaners make you feel like the sky is black and low and you'll never see the sun again.

'I'm sorry you didn't get to meet my mum,' she said. 'I mean ... well, she taught me not to complain about ... my life ... to count my blessings. And my dad, well, he was a lovely man. Not like Bernie's dad, he was horrible.' She leaned forward, determined now to tell. 'I knew he was nasty the first time I met him. He didn't talk to me, he didn't even look at me. He just gobbled down his food and rushed off to watch TV.'

She could still see it so clearly: his head down, slopping his food like a pig.

'If my mum had been alive,' she said, 'she would have given him an earful. She would have stomped into the room and called him a rude old fucker, pardon the language. Him and his schnitzel, thinking he was so grand.'

Meg laughed. She actually laughed. Well, maybe it was a bit funny, after all these years.

'You tell a great story, Gloria.'

But Bernie didn't stand up for me. That's what she really wanted to say. He didn't tell his father not to be so hurtful, he didn't even say sorry to her on the drive back home. Or ever. Couldn't he tell how bad she was feeling? She could still see him opening the front door for her, walking from the house, opening the car door for her. Easy things like that.

But she had to get away from that moment.

'How is Ella?' she said. 'Where is she today?'

'With my friend Hanna. You remember Hanna?'

'The woman who waves her hands a lot?'

Meg laughed. 'That's her. Ella's having a good time on her holidays. She has two lovely friends, and she's doing lots of swimming in a friend's pool.'

Gloria didn't know these friends or the pool, and the two of them went quiet again.

'Is there anything she'd like for school?' Gloria asked. 'Does she need a new schoolbag? A pencil case? Maybe a box of those lovely coloured pencils?'

She remembered a box with the picture of a lake on the lid, and colours inside that she'd never seen before, names she'd never heard of. Oriental Blue. Yellow Ochre. A special present from her mum and dad, for her birthday.

'That's generous of you, Gloria. But ... well, thank you ... Ella's right for the moment.'

Meg was smiling again, but not showing her teeth this time.

'Have you been into the garden?' she said.

'I've only been for a small walk inside.'

Where had she been? There was a room for eating and a room with a piano, but she hadn't gone inside either one. But then she remembered seeing something else, something dreadful, and she had to say that too.

'There's a young girl in here. She looks so young and so sad and ...'

'You don't have to talk about it, Gloria. Don't upset yourself.'

But she had to say, now that she'd started. 'She was so thin, so thin, she looked like she was going to break.'

'Just focus on yourself, Gloria. On getting better.'

'I don't understand, Meg. The girl. It's like she wants to disappear.'

She had bruises all over her legs, hobbling along with a drip on her arm, like walking to the end of the world. But Meg was leaning forward now and saying in a quiet voice, so quiet you could hardly hear her, that Bernie was asking about her. So quiet and careful, like she was treading on eggshells. But Gloria didn't care about eggshells and *Bernie doesn't care about me, he only married me because I was having his baby*.

'I don't want to go home,' she said. And then, in a rush, as if the words had a mind of their own: 'I could come and live with you and Ella.'

Meg just sat there, blank, so Gloria said it again. That she could help look after Ella, drive her to school and pick her up. She could keep the house clean and tidy while Meg was busy with her studies. She saw Meg's face go tight but Gloria couldn't stop herself, she could cook dinner too, she said, she could do the shopping and—

'Oh Gloria ... I understand how you feel. It's ... it's just ...'

What did that mean: *it's just*?

'Shall I bring Ella to visit?' Meg said. 'You'd like that, wouldn't you?'

What would I like, Gloria thought. What does anyone care what I like? Bernie and Karl and now Meg, and Ella far away with her friends, and the neighbours with their yapping dogs and phony flamingos and pills that didn't help me sleep. What do any of them care?

She felt a hand on her shoulder and then a space and she knew that Meg had left her.

Meg

She'd left Gloria staring into space. She'd touched her shoulder and made her flinch. She'd seen the hard, grim line of her mouth. A broken, lonely woman asking another woman about her life, asking if she'd wanted another child. Years ago Gloria had held Ella in her arms and the tears had flowed and *She's beautiful*, she'd said. Not like Meg's mother, who'd declared that babies were naughty and needed to be disciplined right from the start. But Gloria had taken pleasure in her grandchild, in her chatter, in her dress-ups, in the stories Ella had conjured about all kinds of creatures. But living with her? Impossible.

Meg slumped onto a garden bench, feeling tired and hollowed out. What would Ella think if her Nana came to live with them? What would Bernie think if his wife up and left him? Why did Gloria keep turning him away? And where was Karl in all this mess? Meg had been on the point of phoning him, but it wasn't her place to be asking him to visit and nothing was her place and yet she wanted to help and she was meant to be having a break, for fuck's sake.

She needed to make a move. Maybe she should get off the bench and walk back inside the clinic. Ask for pills to calm her down.

She checked her watch. Two pm. An hour before collecting Ella from Hanna's, an hour before she saw her daughter's open, trusting face. She took a deep breath, tried to settle down. She would pick up Ella and suggest take-away pizza for dinner, plus something disgustingly sweet. She would—A shadow crossed her path. She looked up to see a man stop in his tracks, turn around, stride towards her. It was the coffee man. Hal.

'Meg.' He smiled. 'I can't believe it's you. It's Hal, remember? The idiot who—'

'Yes. I remember.'

Did she sound annoyed? Nervous? She was suddenly nervous.

'Mind if I sit down?' he said. 'You look like you could use some company.'

His voice was quiet, gentle, and for an instant, she wanted this stranger, this Hal, to take her in his arms. Hold her. She really was losing the plot. Thinking she mustn't be late for Ella, as he sat down on the other end of the bench. Looking at her as if he could see straight through her, and *I'm OK, really*, she said.

'Well, your face tells a different story. And look at your hands. So clenched.'

She looked down at those hands, then up into his eyes.

'Do you work here?' she said. 'I mean, are you a doctor?'

'Hell no,' he said, and laughed. 'I'm a mechanic. What made you think I'm a doctor?'

She felt her cheeks redden. 'You're ... you have a kind manner.'

'Really? Well, I hope it helps my wife. I'm visiting her.'

She heard the thud of those words: *my wife*.

'Ex-wife, actually. Old habits die hard.'

Was he giving her a message? Get a grip, Meg. The man had a suffering ex-wife; he wasn't doing a chatting-up routine.

'Why is she here?' she said. 'If you don't mind me asking.'

'She's an alcoholic. Well, a recovering alcoholic. That's the name the counsellor insists on.'

'Oh. I'm sorry. Has she ...'

'It's been years. But she's finally acknowledged her problem. They say that's the first step, the hardest step.' Then his face—suddenly, unexpectedly—lit up with a smile. 'It's the weirdest thing, meeting you here,' he said. 'The day I spilled coffee all over you ... how many days ago now? You said you'd been to visit a friend here, and then a few days later, Rachel ends up in the same place.'

Meg wondered how long he and Rachel had been married. Not married.

'Well, it's good of you to visit,' she said.

He shrugged. 'It's the least I can do. I didn't ... well, I should have helped her more.' He shuffled in his seat, moved a fraction closer. 'But tell me about you,' he said. 'Why you're looking so tense.'

'Well. What can I say? I just made my friend unhappy.'

'But you didn't *make* her unhappy, did you?'

'I know that, I know. But she's so fragile. She asked to come and live with us and I had to say no. Not exactly in those words, but she looked so sad when I said it.'

'But she asked you, right?'

'Yes.'

'You had to give her an answer.'

'I want to help her but ...'

He turned away, scanned the garden with a steady gaze.

'I hope your ... ex-wife ... recovers soon,' she said.

He turned to face her again. 'Well, she's taking an interest in other patients,' he said. 'Not in a gossipy way, it's just good for her to think about others. And just now she told me something strange. Apparently there's a woman in here who thinks she's dead.'

'Really?'

'I know. Sounds hard to believe. But yesterday she went

shopping and came back with a pair of red high-heels and a massive leather handbag. So Rachel figures the woman must be on the mend.'

Meg couldn't help laughing. Felt terrible for laughing. But Hal was smiling too.

'It *is* kind of funny,' he said. 'The cure for thinking you're dead is shopping for pointless stuff. Crazy, isn't it?'

'That's one theory,' Meg said. 'And that the so-called crazy ones are actually sane because they understand the madness of the world.'

'But that doesn't stop them from suffering, does it?'

Meg nodded. 'True. But that theory changed the practice of psychiatry. It encouraged doctors to listen to their patients, try to understand what didn't seem to make sense.'

Meg could see him watching her intently.

'Whose theory was that?' he said.

'A doctor called Laing. R. D. Laing. He thought the family played a big role in creating mental illness.'

'Ah. The family.' Hal laughed. 'It gets a lot of stick, doesn't it?'

'And the funny part is—well, it's not funny, really, it's sad. Laing often treated his own children badly.'

Still his gaze was on her. He had a beautiful face. And she had to leave. She checked her watch again, conspicuously.

'You have to get going,' he said.

She nodded. 'To pick up my daughter.'

'Again?'

Should she phone Hanna and ask for more time?

'I'm a single mother,' she said. 'What some people call a blight on society.'

She thought he might laugh, but he didn't. And why couldn't she summon the courage to ask him for a coffee? Not let him slip away. Or maybe he was with someone. Since he was no longer with Rachel.

'So ...' Trying to sound casual. 'Would you like to have coffee sometime?' she said. 'Just ... you know ... only if you're not ...'

He gave her a tight smile. 'I'm on my own,' he said. 'If that's what you mean.'

He turned away again, looked at the garden, didn't say another word.

Meg felt herself shrivel. It was one of those I-wish-the-ground-would-open-up-and-swallow-me moments, a man looking away or down, preparing some kind of excuse.

He turned to look at her at last. Unsmiling. 'Why not?' he said.

Not exactly brimming with enthusiasm.

Another awkward pause. Should she nominate a time? A place? But because he was saying nothing, was giving her nothing, she rummaged in her bag for an old business card.

'Call me,' she said.

Call me: like a sassy woman in a movie. A straight-to-video movie, judging by the tightness of his face.

She handed him her card. 'I don't work there anymore,' she said, 'but my mobile's the same. I've gone back to study. But I'm on a break from study. I'm going to paint the house.'

Why the hell had she said all that? To let him know she had time on her hands? Didn't mind working with those hands? That she wanted him to put on some overalls, paint a few walls?

'I'll call you,' he said, flatly.

She needed to find her car in a hurry. And she wouldn't look back, she mustn't.

She could picture him when he got home, taking her card from his wallet and staring at her name. *Margaret R. Flynn,* a woman he didn't know and didn't seem keen to know better.

She might have told him that her mother had named her Margaret Rose, to honour the sister of the Queen. Would that have made him laugh? Would she have promised not to make him meet her mother?

ΔΔΔ

That night she phoned Bernie to give him an update. Well, more like a highly censored report. *Gloria's sleeping,* she told him, but the clinic had already informed him. *Gloria's speaking freely.* But he knew that too, although judging by the flatness of his voice, maybe he'd given up caring. And then, after her telegraphic messages, the things she didn't, couldn't say, he thanked her for taking the trouble, said goodbye in a quavering voice.

She'd never really warmed to the man, had always found him rather aloof. This father of a man no longer bound to her by law. Over the years he'd given her scraps of stories about coming to Australia as a child: the heat and the flies, the horrible taste of Vegemite, the usual banal observations. A few fragments about studying at uni before getting married and starting a family. She'd tried drawing him out about his studies, but he'd said it was a long time ago. *He swept me off my feet,* Gloria had once said, and Bernie had looked away.

She remembered Gloria's stony face in the clinic, her resentful declaration: *He only married me because I was having his baby.* A shotgun wedding, they used to call it.

She understood that Gloria could drive a man crazy with her talking, and she knew she'd left school at fifteen. But she took an interest in other people. She cared about their feelings. She didn't feel sorry for herself. Had Bernie missed the best of her because he couldn't see past the worst?

But still, Meg didn't have to live with her. She *couldn't* live with her, could she?

ΔΔΔ

Checking the colour cards in Bunnings, Meg was feeling more and more adrift. All those pointless gradations of white paint: Hanna's Ivory, plus Snow, Vivid, Polar, Silver Tea Set, for crying out loud. Hog's Bristle, for crying out even louder. Holding the cards up to the light, muttering under her breath, with Ella sounding bored, then fractious, waiting for her mother to make up her mind. Vivid? Snow? What did Ella think? Ella just wanted to go home, and why couldn't she stay home by herself, she was turning twelve in March and why couldn't she have her room painted black and why couldn't she have a mobile, all her friends had mobiles and Bunnings was the most boring place in the world and why did she have to get dragged along—

'Because I'm your mother and I said so.'

Meg couldn't decide on a colour in the end. And of course the kind man hadn't been in touch. What had she been hoping for, anyway? Some attention? Some kind of connection that might lead to something else? Maybe he didn't like women taking the initiative. Or maybe he didn't like women, full stop. Sexually, that is. It only now occurred to her that the man might be gay. Maybe that's why he and Rachel had divorced. No wonder he'd been so awkward when she'd asked him for coffee.

Or maybe he didn't find her attractive. She thought about those extra kilos and hated herself for thinking it.

At least Ella was more civilised after spending the afternoon with Lola. She'd spent *hours* swimming in the pool, and the rest of the time playing a video game in which—who would have thought—a princess locked up in a castle was rescued by—who would have thought—a dashing prince. Which was marginally better than the games in which men routinely slaughtered women who challenged their path to success. Still, Ella was proud of swimming so many laps, and she was getting some exercise, at least. More than her mother, whose only exercise in the last few days was labouring under the delusion that she might, just might, try again. As Ella opened the fridge door, crouched to see what she could find (and she'd only had lunch half an hour ago), Meg apologised for taking so long in Bunnings, and for barking at her too. Ella turned, smiled, reached out to hug her.

Meg stroked her daughter's curly hair, felt the bones in her hips.

'Will that ever happen to me?' Ella said, muffled into her mother's chest.

'What do you mean?'

'That I'll spend my life looking at colour cards?'

ΔΔΔ

Tuesday night, six o'clock. Meg was pretty sure that Bernie would be home. The shop would have shut by now, and he didn't strike her as one those high-powered men who stayed back at work or took his work home, mobile attached to his ear. At least Karl hadn't done that. She assumed that Bernie wouldn't be out on the town, either, painting it red, or whatever it was that a man liked to do when his wife wasn't around. Bernie didn't seem like the type. Not that a woman could always tell; she often couldn't tell. Maybe Bernie didn't have friends, either; maybe he was a loner, or one of those tagalong husbands who was dragged along to meet other couples for dinner.

What did she know about him, after all?

She stepped out of the car, waited for Ella to do the same. The air was still sticky with heat.

'The garden looks kind of dead,' Ella said.

'Well, maybe Pop's saving on water. I hope he doesn't mind us surprising him like this.'

She'd heard the sadness in his voice. She should make an effort.

She knocked on the door. No answer. Then she heard footsteps inside. The door opened slowly and there was Bernie, looking as dejected as his garden. They trailed into the house as he mumbled apologies for *the mess, sorry, sorry, please sit down*. But the room didn't look messy; it looked neat but unoccupied. There was furniture, a book on a coffee table, drapes and a rug, but the place had the air of a motel room that no-one had rented for a while. But then Meg saw the loveliest thing: Ella giving her Pop a hug, his smile bright with surprise. He looked quite handsome when he smiled. He'd lost weight, too, you could see it in his face. Had he been trying? Or maybe he couldn't cook. Or maybe he wasn't coping.

He turned to Meg, looking sheepish. 'I can't ask you to stay for dinner,' he said. 'There's ... I haven't had time to shop.'

'But we didn't come to eat,' Ella said, being the perfect guest. 'Mum said you could show us your photos.'

'Photos?'

'You know. In your fancy dress costumes.'

His face went blank. 'I don't know if I have any.'

'Nana has a big fat book somewhere,' Ella said.

'An album,' he said. 'I don't know where it is.'

'You could look,' Ella said, gently, as if talking to a child.

He left the room abruptly.

'Pop seems a bit lost,' Ella whispered.

'Well, you're doing a great job of finding him,' Meg whispered in return.

Bernie came back with a bulky brown album, muttering something about dust, and they sat down on the sofa. He began flipping backwards past photos of Karl, as if racing past a life that he didn't wish to see. But then at last he found the ones Ella wanted, and she pointed and laughed out loud. Meg was laughing too, at Bernie dressed as a fat penguin with a smooth white belly and flappy little hands, and *Would you look at that*, she said. Ella said she was already looking. Bernie wearing a space helmet much too big for his head. Bernie as Robin Hood, wearing jacket and tights, with a bow slung across his chest.

'My mother made all these costumes,' he said. 'I can still see her, sitting at her sewing machine. It was the first thing they bought in Australia. When they finally had some money.' He looked across at Meg. 'You would have liked my mother,' he said. 'She was a good woman.'

'Hey. Pop.' Ella jumped up in her seat. 'I just had an idea about Robin Hood. You know, taking from the rich and giving to the poor.'

'Go on.'

'You could put poison on the notes, so when a rich person touched them, the poison would seep into their fingers and make them really sick.'

Bernie tugged at his collar. 'An interesting plan,' he said. 'But, well, there are a few problems to overcome.' He looked over Ella's head, gave Meg a smile. 'You had to be there,' he said, then looked back to Ella. 'Keep working on it. You might be onto something.'

Ella nudged Bernie's arm. 'Show Mum the photos of Nana in her wedding dress,' she said. 'She's shown me heaps of times, and she looked like a princess in a fairy tale.'

Meg had to smile. One minute her daughter was tackling social inequality, the next she was colluding in the oppression of women.

'Look, look,' said Ella, pointing.

The only image on the page: Gloria with pale hair down to her waist, and wearing a loose, long white dress. Loose, no doubt, to make the bride look respectable. Pure. These days, out-of-wedlock children were flower girls or pageboys, proudly displayed in parental arms.

'Isn't she beautiful?' Ella said.

'Yes. She is,' Bernie said. 'She was. Gorgeous.'

Gorgeous? Maybe he was once a romantic, Meg thought. Maybe he'd been a great lover. But that was hard to imagine, looking at this careworn man, who was standing now, wearily, offering tea or coffee in a toneless voice. And what would Ella like to drink? Ah. He only had water, he remembered. Meg found herself standing and following him, unsure of what to say.

He opened the fridge, then turned around to face her.

'I phoned Karl,' he said, quietly.

'And?'

'I said it's been a while. The clinic, you understand. He ... he offered to pay.'

'Oh. That's good, isn't it? That's kind of him.'

'I guess so.' He cleared his throat. 'I don't mean to sound ungrateful.'

'And you don't need to feel ashamed.'

He ducked his head, as if she'd delivered a stinging blow.

'I'm sorry, Bernie. That isn't what I meant.'

'But it's true.'

'But it's only money. Some people have more of it than others, and well, the distribution ... it's not always fair, is it? It's often not fair.'

Bernie sighed. 'And it's not always that simple,' he said. 'But thank you.'

He turned back to the fridge, stood at the open door, turned back to look at her again.

'I don't have any milk,' he said.

'I take it black,' she lied.

'I don't have any biscuits, either,' he said.

He sounded so weary, so helpless, that Meg wanted to give him a hug. But he was filling up the kettle now, then turning to her with a sad kind of smile.

'You've gone back to study, haven't you?' he said.

'That's right. Speech pathology. It's hard work. So many new things to learn. But ...'

'You love it,' he said. 'It's written all over your face.'

Hanna had asked to come round for a drink. Drinks at noon? Hanna never drank wine before five o'clock because then she'd soon start drinking at four, she said, then three, then lunchtime, then breakfast. It made Meg remember the ex-wife. And the man who still hadn't called. So what? It could have been worse: they might have gone on a date and discovered they had little in common. Nothing in common. She might have ended up fleeing from the cafe. Ah, but here was Hanna, opening the door without ringing the bell, making herself at home. She was wearing a stunning dark blue dress, fitted at the waist. *She* hadn't put on an ounce in years. She waltzed into the kitchen—tarantella-ed, really—carrying a bottle of red, opening a cupboard for glasses.

'Where's Ella?' she said.

'In her room. Listening to some crash-bang music.'

'Ah. You've banished her.'

'Not exactly banished, Hanna. Anyway, what's with the wine? With the dress? It's spectacular.'

She took the glass from Hanna's hand, watched her pour the ruby red. She took a gulp of wine. Full-bodied. Wonderful. She saw Hanna staring at her.

'You're going to tell me—again—that I look terrible,' she said. 'The short version is that I disappointed Gloria. She's getting better, but ... well, she asked to come and live with me and Ella.'

'Oh, dear. I'm sorry, Meg.'

'I didn't handle it well.'

'I'm sure you were tactful. And anyway, how could you possibly agree?'

This didn't make Meg feel any better.

'Has Karl been to visit her?' Hanna said.

Meg had been waiting for that question. Hanna was predictably, relentlessly, savage about Karl. She'd told Meg before the wedding that *He keeps checking out other women,* but Meg had laughed it off. She was madly in love, or had thought so at the time, and had badly wanted a baby. To be the mother that her own had never been. There were worse reasons, weren't there, for wanting to have a child?

'He's probably too busy with his wedding plans,' she said.

Hanna scowled. 'Don't try to make excuses.'

'But you know he's not close to his parents.'

'*Close* has nothing to do with it, Meg. It's just common human decency for a son to visit his mother when she's so ill.'

Meg shrugged. 'Some people can't handle a breakdown.'

'What does he think Gloria will do? Bite him and draw blood?'

'Well, maybe he's busy with work.'

Hanna snorted. 'If I had a dollar for every man who used that as an excuse to be an arsehole, I'd be able to start my own business.' She looked Meg in the eye. 'Why do you keep defending him? After all he did to you.'

Because I know I was also to blame, Meg thought. And because I know you'll berate me if I find the courage to confess.

Hanna perched herself on a bar stool. Meg perched herself on a bar stool. They both took a slug of wine.

'You could cut Karl a bit of slack,' Meg said. 'Bernie told me he's paying for Gloria's treatment.'

'Big deal.' Then Hanna leaned forward, intent. 'I keep hinting and nudging, so now I have to say it plain. You need to find yourself a man.'

It was Meg's turn to snort. 'You sound just like your friend Cherie.'

Hanna set down her glass. 'She's not a friend, Meg, I told you. My point is that you've become a drooper. A woman who droops her way through life, instead of embracing it.'

A drooper? Meg felt her self-possession flare. 'For your

information, Hanna, I've just met a man. I'm attracted to.'

Hanna narrowed her eyes. 'Well, I can see he's transported you to a state of heavenly bliss.'

'Well ... he was going to call me, and he hasn't.'

'And you can't call *him*?'

'I don't have his number. I met him at Gloria's clinic. We were both visiting. Well, I met him a few days earlier, actually, in a cafe. He spilled coffee all over my shirt.'

'That old trick?'

'It was an accident.'

'Well, there must be a reason he hasn't called,' Hanna said. 'Apart from being a man, I mean. Because you're the loveliest of creatures, you know. Any man who—'

'Enough.'

Meg didn't want a pep talk. Right now, she didn't want any kind of talk about men, and where they might take you, what they might take you for.

Hanna placed a hand on Meg's arm.

'Hey look, I'm sorry about Karl,' she said. 'I just worry that he's still in your head.'

Meg shrugged. 'You'd think I'd be over it after all these years. I'm pathetic.'

'You're not,' Hanna said, her face softening. 'There's no statute of limitations on grief.'

Was it grief, then, after all this time? Or was it the *what if* that might have saved her marriage? What if she'd sat down and talked it through with Karl, instead of railing and cursing and throwing him out? What if she'd tried to imagine how it felt to be cheated into fatherhood? Well, not exactly cheated, since she hadn't secretly stopped taking the pill. But then his words came back to her: *It's only sex, Meg, why are so upset?* As if having sex with a woman who wasn't your wife was no different from eating a gourmet meal or quaffing a glass of good red.

Or what if she'd taken the high moral ground because she'd wanted an excuse to get rid of him? Since she no longer had much use for him: the sower of the seed.

So long ago now, and still these questions rattled in her brain. What had she learned from Freud? That we could never arrive at the truth of our past; that all we had were stories.

She snapped out of it, asked Hanna what they were celebrating. Hanna grinned, like a mischievous child.

'I got my pay rise,' she said.

'Well, good for you, Hanna. Your boss finally realised how valuable you are.'

'Well ... in a way. I asked my friend Gina to tell him she was poaching me, and she'd pay me a hundred more bucks a week. Ha! She couldn't afford that in a fit.'

'Hanna. That's unethical.'

'It was effective.' Hanna raised her glass. 'Here's to women friends,' she said. 'Much better for your health than a tight-arsed boss. Or cheating husbands.'

Ella

She'd been best friends with Lola and Fern since kindy and they called themselves the Elves, because the first letter in Ella, Lola and Fern spelled ELF. Ella had made up the name when they were little, and it was just right for them because ... well, because elves were little. But they didn't have any magic powers, except for maybe the time when Fern stirred curry powder in her brother's milkshake and his skin turned purple. The Elves didn't help any poor shoemakers, either, like the ones in the fairy tale, because they didn't know any shoemakers, although Lola said they could help poor people by donating their old clothes to Vinnies. They all did it together, and it made them feel even more like a band of sisters who *belonged* to each other and would always help each other and not care too much about boys, like a lot of the other girls in the class who talked about them all the time and gave them stupid giggly looks.

But the minute Naomi stepped into Lola's bedroom, everything changed. Naomi looked a lot older than she did at school, wearing a halter top and tiny shorts and bright pink lipstick, her blonde hair loose on her shoulders, not in her usual two thick plaits. She looked a lot older than the Elves, as well, and she called them a gang: *Hi, gang, thanks for inviting me to join your group.* Before anyone could speak, she pointed at the stuffed teddy bear on Lola's bed and said that people started stuffing animals in ancient Egypt and the teddy bear was named after an American president called Theodore and people who loved teddy bears were called arctophiles. Just like that. All this stuff that Ella didn't know.

'*Arktos* is Greek for a bear,' Naomi said. 'And *philos* means love of.'

Lola frowned. 'So I'm an arctophile?' she said.

'Not exactly. You only have one teddy bear, and even though you might love it, you have to love *collecting* them to be an arctophile.' She looked around Lola's bedroom. 'I like your purple beaded curtain,' she said. 'It looks bohemian. You know, creative in an edgy kind of way.'

Lola looked pleased. 'I like your hair like that,' she said.

Ella hated her own hair: thick black curls, like a mop plonked on top of her head.

'My mom likes it this way, too,' Naomi said. 'She says it makes me look more grown-up.'

'I like the way you say *mom*,' Ella said. 'It's like you have a *plom* in your mouth.'

Oh hell. Did that sound rude? But Naomi was laughing, Lola and Fern were laughing, and Ella felt a rush of relief.

'That's why some people think I'm American,' Naomi said. 'But Canadians don't sound so harsh.'

'And they love peace,' Ella said, 'but Americans love war.'

Naomi beamed at her. It made Ella feel a bit tingly.

'What does that even mean?' Fern said.

'Well ...' Naomi gave them a serious look. 'My mom told me all about this war that America was fighting but Canada wasn't because we thought the war was wrong. So lots of American men jumped across the border to my country. We gave them a safe home.'

'Why they were running away?' Fern said.

'Because if they refused to join the army, the government would throw them in prison and keep them locked up for years.'

'But why?' Ella said.

'Because they needed lots of soldiers to win the war,' Naomi said. 'Cannon fodder, my mom calls it.'

'Cannon fodder?' they chorused.

'It's an expression. It's like the powerful people, the government and the generals, they use ordinary soldiers to fire them out of cannons. Not actually, because that would be dumb. It means using soldiers as weapons, because the people who start the war don't care if the soldiers die. They only care about getting more soldiers so they can win the war.'

'That's awful,' Ella said.

'So not right,' Fern said.

Lola suddenly sprang from her bed and did some scissor jumps. Then she stopped, plonked down on the bed again, and they all kind of looked at each other for a bit, like they'd run out of things to say. But then Naomi pulled out her phone, checked out something, shook her head, looked up at the gang.

'Don't you guys have phones?' she said.

Ella felt herself go red. Her friends didn't check their phones when she was around because ... well, they were her friends.

'My mum says I spend way too much time on my phone,' Lola said.

Ella didn't think this was true.

Then they all went quiet again. Until Fern reminded them how they'd be the big kids at school and wasn't that great, only she'd heard there'd be *piles of homework*.

'Homework's pretty useless,' Naomi said. 'The teachers hand it out so they look good.'

'Did your mum tell you that as well?' Lola said.

Naomi shook her head. 'I read it in one of her magazines.'

'But our teacher's going to be cool,' Fern said. 'The year sevens said she gives them half an hour every day to do whatever they like, as long as they stay in the classroom and don't hurt themselves or anyone else.'

'My mom went to talk to her,' Naomi said. 'She wants us to study critical literacy.'

This was too much. It was doing Ella's head in.

'It means learning to think for yourself,' Naomi said. 'It's different from knowing how to read and write. That's called functional literacy.'

They all nodded in a vague kind of way.

'Do you know ...' Naomi shook her head again. 'There are adults who don't know how to read or write because no one's ever taught them. It makes them feel ashamed because people might think they're stupid.'

'But it's not their fault,' Ella said.

'I know,' Naomi said. 'And even worse, people who can't read or write have to pretend. Like, they'll go to a supermarket and tell someone they left their glasses home, so could they please read out the labels for them.'

'That's way bad,' Fern said.

'If you couldn't read or write, you'd never get to be a doctor,' Lola said. 'Like my mum.'

'And my dad,' Naomi said. 'Or a lawyer like my mum. Both of them noble professions. Doing good in the world.'

'My mum's a rotten speller,' Fern said.

Lola did some more jumps. Then she announced it was time for a swim. Ella's heart seized up. This was the moment she'd been trying not to think about. Getting into her bathers. It didn't matter when it was just the Elves, but now that Naomi was here, she felt all knotted up inside, hating her skinny, bony body. Maybe she could pretend she had a stomach ache and didn't feel like swimming. Or maybe she could pretend she'd left her bathers at home.

'Last one in is an idiot,' Lola said.

Ella knew she had no choice.

So they took off their clothes and there was Naomi in a dark blue one-piece. She was tiny in the waist and hips but curvy too, and it made Ella feel even worse. She wished she wasn't so tall, either, so she didn't stand out so much, but Naomi was looking her up and down and smiling and saying *What pretty bathers, Ella.*

Pretty bathers.

'I love the ruffles round the hips,' she said.

Ella took a deep breath. 'I like them too,' she said. 'The huffles round the rips.'

Which made everyone laugh, even though she hadn't meant to make a joke.

'There aren't any rips in a swimming pool,' said Lola, and stretched out her arms like she was doing a dive.

'Or sharks,' Fern said.

'Or sand in the bottom of your bathers,' Ella said.

Naomi laughed. 'You guys are crazy,' she said.

ΔΔΔ

Ella thrashed about in the pool, splashed the other girls—her friends, her gang—and later, sitting on a deck chair, she drank freshly squeezed orange juice that tasted tangy and bright. No-one was saying much anymore, all of them exhausted from thrashing and splashing, their brown legs stretched out, their hair flattened by water. Ella lounged in her deck chair, thinking what a cool day it had been so far: learning all those things from Naomi, swimming so hard that her arms ached in a proud kind of way, Naomi telling her she had pretty bathers, and now this yummy juice, with an umbrella in the glass just for fun. And Nana was getting better, too, her mum said.

Ella realised that Nana hadn't been in her head for a while. Were some people only a night-time thing?

Naomi's voice came drifting into the quiet. 'I'm the only

person here who lives with their dad,' she said.

No-one said a word.

'Do you guys miss not having a dad around?' Naomi said.

The Elves stayed silent.

Then Lola suddenly burst out: *My dad is an arsehole.*

Ella jolted. She'd never heard Lola talk like that about her dad, about anyone or anything. Her mum would have called it *crude.*

Naomi leaned forward. 'That's too bad,' she said. 'Do you wanna talk about it?'

Lola shook her head, looked away, and everyone went quiet again. Ella wanted to speak, say something to Lola, but her friend didn't look in the mood.

'My mum and dad just argued,' Fern said. 'Like, all the time.'

Naomi turned to Ella. 'And what about you?' she said.

Ella swallowed. 'My mum said they just drifted apart. She and my father.'

'You called him *father,*' Naomi said. 'Not *dad.*'

Ella hadn't noticed this before.

'It's because I don't know who he is,' she said.

'Good answer,' Naomi said.

Ella didn't know there'd been a question.

Lola's mum came out onto the deck, carrying a big bowl of fruit.

'You must be starving, girls,' she said, and bent down to place the bowl on the table.

Naomi sat up. 'Ah. Apples, my favourite,' she said. '*Les pommes.* That's French for apple.'

Fern sprang up to reach for some fruit. 'Can you speak French?'

'I've been having private lessons,' Naomi said. 'My mum's taking me to France at the end of the year.'

'Cool,' said Fern. 'Paris has the best boots in the world, really stylish ones like Serena Gomez wears in *Tweens*. And I saw this movie on TV, about some really nice girl in Paris who wanted to make everyone happy.'

'That's *Amélie*,' Naomi said. 'It's *charmant*.'

'And France has cathedrals,' Ella said. She'd seen them on TV as well. 'And there's one great big palace with a room full of mirrors and the biggest bed you've ever seen for one person. The king.'

'It's the Palace of Versailles,' Naomi said. 'And the king got his head chopped off by people who didn't like the monarchy and believed in freedom and equality.'

Ella shuddered. 'He got his head chopped off?'

'The guillotine,' Naomi said. 'It has a really sharp blade that someone drops from a long way up and it slices the person's neck and...whoops, there goes the head, rolling across the ground.'

Ella gasped, and Fern made a noise like she wanted to throw up.

'But Paris is also a civilised place,' Naomi said. 'They have the most beautiful art in the world. Paintings. My mum wants to show me her very favourite painting of apples, by some guy who said he wanted to astonish Paris with an apple.'

'How can an apple be astonishing?' Ella said.

Naomi nodded. 'I know. But my mom said I had to see it for myself.'

More silence. It seemed that Naomi had nothing more to say. It made Ella feel strange in the quietness. It made her feel smaller, yet bigger too: all the talk about soldiers dying and missing fathers and chopped-off heads, even an astonishing apple. None of those things were like purple nail polish or a boy whose hair flicked round his face.

Lola did a few more scissor jumps. Only this time Ella couldn't take her eyes off her, because she'd called her dad an arsehole. She looked exactly the same on the outside, with her strong shoulders from years of swimming. Her eyes were still bright blue and her nose was still cute but now she *felt* so different to Ella. She felt like a sad kind of secret, even though she was smiling as she jumped. Ella wanted to give Lola a hug, ask about her dad, but it wasn't the right place, sitting by the pool, drinking juice with a paper umbrella in the glass. It wasn't the right time, either, with Lola doing jumps as if nothing bad had ever happened.

Ella reached for an apple, took a small, careful bite.

Bernard

He'd found an apple in the fridge, behind a jar of pickles. It must have been there for weeks because it was bruised-black and ugly. And as for feeding unexpected guests! He didn't have apple juice, or any kind of juice, for Ella. He hadn't been able to offer cake or biscuits, either, when Meg tried to lift his spirits. What had she told him? How the distribution of wealth wasn't always fair? But still, Karl had earned his money. He'd studied hard, worked hard to build up his practice, while his father had languished in sales until the selling stopped. A father who'd hinted at the exorbitant cost of the clinic. Karl hadn't blinked. He'd even offered to pay more *if you need it*, offered with a heavy dose of condescension. It was one of the most humiliating experiences in Bernard's fifty-nine years of waning self-respect.

Should he have gone back to uni? He'd been young enough to start again, and there was only one child to support. There was only one child because he was much more careful with condoms and increasingly indifferent to sex. Money was no excuse either: universities were free back then, because the party of the worker had once believed in higher education for all, including the son of a plumber. Was it a lack of energy or drive that had held him back? Or the fear of more humiliation heaped on his mature-aged head? And what was he left with now? Hours of checking online for jobs, but everything was high-tech this and executive that and something called human resources. By the time he moved on to less skilled jobs, he wasn't feeling resourceful at all. He couldn't drive a forklift, or a truck in the mines, and he was far too unfit to crawl into the bowels of the earth.

He knew he couldn't put it off any longer: he had to check the Centrelink website. He made his way stealthily, like a thief, to his laptop, steeled himself for a long and tortuous set of instructions. Sure enough, there was page after page of information, with highlighted titles to trick you into thinking that your future could be managed. He ignored the first link: *What is it like to lose your job?* He didn't want to be reminded of his feelings: anger, gloom and bouts of despair. He scrolled down to the next link: *Coping emotionally*. He found *depression, loss of direction, social alienation.* Grander words. They didn't change the way he felt. Then he came to an injunction: *Be kind to yourself.* Was he meant to book himself into a grand hotel, order a massage, drink champagne? He returned to the section on *Coping*, skimmed through *new skills, effort* and *persistence*, until, hobbling to the finish line, he learned that help was just a phone call or email away.

Oh, he knew he should be grateful. It was taxpayers' money, after all. But confronted by so much sharing and caring, he just couldn't find the strength to hack through the jungle of *How to Contact Centrelink* and *When to contact Centrelink*. He was fifty-nine years old. He'd dropped out of uni. He had a narrow range of skills. The final instruction—to have a pen and paper ready with his details—seemed to him entirely superfluous.

He needed to call the clinic. It was a fortnight since Gloria had been admitted, and she was sleeping every night, it seemed, and sometimes during the day. He was told that sleep was good. It was necessary. She was eating as well, and the voices hadn't come back. That was also good. In sum, the new pills seemed to be working. Her husband wasn't.

He looked around the kitchen: one mug and one spoon in the drying-up thing. A rack. A rack was an instrument of torture. His wife was refusing to see him, talk to him. But how could he blame her, really? When he'd used her to discover the vigour of sex: in the back seat of his car, in her bed when her parents were out. He should have been warned in that house: there wasn't a single book to be seen. But he'd been mad for her, mad for the pleasure she'd given him, and for the pleasure she'd taught him to give. It had made him feel like a man, to make her cry out for more. But she'd been tender too, and gentle, her golden hair down to her waist. The way she'd gazed into his eyes, told him she'd never met a boy like him before.

He drew himself up. He should make some dinner, he supposed. He checked the pantry, spied a packet of Sultana Bran, then remembered that there wasn't any milk. How hard could it be, to drive to the shops, buy a carton of milk, a loaf of bread? Spread margarine on a slice of bread and shovel it into his mouth? He'd read somewhere that margarine was originally a white, pasty colour that made it look like lard, but then the market gurus had come up with a brilliant idea: let's make it look like butter, folks, bright yellow and dreamy-creamy.

Did other people know this? Should other people care?

Gloria

She was eating again. Taking her time, rolling the food in her mouth, swallowing slowly. Orange Creams with her cup of tea. Tangy rock melon, with three plump strawberries in a pretty blue bowl. The juice of those strawberries, even the tiny bumps on their skin, all of it, everything, was delicious. Fourteen days she'd been here. Two whole weeks. Because time had come back to her too, and the colour in her room, it must have been there all along: an emerald green rug on the floor, pink floral curtains, and cheery yellow sunflowers from Meg. Her sorry-I-can't-help-you flowers, left on her bedside table when Gloria was asleep. But how could she still be mad at Meg, when she'd come to see her, tried hard to cheer her up? She'd always known that Meg would help her. She'd always seen the softness underneath the stony face.

Gloria stretched out her body. How wonderful to feel glowing again, in this quiet, special place. That must be costing a fortune. She hadn't thought of that before. So. Bernie must be paying. A fortune.

She didn't want to think about that.

Knock knock.

That couldn't be Meg again? Or one of the neighbours? After all this time. The friends who hadn't once knocked on her door, hadn't even picked up the phone to call her.

'Come in.'

It was Dr Gray again. Connie. Closing the door behind her. She was wearing an orange top that made her face look orange too, or maybe it was her make-up.

'Do you feel up to talking, Gloria?'

'I guess so.'

She could still feel words coming fast into her brain but she didn't feel the need to speak them all. Maybe she was storing up her energy, but what she was storing it up for she couldn't really tell.

The doctor sat down. 'It's good to see you out of bed, Gloria. Not that it's bad to sleep. Sleep helps boost the chemicals in your brain. It's called serotonin.'

Gloria was trying hard to listen. It was strange to think of having chemicals in her brain that seemed to work without her, as if they had a mind of their own.

'I've been walking, too,' she told the doctor. 'In the garden.'

'And how did that feel?'

'It was noisy. All the cars. They jangled my nerves a bit.'

The doctor nodded. 'You've been inside for some time,' she said. 'The outside world can seem too much at first, but you'll get used to it when you go home.'

Home.

'Let me explain your medication first,' the doctor said.

She talked about the old medicine, how it had made Gloria feel worse, but the new one seemed to suit her, it was an older kind. The doctor gave it a name, it sounded like a tricycle. So this new medicine was an old medicine. It was all a bit confusing. But what Gloria really wanted to know, what she needed to know, was the voice she'd heard in her head.

'I thought it was the devil inside me,' she said. 'It really frightened me.'

'And what did that voice tell you?'

'That I'm a bad person, an evil person. Who deserves to die.'

'You know that's not true, don't you?'

'But I'm not religious, doctor. I go to church on Christmas Eve but that's the beginning and the end of it.'

'It's a strange thing, Gloria. Those voices can happen to people who don't believe in God or the devil. We don't really know why.'

Gloria had a think about that. 'It's just like the flamingos,' she said.

'Flamingos?'

'No-one knows why they stand on one leg. Not even the experts.'

The doctor smiled. Gloria liked her smile, it made her look less stiff.

'The mind is still a great mystery,' the doctor said. 'Some scientists call it the new frontier. You know, a place we need to explore. So maybe we can start by you telling me why you think you're a bad person.'

'But I don't think that anymore.'

'I mean, why did you think that before? Maybe you could tell me about your family.'

'My family?'

'Let's start with your mother, shall we? How would you describe your relationship with her?'

Gloria sat up in the chair. It was another question no-one had ever asked her.

'My mum died a long time ago,' she said.

'And how did that make you feel?'

'Well ... I cried for weeks. She never even got to see her grandchild. But ...'

'But what, Gloria?'

'It was a long time ago now, but she was the best mother.'

'How so? The best?'

'Well, she always made me feel loved.'

The doctor nodded. 'And your father? How do you feel about him?'

'Well, he's dead too. He died a year after my mum, and he loved me too. I was his special girl.'

'Really?'

Gloria heard something sharp in the doctor's voice.

'Why did he think you were special?'

'Well, I had two really rough brothers, they were always in trouble with the police. Dad, and Mum, too, they thought I was a godsend because I got a job and gave them money for my board and helped a lot around the house.'

'And where are your brothers now?'

'They're dead.'

'Oh dear. What happened?'

'They smashed their car into a tree. Trev was driving.'

'How terrible.'

'Well … they weren't very nice people. They broke into someone's house and they got time for that.'

'I see.'

'And then they got worse. They bashed an old man in the street and stole his wallet. They got a *long* time for that.'

The doctor shook her head. 'That must have been so traumatic for you. What a dreadful thing to experience.'

'Well, *I* didn't experience it. It was the old man in the street. And when my brothers died, all the neighbours said good riddance to bad rubbish.'

'But were you able to forgive them?'

'Trev and Mick? No. They drove my mum to an early grave.'

The doctor leaned forward. 'There were a lot of deaths in your family, weren't there? Do you think this might help to explain things?'

'Things?'

'Your depression.'

'But I'm sleeping now, and eating. And I don't feel all knotted up inside.'

'That's because the pills are helping you. And it might help you even more to talk about your past.'

Gloria felt herself sinking but she needed to sit up.

'Tell me more about your husband, Gloria. I believe you've made it clear that you don't want him to visit.'

'That's right.'

The doctor nodded again. She was doing that a lot, and Gloria couldn't tell if she was agreeing, or whether she just liked to nod.

'Last time we spoke … you told me that he made you feel stupid.'

'Yes.'

'Have you ever told *him* how you feel?'

Gloria shook her head.

'The way your husband treats you …' The doctor was edging towards something, her eyes narrowed. 'You know that's a form of abuse, don't you?'

'Abuse? But …'

'A person doesn't have to use their fists, Gloria. They can be emotionally abusive. Psychologically abusive.'

Gloria felt the thud of those words in her chest.

'Maybe you need to tell him how you feel,' the doctor said. 'Maybe he doesn't realise he's doing it. I'm not trying to excuse him. I just mean that if you told him how you felt, it might make him think about his behaviour. How he treats you.'

Gloria gave this a long, hard look. 'If I have to tell him …' She sniffed. 'If I have to tell him, it's not really worth it, is it?'

The doctor nodded, slowly. 'I understand,' she said. 'But sometimes people need to have things spelled out for them. If you want things to change, you might need to be the one to—'

'Do the spelling.' Gloria sighed. 'I don't know … the truth is …'

What was her truth, after all? That she was miserable in her marriage. And then it just became easier to stop wanting and hoping.

'I don't want to go home,' she said, and slipped back on her pillow.

'I understand, Gloria. I really do. But—'

'I don't have any choice.'

The doctor raised an eyebrow. 'People always have a choice, Gloria. Don't you think so?'

Gloria could feel the beginnings of a headache. All these questions with no answers.

'So tell me what to do, then,' she said. 'What choice should I make?'

The doctor smiled, showing her pearly teeth. 'I'm not here to tell you what to do, Gloria. I'm here to suggest some options.'

Gloria breathed deeply. 'OK. Suggest some options.'

'Have you thought about living with someone else?'

'I don't have someone else.'

'Don't you have friends?'

'Well, they have their own lives, don't they? And I wouldn't want to be a burden. I want to keep them as my friends.'

'What about living by yourself, then? Would you like living on your own?'

'I don't have any money.'

'Surely your husband—'

'Doesn't earn much. And I wouldn't take it if he did.'

'You don't have a job, do you? I read on your form that you're a housewife.'

Gloria felt something flare inside her. She knew it wasn't good for her nerves but she just couldn't help it. You couldn't swat away your feelings like a fly.

'I've worked all my married life,' she said. 'But no one pays me a thing for all the work I do, the cooking and cleaning and—'

'But your husband supports you, doesn't he? So you can buy food. Things for the house.'

'Well, he's meant to. It wouldn't be fair otherwise.' Gloria would have stamped her foot if she'd been standing. 'I've paid off the mortgage, make sure all the bills get paid.'

'That's wonderful, Gloria. It means that you're capable.'

'Of what?'

'Well ... I mean, you're able to take on responsibilities.'

'Well, of course I am.' What did the doctor think? That she'd spent her whole life floating on one of those blow-up beds in a swimming pool? She wouldn't have done that even if they had a swimming pool.

'And another thing, Gloria. I'd like you to think about this. You've been managing the money, which is often the man's job. It means you're prepared to be flexible, you and your husband.'

'It means he's hopeless with money.'

'No, I meant ... you're not stuck in the usual gender roles.'

Gender roles? Gloria remembered that from TV, and it had made her laugh, thinking gender rolls were something you'd eat for lunch. Only now it wasn't funny anymore.

The doctor looked down at her clipboard, looked up again.

'Have you ever tried visualisation?' she said. 'It means making pleasant pictures in your head. To give you a sense of agency.'

'What's that?'

'It's believing you can change things.'

'Things?'

'Your life, Gloria. Or if you can't change your life, you can change the way you feel about it.'

Gloria had had enough now. Really truly.

'I'm tired,' she said. 'I need a nap.'

The doctor looked like she was going to say more, but then she sprang from her chair, like a jack-in-the-box, and said she'd come back tomorrow with a plan.

Finally, thank goodness, she left.

Gloria's plan was not to see that woman again, with all her questions and her talk about pictures in your head, things to be grateful for. Well, she'd be grateful for an axe right now, she was feeling so worked up all of a sudden. An axe for Bernie and Karl, even Karl, her only child, and for her brothers who'd been so mean and cruel to her mum and dad, to an old man in the street. And that's when she saw it. She saw herself as a girl again, a fighting girl, telling her brothers they were rotten human beings, she was ashamed of them, they'd ruined a man's life and their mum's life and how could they do such a terrible thing. They'd called her names but she didn't care. They'd tried to hurt her but she didn't care, beating her fists against their chests and laughing, because what could they do to hurt her when she had so much rightness inside her? And then she was an older girl who knew what she wanted, so she let boys put themselves inside her. But after, when they called her terrible names, she said she hoped their dicks would drop off. And the girls who called her names, she'd shouted back at them too. But then she'd stopped going with boys after that, even though they still wanted her, because she found out it wasn't her they wanted.

She sat hard and cold in the chair. She wished she hadn't remembered all that, but there it was, there she was. She'd been a fighting girl. She'd met Bernie and become quiet and gentle and soft. But he didn't want that girl either.

What was she left with, then? Who was she left with?

Maybe all she had was herself.

ΔΔΔ

She jumped. It was a phone. Ringing. It was next to the bed with a number to call if she needed anything.

'Hello?'

It was Wendy, sounding upset because she didn't know ... something about Bernie ... she wished Wendy would slow down... *Bernie said you were having an op but then I wormed the truth out of him and how are you holding up, you poor thing?* Gloria said she was feeling much better. Wendy's voice came back again, saying she hoped it wasn't their puppy barking all the time, she hated to think it had made Gloria unwell. They were going to train Gypsy not to bark.

'Are you feeling up to a visit?'

Gloria felt her heart swelling. She thanked Wendy, but she also had to say that she was ready to come home. What choice did she have? Options, the doctor called them. And then, searching for the best words she could find:

'It wasn't your puppy, Wendy. Honest to goodness.'

Mind you, she wouldn't mind if that hound stopped barking. Since she had to go home. She heard Wendy sending her husband's love, and Donna's love, Donna wanted to visit too. And Trudy, lots of love from Trudy, she'd been so upset when she heard. Gloria tried not to cry because she'd already done a lot of that, and she didn't want to upset Wendy. She put down the phone, the kindness still humming in her ears, but then she remembered ... Bernie had told Wendy a lie. He was ashamed of her. The breakdown. Not a single smudge of kindness in his heart. Karl hadn't called her either. Had Bernie told him not to call? Had he told him his mother was crazy?

She needed to get out of bed, move her legs. She pulled back the quilt, slowly rose to her feet, wrapped her cardigan around her shivering body. Why was she cold all of a sudden? She needed to get out of the room and walk in the garden, into the sun, even if the cars were noisy. She could choose that much, couldn't she? She opened the door and peeped outside. She didn't know why she was peeping, no-one was going to hurt her in this careful place. But she took it slowly, step by step, and as she walked she thought she heard sounds. Voices. Singing. She kept on walking and the voices came closer, coming to meet her, the high and the low, mixing together. She stopped. The voices were coming from inside a room. She opened the door slowly, just a bit, and she could see it now, through the smallest chink of light: five people standing in a circle, their heads high, their mouths open wide, making these lovely sounds. She saw a woman waving her arms, keeping the voices together. She saw a woman in a flowing red dress, and two men wearing purple beanies. A plump woman wearing big glasses, and a young girl dressed in bright blue pyjamas. It was the girl she'd seen in the hallway, so thin she could hardly walk, but now she was belting out a song much stronger than her bones. Gloria didn't know any of these people. She didn't know what had made them ill and what might make them better. Maybe she could have got to know them, could even have made new friends. But then, as she listened to their voices ringing out, watched their bodies swaying, she could tell that they wouldn't want to talk, share their problems, get to know. That's what she saw: how they were free in the music, all of them, free from needs and talking and troubles, before the music died.

Meg

She could barely hear the Bartók on the radio, with that insane leaf blower blasting outside. Bob Watson, her anally retentive neighbour, used that damn machine every single week. It was plain crazy, when the leaves kept right on falling, just as they damn well should.

'What's that noise?' Ella said, mooching into the kitchen, opening the fridge.

'A leaf blower.'

'No. What you're listening to.'

'It's not noise, Ella. It's Bartók. A violin sonata.'

'It sounds like someone's in pain and no-one's answering their cries for help.'

Her philistine daughter. Meg had taken her to classics for toddlers, encouraged her to play recorder (badly) and then guitar (even worse). She'd let Chopin and Debussy drift through the house, but Ella had never stopped to listen, had indeed been conspicuously bored by talk of nocturnes, preludes and sonatas. And now she was crunching an apple, as loudly as a sonic boom. Meg felt a stab of irritation, then pulled herself up. It wasn't Ella's fault that the man hadn't called.

Ella stopped crunching, held the apple in front of her, turned it from side to side.

'Do you know about astonishing apples?' she said. 'Some

painting Naomi told us about.'

'Ah. Yes. The painter was Cézanne. He famously said *I will astonish Paris with an apple* because ... well, he wanted to make people sit up. To surprise them with his painting.'

'Of an apple?'

'Yes. So people would be amazed by the beauty of everyday things. I'll show you some pictures, if you like.'

'So how come you know this stuff?'

Meg laughed. 'You'd be surprised at all the things your mother knows.' Her parents had taken her to galleries and concerts. She supposed she should be grateful. 'And ... well ... one time ... many years ago, I wanted to be a painter.'

'Why did you change your mind?'

'I realised I wasn't any good.'

'Well, that's a bit sad. You could still paint now if you wanted to.'

Meg shrugged. 'I don't want to, that's the thing. I don't *need* to anymore.' She turned down the volume, looked around. 'The only thing I need to paint right now is this living room.'

What was the point of dabbling when millions of dabblers throughout history kept producing hideous art? But she was pleased that Ella was taking an interest. Why hadn't she nourished it before? Meg dug out an old art book from her bedroom and found those images she'd studied, tried hard to reproduce. Her favourite had always been *Still Life with Apples*; she was nothing if not predictable. And there it was: a cluster of colourful apples nestled in a bowl.

She sat next to Ella on the sofa, the book on her lap.

'It's called *nature morte*,' she said. 'Nature made still. But see how the painting seems to move. It looks vibrant. Alive.'

Ella looked closely. 'But it's not finished,' she said, and pointed. 'There are bits not filled in.'

'That's right. And see how the edges of the apples are

undefined? They look like they're shifting. It makes them look radiant.'

'And look at the table, Mum. The right and the left side are out of whack.'

'Well spotted. The perspective is wrong.'

'So why didn't he fix it up?'

'He wanted it to look unfinished, so people could see it was a painting and not real life.'

'Why?'

'To show you the power of art. That it can open your eyes to the world around you.'

Ella nodded. 'Well, I like *these* apples,' she said. 'I didn't know they could have so many different colours. And they're so shiny, so beautiful, you wouldn't want to eat them.'

'There you are, then.' Meg smiled, pleased. 'There were also practical reasons for choosing apples. They're easier to paint than other kinds of fruit, and they don't spoil quickly. It could take a long time to do just one painting.'

'That's cool.' Ella sat back. 'I've learned a pile of new stuff today.'

Meg didn't tell her how Cézanne became a tormented, reclusive man. That he saw women as the enemy, intent on punishing his pitiful, quivering self. For the moment, at least, she didn't want to spoil those apples.

'So is this painter still alive, Mum?'

'He died in the early 1900s. So, more than a hundred years ago.'

Ella gave her an eager look. 'I'd like to go to Paris one day,' she said. 'Naomi's going with her mum at the end of the year.'

Meg kissed the top of her daughter's head. 'Maybe *we* can go together,' she said. 'And I can still remember some French. I can teach you, if you like.'

Ella was wide-eyed. 'Really?'

'Yes, really. We can go in a few years, when I've finished my degree and started working again. And first up, I'll take you to the Musée d'Orsay. It has magnificent art, including these apples. I'd like to go back and see them, properly this time.' She laughed. 'When I went, there were so many tourists in front of me that I could only see glimpses of flowers and fruit. A few rooftops.'

It had felt like the bulk of the western world standing in her way, and half of Japan as well. Karl hadn't minded, though: he was six inches taller than his wife.

'Did you go with Hanna?' Ella asked.

'No, with your father. We were on our honeymoon.'

Ella pulled a face. 'You could've waited till I was old enough to go.'

'I promise I'll make it up to you,' Meg said, and put an arm around Ella's shoulder. 'Imagine if I hadn't had you, sweetheart. My life would be so much poorer.'

'But I could have turned out to be horrible, and then you'd be saying, imagine if I hadn't had Ella, my life would be fantastic.'

Meg smiled. 'You're being completely logical. And I'm being sentimental. Sloppy with my feelings.'

Ella moved away. Looked up at her mother.

'Why did you and my father split up?' she said.

Meg tried not to look surprised. She knew this day would eventually arrive, and she wanted to take it calmly.

'Well, like I told you, we drifted apart,' she said. 'We didn't have a lot in common, really.'

'But you went to Paris together. And you decided to have me.'

Meg felt the strain of her smile. 'We were both busy people, Ella. Looking after you, working long hours. We ... well, we just spent less and less time with each other.'

'Why?'

'I guess we didn't feel the need to make the time. We cared

about each other, but we didn't care enough.'

She waited for another question. Nothing.

She felt relieved, and vaguely ashamed at the ease of her dissembling.

ΔΔΔ

Meg had offered to bring Ella for a visit. Since she couldn't offer Gloria a home. As she drove along a mercifully quiet highway, she tried not to think about Gloria going home. It was none of her business, anyway, and besides, she needed to get her head back into study mode, start thinking about her future: lectures and assignments and three more placements, dealing with actual people instead of problems on a page. Where would she be placed next time? Maybe a school, or another hospital? She remembered not knowing whether to laugh or cry when an elderly stroke survivor told her that *My moodle spunkered and I want to go mangling like I used to.* You might learn the science, follow the drill, but you also had to learn that you couldn't always help. That broken couldn't always be mended. Meg sighed, gripped the steering wheel more tightly, hoped she was ready for the challenges ahead. Wished her break had been more relaxing. More fun. When was the last time she'd had uncomplicated, even riotous fun? Was that too much to ask before she knuckled down to study?

'Can I go to Paris this year?' Ella said. Out of nowhere.

'What do you mean?'

'With Naomi and her mum.'

'Did they ... I mean, did they ask you?'

'No. I just thought maybe ... so I don't have to wait a few years.'

'I don't think so, sweetheart. For a start—'

'I've got heaps of Christmas money and some birthday money and—'

'We're talking *big* money here, Ella. It will cost thousands, not a few hundred dollars. And besides, you can't just bowl up and ask people you hardly know—'

'But I know Naomi and I really like her and I know she likes me.'

Meg pictured Ella at the airport, madly excited about stepping on a plane as her mother looked on. She pictured Ella walking the streets of Paris, holding another mother's hand.

'Mum, I—'

'Ella. Why can't you wait? What's the big deal, all of a sudden?'

'I just thought it would be fun.'

'Fun! Great! I'd like some fun, too, for a change.'

She heard how that sounded and immediately felt guilty. Ella wasn't to blame for her mother's choices.

'I'm sorry for snapping at you,' she said. She turned into the car park. 'And thank you for coming to see Nana.'

'It's OK,' Ella said, quietly. 'I shouldn't have asked about Paris. And it's OK about seeing Nana. I know it's the right thing to do.'

Meg's heart melted. Her sensitive, lovely child, how could she not adore her? And when would she stop beating herself up whenever she lost her patience? Ah. An empty space in the car park. Meg glided in, came to a halt, and Ella sprang from the car, slammed the door. No matter how many times her mother told her not to slam the door. Meg stepped out, looked around. Hoping not to see a certain person.

'The garden looks really neat and tidy,' Ella said. 'Like it has a hundred gardeners.'

'Just remember to be quiet, Ella. People here need rest. Peace.'

Meg took her daughter's hand, in order to keep her steady. To keep *herself* steady, just in case. But Ella pulled away from her and looked straight ahead. Making some kind of statement. It only seemed like yesterday that a mother could grab her daughter by the waist and swing her round, but Ella was growing so fast, her dress getting tight under the arms, and her shoes—Damn. Damn and blast. She could see him up ahead. Standing by the entrance. Should she just walk past, avoid his gaze? Pretend not to feel embarrassed? But she could already sense him watching: a tall, lean man in a dark brown shirt, dark blue jeans.

'Hello, Meg,' he said.

He looked embarrassed, too. As well he might.

Ella looked up at him, then back to her mother. Unsure.

'Ella, this is Hal.' Hearing the stiffness in her voice. 'Hal, this is my daughter, Ella.'

To Meg's surprise, he held out his hand and shook Ella's hand firmly, said he was pleased to meet her. She could see Ella watching him closely, as if trying to work him out. That makes two of us, she thought, needing to make a move. But Hal was looking at her daughter now, steadily, carefully, it seemed.

'Are you visiting someone sad?' Ella said. 'With depression, I mean.'

'I'm visiting someone who's getting better,' he said.

'So their brain must be getting fixed,' Ella said.

An amateur psychiatrist, looking pleased with herself. But Meg didn't want to hang around; she certainly didn't want to look desperate. She could see Ella looking Hal up and down, then turning again to her mother, as if trying to make a connection.

'Mum's going to teach me French,' she said.

What was that about, Meg thought.

'Just for the fun of it?' Hal said.

Ella smiled. 'Mum's taking me to Paris, so I have to know how to speak to people there.'

'A great idea,' he said. 'It's respectful to speak the language of the country you're visiting. To try, anyway.'

'I'll have a long time to learn,' she said. 'We're not going for a few years.'

'Then you'll enjoy it all the more. How old are you, Ella?'

'I'll be twelve in a couple of months,' she said, proudly.

Meg gave her daughter a nudge, but it seemed that Hal wasn't done yet, giving Ella a crafty kind of look.

'So here's a riddle for a nearly twelve-year-old girl,' he said. 'Guess what this is?'

He made a tiny wave with one finger. Ella looked puzzled, watched as he made the sign again.

'I give up,' she said.

'It's a microwave.'

'Ha ha.' Ella's eyes were shining with the joke. 'My friends will like that, especially Fern. She wears T-shirts with jokes on them, like *4 out of 3 people struggle with maths.*'

'I had a favourite when I was kid. *I may be wrong but I doubt it.*'

Ella took this in. 'That's very deep,' she said.

Meg told her daughter, firmly, that it was time to go. They'd come to visit Nana, remember? She was still feeling edgy, and a touch resentful, too, of Hal's easy banter with her daughter. But now he was turning to look at her, his blue eyes intent.

'So you know French?' he asked her.

'I did a couple of years at uni, but I'm rusty.'

'Do you know *je suis désolé*?'

'Yes.'

'What about ... *un autre chance*?'

She wasn't sure.

'I have .... there's been ...' He stopped.

She waited.

'*Ma femme,*' he said. 'Formerly.'

Meg could have kicked herself. How could she not have seen this? She'd been insensitive, selfish, thinking only of herself instead of his difficult situation. Not that he'd sounded concerned about his troubled former wife. But still. Things must have happened. Rachel must have needed more help.

'*Je vous aime bien,*' he said.

Meg suppressed an urge to laugh.

'And you're *belle.*'

She did laugh this time. 'And you're very ... *ringard.*'

'*Ringard*?'

'Corny.'

And when would she be free? Tomorrow. Ella was going to Lola's.

'Is tomorrow any good for you?' she said. 'The cafe round the corner?'

'How could I forget?' he said.

She was on the verge of saying: but you did. You did forget me. But he'd said he was sorry. He had a problem. He'd told her that he liked her, told her she was beautiful. And she'd called him *ringard*. She'd been flirting. She wasn't nearly as rusty as she'd thought.

She glanced at her daughter, who was looking from Hal to her mother, then looking back again. Smiling with the newness of it all.

ΔΔΔ

The visit didn't happen because Gloria wasn't in her room. She was having her hair done, according to a spritely nurse, a shampoo and cut in the clinic's salon. Meg wondered if this was a good sign. Was Gloria preparing to look her best because she was going home? But as soon as she closed the door on Gloria's empty room, Meg found herself hoping to catch another glimpse of Hal. In the corridor. Around a corner. Out in the garden. What perverse creatures we are, she thought. Concerned for Gloria one moment, and then, in an instant, fired up with desire. Ella must have sensed it too, peppering her mother with questions as they slipped into the car. *Where did you meet him, Mum? Are you going on a date? And belle means beautiful, doesn't it?*

'Oui.'

Ella gave her a huge grin and Meg looked away, knowing she was smitten with the man. Like the first time she'd laid eyes on Karl. That first kiss which made her catch her breath. Holding hands in the darkness of the cinema; that ordinary, ecstatic gesture. Did Karl ever remember the happiness? Their holiday in Rome, when they'd stood at the edge of an insanely busy road, waiting and waiting to cross, staring at all the chaotically swerving cars, the recklessly weaving motorbikes. Waiting, looking, still waiting. And then out of nowhere, a nun, all trussed up in her habit, had bobbed up beside them, made a conspicuous sign of the cross, strode into the traffic, held up a hand, waved at them to follow. She'd disappeared just as quickly. Karl had cracked a joke about God moving in mysterious ways and they'd laughed, mockingly praised the lord for small miracles. Because they were young and safe and happy, with a great story to tell their friends back home.

Bernard

Every man has a story, he thought, to hand down to his son. But as Bernard stood at the window, where he seemed to stand more and more these days for no discernible reason, he wondered what his story might have been. Had he been more willing to talk, or his son more willing to listen. He might have said he was the child of migrant parents urged to speak English as soon as they disembarked, to eat meat and three veg for dinner, to get excited about Aussie Rules football. He might have said that he'd once been a child who'd felt flurries of snow tickling his face, heard the echoing of church bells on frosty mornings. He might have mentioned his friends: how he'd written to Hans and Klaus, and they'd eagerly written back. Until the letters petered out, then stopped altogether. He could no longer remember who'd stopped, or even what they'd written. Was that the real story of his life, then? People left behind, friends fading with the years?

Then the clinic called. A woman called Sasha, trilling like a bird, informing Mr Newman that his wife was ready to come home. She wanted to be picked up at 2 pm, would that be convenient? Maybe that was protocol, ringing on a patient's behalf, but Sasha sounded too cunningly upbeat to convince him that all would be well. He went in search of the car keys, knowing he should phone Karl. He'd coughed up the money, after all. Karl was *pleased to hear the news, good to know life's back on track*, sounding suave and smooth, as though he were wearing a smoking jacket and holding a martini. And Meg. He must phone Meg, although Bernard suspected she'd already heard. *How wonderful, great news*, sounding just like the breezy receptionist, trying to disguise an uncomfortable truth. And he really should ring Wendy, who'd cornered him one morning at the letterbox, had more or less bludgeoned him to confess. Insomnia, he'd said. Not eating. He'd given Wendy the name of the clinic, and the woman had actually touched him on his arm, actually asked him how he was coping. Not bad, he'd said. Fine, really. Words to that effect.

He left a message on her answering machine, to say that Gloria was coming home. That he was sure she would be in touch.

When was the last time he'd touched anyone? When was the last time he'd given anything to anyone, except advice on sucking up dirt?

He set off early for the clinic. He didn't want to be late, in case Gloria was fretting or confused. She'd been away for sixteen days, after all. But as soon as he pulled into the car park, he could see her waiting at the entrance, staring into the distance. No wave of welcome, no wave at all, her arms jammed by her sides. No smile, not even the tiniest hint. He leapt out of the car, jumped to the ready, hoping to show her ... what was he hoping to show her? That he was trying. But she didn't even look at him, didn't thank him as he hauled her case into the boot, opened the car door for her. He noticed she'd lost weight, and yet the obstinate set of her body made it seem like there was more of her: stronger, a little forbidding. And once seated in the front—at least she was sitting next to him, that was something, wasn't it?—she turned her face away, as if he wasn't there. He wanted to say that he was glad she felt better, but not glad about losing his job. He wanted to say that he'd like a touch of sympathy, if that wouldn't put her out. But instead he told her he was taking a break because business had been rather slow. A two-week break, he added, hoping to prompt a response. But all she did was look through the window, as if row after row of dull brick houses was a source of endless fascination. Should he shout it out and be done with it? I've lost my job, Gloria, and I don't know how we'll manage because the chances of me getting another one are small and I'm feeling small, too, almost invisible. Would that nudge her? Make her scream with frustration?

He pulled up in the driveway. He'd brought her safely home. Home: a garden in need of weeding, and junk mail stuffed in the letterbox. At least he'd cleaned the bathroom and vacuumed the carpet.

He turned off the engine, sprang from the car, hurried to open the door for her. But she was one step ahead of him, brushing him aside, standing with her hands on her hips. Glaring.

'You lied to the neighbours about why I was away,' she said.

He felt his jaw twitching. 'I was trying to protect you,' he said.

'I don't need your *protection*,' she snapped.

Then she headed for the house, without looking back, without saying another word.

ΔΔΔ

All she said that afternoon was *close the curtains, give me your washing, where did you put the TV guide*. Not a solitary *please* or *thank you*. Bernard felt too slapped down to fight back. Then she discovered an empty fridge, fumed at him some more, drove off in a hurry. She returned with laden shopping bags, refused his offer of help with a scornful twist of her mouth. He retreated to the bedroom with a book, until she stormed in and demanded that he take the car to the garage, it was leaking oil, she said, didn't he know about leaking oil? Didn't he know about anything?

At dinner she ladled out the food, then munched away in silence. She polished off everything on her plate, then ordered him to move the TV into Karl's old room. She made up the bed in that room. After a restless night in which he heard her snoring in the distance, he woke to see her standing at the letterbox, chatting with some neighbours. Then she disappeared, presumably into those neighbours' houses, drinking tea, eating cake. Would she denounce her heartless husband because he hadn't come to see her? Would the neighbours denounce him, too? Cast him flinty glares if he ventured outside? He slunk back to his armchair, retreated to his magazine. He read about a gang of feral youths in some New South Wales border town, a man's front yard strewn with rotting prawn shells, smashed eggs, newspapers, empty bottles, used sanitary pads. He read about a critic re-reading *The Female Eunuch*. Bernard hadn't even read it once, although he did remember seeing the author on TV: statuesque, imperious, denouncing the world of brutish men.

That afternoon Gloria fronted up to him and declared that he'd been *sprung*. She had a feeling something was up, she said, so she'd called the shop and discovered he'd *got the sack*. Bernard was aghast, hugely embarrassed. *How are we going to pay the bills, then?* she said, but it didn't feel like a question. She'd checked their bank account: how long did he think they could manage with no money coming in? How could they pay for the clinic when the Mastercard bill came through? Had he bothered looking for a job? Had he bothered contacting Centrelink? Did he even *know* about Centrelink? On and on she went, and she was right, and so wrong, because she could have said how awful, Bernie, how terrible, to be cast aside like that. She could have said. But instead she just shook her head and walked off to Karl's old room. Maybe she railed against him in that room. Maybe she sat staring at the walls. Maybe she thought about leaving him.

That night he made himself dinner from a can: sad spaghetti circles drowning in some kind of sauce. He couldn't bring himself to eat a mouthful.

He showered, brushed his teeth and slumped into bed. And as he threw off the sheet in the hot, sticky night (no turning on the air con anymore), he asked himself the question he'd been asking since Gloria came home: what had they done to her in the clinic? He'd been informed about new pills, and Mrs Newman's progress; the doctor, at least, had shown him some respect. But surely no pill could explain her cutting disdain, her withering disregard. The eyes that told him he was worthless.

He hadn't dared to ask her about her treatment, or how she was feeling now. He felt too cowed to ask her anything.

He turned over in bed, turned back again. He had nothing else to do but wait for the darkness in a house that at least was fully paid for because his wife could manage money. Should he tell her that? Should he say: you've always been good with money, Gloria, and I'm sincerely grateful for that. Should he tell her how useless he felt, having lost the only thing that had given him a smidgeon of self-worth: ringing up the sales and bringing home a wage.

Would any kind of talking offer some kind of cure?

Meg

Would they talk, she wondered. Gloria and Bernie? As Meg drove along the highway, ignoring the honking behind her when she stopped at orange lights (at what point in history did an orange light mean plant your foot on the accelerator and not give a stuff about killing other people), she found herself hoping they could make some kind of start. Have an honest heart-to-heart. The conversation she'd refused to have with Karl because she couldn't, wouldn't, try to understand. Oh, give over, Meg. What it did matter, after all these years, when she was open to meeting a different kind of man. A man who'd been kind to her, who'd enjoyed talking with Ella, had taken a genuine interest.

Meg turned to glance at her daughter, who was looking decidedly grumpy.

'It's a shame Fern can't make it,' she said. 'What's the matter with her?'

'She's got some kind of bug. Vomiting and stuff.'

'That doesn't sound good.'

Ella shrugged.

'But you and Lola will still have a great time.'

Ella shrugged again. What was wrong with the child, Meg thought. She and Lola had been best buddies for years, and they were off to Cat Haven tomorrow, to choose a kitten. Maybe she was getting her first period. But wouldn't she have told her mother, asked for some reassurance? Not like Meg's mother, who'd merely handed her a booklet called *You're a Young Lady Now*, full of stern advice about personal hygiene and keeping your distance from boys.

'Are you OK, sweetheart?'

'I'm just thinking.'

'About anything in particular?'

'Just stuff.'

Meg slowed down at Audrey's driveway, knowing it was pointless to push her daughter any further. Ella hadn't asked about *the date*, either, with a man who'd made her laugh, told her mother she was beautiful. And no goodbye, either, as Ella stepped out of the car, not one backward glance. So why the cold shoulder, Meg thought. And would it get worse once the hormones kicked in harder? There was nothing to do but have a few quick words with Audrey, who was still *recovering*, she said, from a patient who wanted to reduce the size of her thighs.

'Perfectly normal thighs,' she said. 'Honestly Meg, what could I say to the woman? Forget about a referral, try thinking about media manipulation. Try thinking, full stop.'

Meg laughed. 'Did you actually say that?'

'More or less.' Audrey leaned on the car door. 'But she insisted, so I referred her to a surgeon with zero people skills. An emotional zombie, really.' She shook her head. 'More and more women want cosmetic surgery these days, noses and chins and tummy tucks. Men too. I had a guy last week, all of twenty-five years old, wanting botox to make him look younger.'

She shielded her eyes from the sun. She looked tired. Fed up. Her red hair ragged at the ends.

'And did I tell you about my ex?' she said. 'Last week he sent me a photo of his new girlfriend.'

'You're kidding me!'

Audrey laughed. A trying-too-hard kind of laugh.

'And I do mean *girl*,' she said. 'Barely over the age of consent by the looks of her. He even wrote on the back, letting me know what a great time they're having. *Me and my honey lounging by the pool in Phuket*. Pathetic, isn't it?'

'Did you tell him where to get off?'

Audrey laughed again. 'No, I just tore up the photo and flushed it down the loo.' Her eyes suddenly brightened. 'You're looking lovely, Meg. Doing something special?'

'Just catching up with an old friend.'

Because it was just a cup of coffee. A conversation. And because Audrey's ex was clearly a nasty piece of work. Any mention right now of meeting a man would have sounded like sleeping with the enemy.

'You know, I almost feel sorry for the guy,' Audrey said. 'He doesn't mean to be cruel, he just has the brain of a twelve-year old boy.'

'You're being very generous.'

'I'm being a scientist,' Audrey said.

As Meg started up the car, waved goodbye, she couldn't help thinking of the greeting on the card: *Lounging by the pool with my honey*. Meg had never liked Audrey's ex, a smooth-talking corporate guy with free-market hands. He'd once glided those hands around her hips and she'd jumped back, sent a tray of canapés hurtling to the ground. She told herself to focus on the Sunday afternoon traffic: people driving to shops and cafes, a movie, a glass of wine. Perth, the land of *no worries*. It ought to be the national mantra. She checked the time on the dashboard. She didn't want to be late, in case Hal thought she could take it or leave it. Him. But she didn't want to be early, either, in case she looked too keen. Twenty minutes to the hour. She was going to be *much* too early. Maybe she'd have trouble finding a parking space, in a trendy suburb jostling with cafes, bookshops, boutiques and gift shops, a pub, at least three wine bars. But no, she found a spot right away, next to the trendy deli. Maybe she could walk in, kill some more time, pretend to check out the avocados.

She paid for her ticket. Walked slowly to the cafe. She checked her watch. She was now fifteen minutes early. She could window shop for a bit, but what was the point, really? She was here now. She might as well go inside. Maybe he was early, too. But no. He wasn't there. She would have noticed him anywhere. She found a spare table in the corner, grateful for the relative quiet, the low hum of conversation, faint music in the background. So what if it was the usual *Four Seasons*? At least it wasn't heavy metal, or the theme song to *Chariots of Fire*. She checked her phone again: ten minutes to the hour. She didn't want to look bored or put out, so she rose to choose a paper from the rack. She could read either *The Australian*, full of right-wing, white-man diatribe, or the *West Australian*, full of 'Dog bites jogger' and first-world gripes about the heat. She chose the *West* as the less offensive, sat down at the table, began to read. Could take in nothing much except the usual reports on the weather and some scandal about a football player … drugs … no excuse … coach disappointed … Why was she even reading this? She stared through the window at an entwined couple, conspicuously gay. She saw a couple of fluffy dogs on leads, and streams of people checking out their phones.

She felt a hand on her shoulder, swung around.

'I'm so sorry,' he said, sitting down, red-faced. 'I got caught up and—'

'You're not late. In fact, you're right on time.'

He smiled, relieved. Had she looked impatient? And should she ask him how his ex-wife was doing? She knew nothing, really, about the experience of addiction. But she didn't want to seem nosy, either. But then, if she didn't ask, would he think she didn't care?

He leaned forward, his eyes suddenly intent.

'Did you know,' he said, 'that only two percent of the world's population has green eyes?'

What was he on about?

'You're in elite company,' he said. 'With those eyes.'

Was he a little too smooth?

'They used to burn green-eyed women at the stake,' he said. 'In medieval times. People thought they were witches.'

'I wouldn't call that thinking,' she said. 'I'd call it misogyny.'

His face fell. 'I'm sorry. That was dumb.' He gave her a strained smile, folded his hands on the table. 'So. Your old business card. You used to work for the ATO. Did you leave because—'

'It was tedious. Pointless. Frustrating. Answering endless complaints.'

And here she was, complaining.

'And now you've gone back to study?' he said.

'Yes. A degree in speech pathology.'

'Ah. Is that—'

'Interesting? Yes.'

What else was she meant to say? That she'd be called a speech-language pathologist in America? A speech-language therapist in the UK?

He scratched his head. 'I'm making a mess of this, aren't I?' he said.

But I'm not helping either, she thought. She was being a combative cow. Maybe that was her nature. Karl had certainly told her so, when she'd kept pushing him away.

Hal gave her an awkward smile. 'The truth is, I'm out of practice,' he said. 'It's been years.'

Meg laughed, without meaning to. 'Have you been living in a monastery?'

'I didn't say I'd been celibate. I mean ... I haven't talked to a woman, not properly, since my divorce. Six years ago.'

There was something in his voice—an edge of regret, perhaps—that made her think he was sincere. And wasn't it the voice, and not the eyes, that revealed the truth in a person's heart?

'Well, *I'm* out of practice, too,' she said. 'If that's any consolation.'

He looked down at the table, then up into her eyes. 'It's difficult, isn't it?' he said.

'The first date?'

'I guess so,' he said, awkward again. 'Yes. A first date. If that's what you want it call it.'

Meg drew herself up. 'Well, I'm not looking for a casual fuck,' she said.

Out before she could stop herself.

Hal jolted. Stared at her. 'You don't hold back, do you?' he said.

'I'm not asking you to marry me.'

As if that made it any better.

'I'll keep that in mind,' he said, straight-faced.

She sighed. 'I'm sorry,' she said. 'It's just ... well, like you, I haven't been involved with anyone, not seriously, since my divorce. Eight years ago. And I have a daughter to care for.'

'Who you need to keep picking up.'

'Twice since I met you.' Meg smiled. 'And if anyone tried to hurt her, I'd take a kitchen knife and stab them to death.'

'I take it she's the most important thing in your life?'

'Absolutely.'

He nodded. 'She seems like a good kid.'

'Good?'

'Interesting, I mean. You know. Smart. Funny. And curious about the world.'

Was he laying it on a bit thick? Was he one of those men who wormed his way into your bed by singing the praises of your child?

'And after your daughter?' he said. 'What's important to you?'

'My studies. And then a job, if I can find one after I graduate.'

'So not much time for a social life?'

She smiled, tried to look casual. 'A friend told me I should get out more. But ... well ... it sometimes feels like ... you know, too much of an effort.' She flinched. 'I'm sorry, that sounds rude. I don't mean that ... *you* ... are an effort.'

He was watching her closely. She noticed tiny silver flecks in his dark blue eyes. She looked away, looked down, and saw that his hands looked rather red and shiny. Almost as if he'd polished them. She wondered if he had some kind of skin complaint, the kind of detail that didn't feature in her romantic lying-down novels.

'I gave them a good scrub,' he said. He'd caught her looking. 'They get a bit dirty with grease.'

Meg felt oddly touched by this gesture. As though he was a boy, keen to spruce himself up, make a good impression.

'Did you always want to be a mechanic?' she said.

He shrugged. 'Not really. I was meant to take over the farm but I wanted to go to uni.'

'So what did you study?'

'A bit of French and philosophy. Years ago now.'

'But how does a farm boy ...' *A farm boy*? Who did she think she was? 'I mean to say ... were your parents readers? I mean ...'

He laughed. 'You've got me,' he said. 'I have to confess. They shipped me off to boarding school when I was twelve, where I promptly fell in love with the French teacher.'

'Ah. The schoolboy crush.'

'It was her voice, more than anything,' he said. 'She could even make the word *cauliflower* sound romantic. Only I can't remember what it was.'

Meg knew it was *choufleur*. She also knew that the verb to wish— *souhaiter*—sounded like *sweat*.

'My teacher sounded a bit like you,' he said. 'It's a classical music kind of voice.'

Meg laughed. 'You mean a snob's voice?'

'No. Not at all.' He looked her straight in the eye. 'And you're sitting here with me, aren't you?' he said.

She shuffled in her chair. 'So why did you study philosophy?' she said. 'And I don't mean because you grew up on a farm and so by definition, you must be an ignorant bumpkin.'

He grinned. 'The sheep seem to like the farm,' he said. 'Although sheep are pretty dumb animals.'

So, he had a sense of humour. That was something, wasn't it?

'Studying philosophy was a mistake,' he said. 'I thought I was going to a politics lecture but ... well, it all came to nothing in the end. I was out of my depth, big time. And I was too busy falling in love with another student. That didn't last long either, because I was ... well ... eighteen years old and selfish. A shallow prick.'

Meg smiled. 'Just the eighteen will do,' she said.

He smiled in return. 'Anyway, enough about the man,' he said. 'Tell me more about you.'

'Ah. You've read the book,' she said.

'The book?'

'The dating guide.'

Hal frowned. 'Hey, I'm doing my best here,' he said. 'And ... well ...' His face softened. 'I really do want to know about you. Honestly.'

Meg knotted her fingers. 'I'm sorry,' she said.

They'd spent the last five minutes saying sorry to each other, sitting in silence now, looking at each other, looking away, looking back.

'So tell me about your name,' he said. 'Flynn. Is that Irish?'

'From way back when. The great-greats, I think, or maybe even greater. I've never even been to Ireland. Maybe I will one day.'

'So you don't feel any Irish in your blood?'

'No. I don't feel Australian, either. I ... well, I don't feel like I belong to any place. I envy people who do, but I've never found it in me. Do you feel Australian? Whatever it is we're meant to feel?'

'It's certainly not about working the land,' he said. 'And it's the miners working the land now, anyway, and the people who keep voting against their interests.'

'So you're political?'

'More cynical than political.'

Was this a sign of something deeper, she thought, something more disturbing? She wanted to probe a little further, but she also had to challenge what he'd said.

'Cynicism is easy,' she said. 'And it doesn't change things for the better.'

'You're right. But it's also useful. You're never disappointed if you expect the worst in people.'

Meg studied his face. Was he being serious, or exaggerating for effect? And what kind of effect was he after?

'I can be cynical, too,' she said. 'But I don't want that to define me. Going back to study has given me a sense of purpose. And having a child ... I want her to feel that sense of purpose too. And to believe that life can be joyful.'

'That's an excellent philosophy,' he said.

She tossed her head, just a little. 'You're making fun of me,' she said.

He startled. 'Not at all. Not a bit. I admire that, I really do. And I'm sure your daughter will be grateful.'

Was he a father? Or wanted to be a father? Had he failed as a father? But just as she was about to ask that simple, complicated question—*Do you have children*—she heard a phone ringing.

Hal grimaced. 'The Mexican Hat Dance,' he said. 'I still haven't changed the ring tone.'

'Please answer it, if you like.'

'Thanks. It might be ...'

Rachel. As if he was on high alert.

She watched him checking his phone. Saw him frown. He looked up at her, almost sadly, she thought. Weighed down.

'I need to go,' he said. 'I'm sorry.'

'But aren't you going to answer?'

'I'll just send her a quick message. Then ... I'll have to be off. I'm sorry.'

'You've already said that.'

And he'd told her that he liked her. He was thoughtful. Forthright. Charming.

'Shall we do this again?' he said.

'If you'd like to.'

'I asked *you*,' he said, and cleared his throat. 'I mean ... Is that OK? You'll let me call you?'

He sounded ... not exactly pleading. A little anxious.

'You make it sound like I'm calling the shots,' she said.

He looked away, looked back into her eyes. 'Maybe you are,' he said.

He rose from the table, pulled back the chair, winced as it scraped the floor. Meg rose too, flustered: everything had changed in an instant. He gave her a small smile but kept standing on the spot. No goodbye kiss, no offer of a hand, just an awkward half-wave, a muttered *See you soon*. He turned around, but then turned back to face her.

'Say hi to Ella,' he said.

'Oh. Sure. I will.'

'You're lucky,' he said.

'Lucky? You mean ...'

'I mean I would have liked a child,' he said. 'But I could never find a woman who wanted one. Not with me, anyway.'

Then he turned on his heels and headed for the door.

Meg stood stock-still. Puzzled by this unexpected, heartfelt confession. By his honesty, his irony, his shifting, awkward moods. What on earth was she to make of him?

Dean had been so much easier.

Ella

She knew it wouldn't be easy, but all the time they were eating popcorn, trying on each other's shoes and listening to the Black Eyed Peas, Ella kept wanting to ask Lola about her arsehole dad. Just the word *arsehole* made her shudder. She wished she'd phoned Lola before, but she didn't have her own phone, did she? She could hardly ask her mum, either: hey Mum, can I borrow your phone, take it to my room and ask Lola to tell me all about her rotten father. And now Lola was dancing around to the music, but she was maybe dancing a bit too crazy, too hard. Then she suddenly stopped, flopped down on the bed, picked up her teddy bear and gave it a squeeze.

'Remember what Naomi told us?' she said. 'About teddy bears?' She patted the bear's head, gave it another hug. 'Do you think she's ... you know ... a show-off?'

Ella took this in. 'Oh. Well, I don't think so,' she said, slowly. 'She just knows a lot of stuff we don't.'

'But she doesn't have to tell us all the time,' Lola said. 'I mean, I feel like I'm in school when she talks.'

Ella wanted to stand up for Naomi, but she didn't want to upset her best friend.

'She *can* go on a bit,' she said. 'But at least ... well, it's about important things, isn't it?'

Lola looked up at her, her big blue eyes kind of brimming.

'Do you like her better than me?' she said.

'Lola. No!' Ella couldn't believe it. 'We've been best friends forever.'

Lola shrugged. 'I don't think I'm all that interesting,' she said. 'I just swim a lot and jump.'

Ella had never heard Lola say stuff like this before.

'But you're the best friend anyone could have,' she said. 'You're always kind to me and you never laugh if I make mistakes and you give me hugs when I don't even ask for them. And I know I can always trust you.'

Lola smiled, feebly.

'Besides, look at me,' Ella said. 'I am definitely the world's most boring person.' She dug Lola in the side. 'We can be the Boring Twins, you and me.'

Lola laughed. She put her teddy bear down and picked up another stuffed toy, a monkey with a drum that she'd had since she was a baby. It used to be fluffy but now its fur was all thin, like it had some kind of disease, and its name was Ali Bongo. Ella had always loved Ali Bongo, but her mum always had a word for noisy toys: *No*.

'Mum loves this toy,' Lola said. 'She told me the noise used to drive my dad *demented*.'

Then she burst into tears, just like that, tears filling her eyes and rolling down her cheeks. Ella froze. She'd seen Lola crying before, but it was always about little things, like getting a bad haircut or a really bad mark in maths. But now she was sobbing like she'd never stop. Ella put an arm around her.

'My dad sent Mum a photo,' Lola said. 'Of his girlfriend.'

'Oh. That's ...'

Lola sniffed. 'I know. I saw Mum ripping something up and chucking it down the loo and I asked her what was going on. So she told me. She said he was just showing off. Like he was saying, see, I've got this hot new chick, ha ha.'

'She *said* that?'

'Not exactly, but that's kind of what she meant.' Lola sniffed again, took a deep breath. 'She didn't call him an arsehole, either, but … she said he cheated on her when they were married. More than once.'

'Oh. That's awful.'

'I know. I used to like him but now I hate him. Mum says there's no point hating him but I do. And I'm glad he lives way over in America so I won't have to see him much and pretend to like him.'

Lola looked up into Ella's eyes.

'Promise you won't tell anyone,' she said. 'Mum said not to tell.'

'Of course not. I won't. Ever.'

'Not even Fern.'

'No. No. I promise.'

Lola flopped back on her bed, and Ella flopped down beside her. She pictured Lola's mum tearing up the photo. She imagined the hurt in her eyes.

'I'm sorry about your mum,' she said. 'It must be really sad for her.'

Lola took Ella's hand. 'Mum says she's better off without him.' She gave Ella's hand a squeeze. 'I'm really glad she told me, even if it was awful. She trusts me. She treats me like a grown-up.'

Ella stayed quiet.

'Thanks for listening,' Lola said. 'It was just all building up inside me and I had to tell you. But you won't tell anyone, will you?'

'I made a promise, Lola. You know I absolutely won't tell.'

They kept holding hands and Ella hoped Lola was feeling better. She *sounded* better, and she wasn't crying anymore.

'Does *your* mum tell you things like that?' Lola said.

'Like what?'

'About your dad.'

Ella wasn't sure what to say. What did she know about her parents, anyway?

'You said your mum and dad drifted apart,' Lola said. 'Like they were far apart in the ocean and didn't have the energy to swim back to each other.'

Ella felt something tighten in her chest. 'Mum said they didn't care enough about each other,' she said.

Lola turned to look at her. 'Like, they just stopped loving each other?'

'I guess so.'

'So how long were they married?'

'A few years. I don't even remember them being married.'

'A few years? That's not long to stop caring, is it? My parents were married for *eight*.'

'Well, it can't have been that bad,' Ella said. 'Mum never says anything awful about him.'

But she'd seen his eyes go all greedy when he stared at the girls in their bikinis. She'd seen it and hadn't told Lola or Fern. She hadn't told anyone. Maybe it was like Lola's secret, hidden inside you, and you didn't know how to unlock it. Maybe her father had cheated on her mum. Maybe he was an arsehole too, even though her mum hadn't said. She felt Lola's hand, warm and soft, and it made her feel a bit teary and weird. Lola's story, the girls on the beach, her father's eyes: all of it made her feel sick. She found herself saying she was sorry but she wasn't feeling well all of a sudden and maybe she had the same bug as Fern and she was honestly sorry but she needed to go home.

ΔΔΔ

Her mum started the engine, turned to her with a smile.

'Not feeling too well, sweetheart?' she said, in her kind-mum voice. It was SO annoying.

'I hope you're not getting Fern's bug.'

Ella shrugged.

And then: 'You and Lola didn't have an argument, did you? You can tell me.'

Well, maybe you can tell *me*, Ella thought. She looked through the window, saw a little kid scooting down the footpath on one of those scooter things where you put one foot on the footpath and pushed like crazy. She couldn't see the point.

'What's wrong, Ella? Something must be bother—'

'You won't tell me why you split up. Got divorced.'

Her mum kept her eyes on the road. 'But I did tell you. I said we grew apart. I said we didn't care enough to stay together.'

'But it doesn't happen for no reason.'

Her mum looked in the mirror, like she was worried about some car crashing into her, but she didn't say a thing.

'Did you just get bored or something?' Ella said.

'Yes. Something like that.'

'What do you mean, *something like that*?'

'Well, it's hard to explain.'

'Try, then.'

'Why are you snapping at me? I don't understand.'

'Because you're always explaining things to me about all kinds of stuff but you won't tell me ...' She stopped. She had to say it. 'He kept looking at girls. When we went to the beach, he just kept looking at all the girls in their bikinis. It was gross.'

'Well ... a lot of men do that, sweetheart. They ... they just like to look.'

'Well it's still gross. And now he's getting married again and what will *she* think if he keeps perving on other women all the time?'

'Don't say *perving*. It's—'

'So did he have a girlfriend when you were married? Did he?'

'No. Look. I don't know.'

'How can you not *know*? How can you—'

'Ella, people can do all kinds of things you have no idea about, even people you think you know well. You'll find this out when you get older.'

'When I'm older. When I'm older. Why can't you tell me now?'

'Because there's nothing more to tell.'

But how could there be nothing when her mum kept edging around, saying stuff about *people* and not about her father. When the truth was perving on girls, even if her mum said a lot of men liked doing that. But her father wasn't a lot of men, and how could he even do that when she was sitting right next to him, shivering in her towel, and he hadn't even noticed she was shivering.

She was silent now, watching other cars flashing by. All the people driving home or off to see a friend or heading for a movie, even a hospital. She would never know where they were going or what they were planning or thinking or feeling, and this made her feel sad in all her bones.

'Would you like to go with Lola tomorrow?' her mum said. 'She's getting a kitten, isn't she?'

Ella sank back in her seat. Why bother answering a dumb question like that?

ΔΔΔ

Ella was curled up in bed, feeling drifty and heavy at the same time. It was a feeling she couldn't really name. And even if she could, would it be the same feeling for her mum? For Lola or Fern? And how would you even know? Even if someone said *I know just how you feel,* how could you be sure they felt the same way as you? It wasn't like two friends wearing a red dress and saying *we're dressed in the same colour* and you could see it right in front of you.

She heard a knock on the door. She said to come in.

'Are you hungry, Ella? Do you want some lunch?'

Her mum, standing in the doorway, her face all creased up.

'Not really.'

'We could go out for a bite to eat. Somewhere special.'

'No thanks. I'm ... I don't know ...'

Her mum stepped into the room, then looked up at the few books stacked between the flamingos. She pulled down a big fat book that Ella hadn't looked at for years.

'Remember this, Ella? *Five Hundred Poems for Little Kids*. I used to read them to you. Every night. Or when you were feeling unwell.'

She sat down on the bed and turned a few pages. She read out a poem about Dr Foster who went to Gloucester and stepped in a puddle right up to his middle. Ella liked the way *puddle* and *middle* didn't rhyme because it made Dr Foster's day sound even messier. Then her mum read out a much longer poem about an owl and a pussycat and Ella liked the way the Pussycat called the owl an *elegant fowl* because the two things didn't go together.

'You used to love these funny poems,' her mum said. 'And I know some great ones, too. Some limericks.'

And then, just like that, she began: 'A creature of charm is the gerbil, its diet's exclusively herbal. It grazes all day on bunches of hay, passing gas with an elegant burble.'

'It's a fart poem,' Ella said.

'But it's clever, don't you think? And you don't expect it to end with passing gas.'

'So why do adults think kids always love fart jokes?'

Her mum smiled. 'I know another limerick,' she said, and took a deep breath. 'There was a young man from Japan whose poems nobody could scan. When told this was so, he answered *I know. But I always try to get as many words in the last line as*

I possibly can.'

Ella laughed out loud. That was much cleverer than the fart poem. It was totally hilarious.

Her mum put the book back on the shelf but when she turned around, her face had gone all creased again. 'I want to say something else,' she said. 'About your father and me.'

She sat down on the bed again. Ella didn't move in case her mum changed her mind. About *something else.*

'We made each other unhappy, Ella,' she said, her voice all quiet.

'But *why*?'

'Well ... we wanted different things. From our marriage.'

'Like what?'

Her mum put her hand on Ella's cheek. Her skin felt really warm.

'Your father did cheat on me,' she said. 'But I don't want you thinking terrible things about him. It was my fault too, because I didn't spend time with him. I ... well, I neglected him.' She brushed Ella's hair back from her forehead. 'You won't understand this, but I want to tell you now. Wanting sex is a very powerful thing for some people. It can make them do things that can hurt other people.'

Ella felt a sinking inside her. Was *this* what she'd come to understand about sex? Not like *The Bold and the Beautiful*, but for real people.

Her mum pulled back the sheet, slipped into bed, and they snuggled up close.

'I want you to know that it wasn't your fault,' her mum said. 'Your father and I splitting up had nothing to do with you.'

'But I never thought that, Mum. Ever.'

'OK. That's good. That's important. But ... well, I don't want you to be unhappy about it. That's all that matters to me.'

'But I'm not unhappy, honestly. Well, I was a bit, but only

because you wouldn't tell me the truth.'

She felt trusted and safe and calm, lying next to her mum.

'I'm happy with just you,' she said. 'And I don't miss my father at all. But ... well, I'll keep going to Sydney if you want me to.'

Her mum snuggled in closer. 'Is it really so bad, Ella? You must tell me.'

'It just feels ... I mean, he stops work and takes me out but ... well, he tries so hard to *entertain* me but I don't feel like it's *me* he's entertaining. If that makes any sense.'

'It does, yes.' Her mum drew away, looked Ella in the eye.

'You don't have to keep going if you don't want to,' she said. 'Your father can come here instead. He's only been a couple of times, hasn't he?'

'You won't mind if you have to see him too?'

'No, not at all. You might have to go to Sydney for the wedding, though. I'm sure he'd like that.'

Ella looked into her mum's soft, kind face. She wished she had her mum's beautiful dark green eyes. The only thing her father ever gave her was a big hooked nose.

'Will he invite you, too?' she said.

'I don't think so. But I won't mind that either. I stopped loving your father a long time ago, and when that happens ... well, a lot of things don't seem to matter anymore.'

'Does that mean *you're* unhappy?'

'Not a bit. I'm fine, I really am. And you're my wonderful girl. You mean more to me than anyone else in the world.'

She felt her mum sighing deeply.

'What made you ask me?' she said. 'About the breakup?'

I made a promise, Ella thought, and a promise is for a lifetime.

'I've just been thinking about things,' she said. 'People things.'

She lay quiet and still and felt the two of them breathing, and the more they breathed in and out, in and out, the more they did it in time. Deep, slow breaths, steady and calm, warm and cosy. Would she keep visiting her father? She didn't know. She only knew that she didn't need him, not like she needed her mum. Loved her mum. Because she always knocks on my door, Ella thought. She tries to help me understand. She makes me laugh.

'Did you really read me five hundred poems?' she said.

'I did.'

'Why?'

'Because you asked me.'

Gloria

She'd left Bernie sitting in his chair, reading, as usual. Well, she wasn't going to sit around watching his miserable face, was she? She'd already prepared dinner and some hardboiled some eggs for tomorrow's lunch. She'd cleaned the cooktop and the kitchen cupboards, and now she'd like a bit of fun, thanks very much. But of course, she didn't say that to the neighbours, sitting in Donna's house and drinking tea, nibbling on Wendy's scrumptious lemon cake. She didn't tell them about all the sadness she'd been feeling for years. She just kept having trouble sleeping, she said, and it made her brain go all wonky, so then she couldn't eat either. So, yes, she'd lost weight, and yes, what a good idea, she could give herself a treat and buy some new clothes because the old ones were too loose now and made her look a bit droopy. But how could she tell them that she couldn't spend money, now that Bernie had lost his job? It wouldn't be right to tell them, even if he was grumpy or ignoring her. She didn't want to shame him. Besides, she wanted to stay cheerful, like her friends made her feel, inviting her round, saying they'd missed her, how brave she'd been and all that.

But then Wendy showed them some photos of her grandchild. Raine. A roly-poly baby with a gummy smile, like Ella used to have, and why hadn't Ella come to see her, why hadn't Meg called since the clinic? Is that what happened when people were over the worst? But she mustn't go down that path, she mustn't.

Couldn't she invite Meg and Ella to dinner, make something special? A tasty casserole and a delicious pavlova. *Crunchy fairy floss*, Ella used to call it. Why not pull out all the stops? And maybe buy just one new dress. She'd always been careful with money, checked for specials, made sure the bills were paid on time. She hardly bought anything for herself except food she didn't need: chocolates, cake, biscuits, potato chips in giant packets, but she wasn't going to buy that empty kind of stuff anymore. Mind you, Bernie had never been one for splurging. He wasn't into fancy cars, like other men, or fancy suits like Lionel, strutting about in the finest Italian something or other. Bernie didn't gamble, either, and he never asked her what she'd bought, poking and prying. Donna once told her how Lionel checked all the receipts to make sure she'd bought the specials, got mad at her for buying takeaway coffees instead of making instant at home. But Bernie wasn't mean like that. He was a whole lot of other bad things but he'd never been mean about money. And he'd wanted to protect her, he'd said. He hadn't been ashamed of her, after all. Not about her time in the clinic.

'Your Bernie's lost weight,' said Wendy. 'I saw him at the letterbox and asked him if he was missing your cooking.'

I bet he ran away, thought Gloria.

'And then he ran away,' Wendy said.

'Well, he's not skinny like he was in the early years,' Gloria said. 'But he's ... yes, he's lost weight.'

It made him look more handsome, too, in the face. Only why would she tell him, when he'd just grunt or say she was seeing things. And why had he lost weight, anyway? Because he didn't know how to cook, had probably been living on two-minute noodles. Or maybe he'd been spending hours in the gym, not worrying about her at all. Or maybe he'd been ill, like her. But Bernie didn't get ill. Bernie didn't believe in people being sick, and he'd only liked her when she was healthy and young and full of life. When she gave him sex. But then at some point, she couldn't remember when, and time had a way of blurring and pulling up sharp and blurring again, it stopped. The pleasure. And so she'd given it to herself, after he'd gone to work, but then it started feeling lonely and sad, leaving her with a tear or two trickling down her cheeks. Looking back on what she'd done, lying on the bed, she couldn't believe she'd been that woman. But then she couldn't believe who she used to be before Bernie came along. She'd wanted boys to make her feel good but they'd taken all the pleasure for themselves. She'd wanted to feel the thrill of them wanting her, but the thrill died the moment they shoved inside her. It was done then. They'd won. When she hadn't even known it was a battle.

'Are you OK, Gloria? You look ...'

She tried to laugh. 'I'm good, Donna. Just ... you know, mulling things over.'

Donna was looking gorgeous in a pale green dress, and showing quite a bit of cleavage, if you don't mind.

'It's a great dress, isn't it?' Donna said, smiling. 'Why don't you buy one like this, Gloria? It will make you feel ever so young, let me tell you.'

Gloria saw herself lying in wet grass, knickers around her ankles. Or in the back seat of a car, a boy fumbling and cursing because her clothes got in the way.

She said no to a second piece of cake because she wanted to keep the weight off.

Bernie's body might have changed but the rest of him wouldn't.

Oh, she knew she was being mean to him but she just couldn't stop herself. Even though she felt sorry for him, losing his job like that. He'd kept all his jobs for years and it wasn't his fault when he lost them. She'd found his references on the top shelf of a cupboard, because he never boasted about his work. So she'd be thinking good things about him and then she'd see his face all closed in and she'd feel cold all over again. Sometimes she wanted to hit him as he sat in his chair reading, pretending that nothing was wrong.

She had to excuse herself and go to the loo. She didn't want to break down in front of her friends, didn't want them worrying or making a fuss. She looked in the bathroom mirror and fluffed up her hair: short and grey and sad. It used to be long before she had Karl, down to her waist, and Bernie had loved it like that. But baby Karl kept pulling and tugging so it really hurt and her golden locks ended up on the hairdresser's floor. Karl. She'd told him, when he phoned, that she was *managing*. Because what would be the point of saying how she really felt? *He* wasn't going to change, either.

She went back to the living room, saw Trudy looking a bit glum all of a sudden. She asked if anything was wrong.

'Indigestion,' she said. 'It's not even worth mentioning.'

Which made them all laugh.

'Well, *I* want to mention something,' said Donna. 'I'm planning to get a new man.'

They all gasped.

'Are you leaving Lionel?' Trudy said. Her little voice had shrunk even more.

Donna waved a hand about. 'He's been having affairs for years,' she said. 'I'm ever so sick of it. So now I'm thinking, why shouldn't *I*.'

'So how ... I mean ...' Wendy's eyes were huge with shock.

'How will I find someone?' Donna said, and laughed. 'There's thousands of men out for a bit of fun. It's ever so easy, you can go to a bar or the casino. Just a glance or two will do the trick.'

'A bit of fun?' Trudy whispered.

'Well, a bit more than that,' Donna said. 'I want someone to notice me for a change.'

'*We* notice you,' Wendy said.

'And I thank you for that,' Donna said. 'From the bottom of my heart. But it's not the same thing, is it?'

Gloria looked around the table at her friends, women she'd known for years. Donna, with her warm heart and tinkling laugh, and a husband who treated her like dirt. Wendy, who liked to tell you all the time about her wonderful Max till you sometimes wanted to scream, but who would give you the shirt off her back. Trudy, who hardly ever spoke, but always listened carefully to what people said, even if their saying was a waste of breath. Like last year's Christmas dinner, when she'd listened so politely to Lionel's endless boasting about his job, his money, his car. She'd listened for Donna's sake. But in all their years together, Gloria had never said a word to her friends about her sadness, because she didn't want to burden them. That's what she'd told the doctor in the clinic. But now that she was sitting here, trying hard to be cheerful, she felt the truth she'd kept hidden in her heart. That she'd been ashamed, she was still ashamed, of her sad, broken marriage. When her mum and dad had made something lovely that lasted for years, that would have kept lasting with so much love if life hadn't been so unfair.

ΔΔΔ

Bernie bothered to look up from his magazine as she walked past him. *The Monthly*, it was called. Didn't they know that was a woman's thing? They might just as well have called it *Tampons*. But of course he didn't ask where she was going, with her handbag draped over her arm. She could have been going out to jump off a cliff for all he knew or cared. She opened the door, slammed it. It made her feel better, then it didn't. So as soon as she started walking, she made herself look up at the big blue sky, enjoy the cool of a breeze on her skin. *Buck up, my love*, her mum used to say, there's plenty more people a whole lot worse off than you. Her dad used to say the same, only harsher, how Aussies were turning into whingers. *Three TVs and holidays overseas and all they do is complain.*

Decent folk, her mum and dad. How she wished they were still here.

She saw Donna waving from her front door. She looked glamorous in a bright red dress and black high heels. Gloria thought she'd feel shocked by Donna's news, but she wasn't. None of them were shocked, not even timid Trudy. They were all pleased for Donna, once they'd taken it in. They'd all said good for you, in their different ways. Donna wanted someone to notice her. Gloria had almost said *And so do I.*

The walk to the shops was longer than she'd thought and she was starting to puff a bit. Maybe she should walk to the shops every day and get fitter. But not to buy clothes. This would be her very last splash. There was only one time in her whole married life when she'd splurged on a special dress, not long after she'd had Karl. It was a pink and shimmery gown with lace around the top, and Bernie had kissed her, undressed her, taken her to bed. But then everything changed, not like a clap of thunder, but like drizzling rain getting greyer and greyer, and before she knew it he was stuck behind a magazine and she was stuck in front of the oven.

One shimmery dress in nearly forty years of marriage.

Then she saw it: *Natalie's Place*. A dress shop. It used to be a kitchen shop run by a woman who always looked at Gloria in that you-can't-afford-anything-in-my-shop kind of way. Gloria was glad the shop had changed hands, and she hoped the woman had lost a lot of money when she sold it. It wasn't a nice thing to feel, wanting some kind of revenge, but you couldn't help your feelings, could you? It's what you did with them that mattered. She didn't look in the window, just stepped right in, before she changed her mind. A young woman was standing behind the counter. She had golden hair, like Gloria's used to be, but she was bony and small, with a darting kind of face. She couldn't be a day over thirty.

Gloria asked the woman if she was Natalie.

'That's me, yes.' She had a darting kind of voice as well. Sweet. 'And you are?'

'Gloria.'

'Gloria. It's nice to meet you. Welcome.'

'I'd like to ...' Gloria stopped, started again. 'I'd like to try on some dresses.'

'Certainly. Did you have anything in mind? Any special occasion?'

'I don't have special occasions. I'd just like a new dress.'

She could see Natalie looking at her, a bit funny, and knew she'd said too much. But she had to make a start. Natalie was beside her now, chatting about styles and colours, helping her to choose. Not being pushy, not pouring phony flattery all over her. Gloria lingered over the pink dresses but couldn't find one she liked. She gave some thought to a red number, but that would have been too ... too glamorous, really. Too Donna. She finally picked out a pale mauve dress, lacy at the top, and swirling. Stunning on the rack, at least. She went into the change rooms and the dress slipped easily over her head and arms. Not like the last time she'd tried on a blouse and got stuck and had to ask the assistant to get her out. She'd nearly died with embarrassment. Now she dared to look in the mirror, turning this way and that, liking the way the dress floated round her legs, the way it clung to her bum. Her bum was still *ample*, her mum would have called it, but not as ample as before. She took a longer, closer look. She could almost look sexy in the right kind of mood. She came out of the change room, a bit flustered.

'What do you think?' she said.

Natalie's face lit up. 'Wow! It's perfect. You definitely need a special occasion.'

Gloria laughed. It felt good to laugh, finding lace and shimmers and pleasure. But—the cost! A dress like this would cost a fortune. How could she have forgotten? That Bernie had lost his job. She'd called him hopeless to that doctor in the clinic. And there, in the middle of this brand new shop, wondering how she could say that she'd changed her mind, she felt her heart seizing up because she hadn't said sorry. I'm sorry Bernie, it wasn't your fault, and the boy who told me you'd lost your job sounded like he didn't care a hoot. Then something else came into her head, from a few years back, how she'd wanted to pop into Bernie's work to say hello, surprise him. How she'd looked through the window and seen him standing at the counter looking miserable, his arms hanging by his sides. She'd wanted to go in and tell him. She'd wanted to say: I see you, I see how unhappy you are. Would that have made him feel better, or worse? Would that have made a difference to how they were, together and not together? She should have said, Bernie, it's not your fault, and you're not a bad man, not really. She knew what a bad person was, you saw it on TV all the time, the bashings and the killing. Like that man who put a pillow over his little boy's head and smothered him to death. The mother was crying on TV and Dr Phil kept asking her all these questions: how did she feel when she found out, how did she feel now, like he wanted her to keep crying. Then the mother put a hanky to her weeping eyes and the hanky had the name of the show embroidered on the corner: *Dr Phil.* Gloria had flicked off the TV. It had made her feel sick to the stomach.

'Are you alright, Gloria?'

She pulled herself together. 'I forgot to look at the price tag,' she said.

Natalie walked round behind her, gently pulled out the tag.

'One hundred and fifty dollars,' she said.

'I'll take it,' Gloria said, before she had time to think. Because she couldn't say it, she just couldn't.

'Lovely. A great choice, Gloria. Let me put it in some tissue paper.'

'I'm going to leave it on.' Relieved that Natalie couldn't see her foolish face.

'Well, why not?' Natalie said. 'Just let me take off the price tag.'

Gloria froze as Natalie snipped off the tag. Wanting to get out quickly now, run from the scene of her shame. She fished out her Mastercard, handed it over, not daring to look at Natalie as she put the old dress in a carry-bag. Nutty woman, she must be thinking, both of them turning to look as a large, hunched-up woman trudged into the shop. Gloria tried not to stare, because she knew that look, she knew how it felt to rifle through clothes, like the woman was doing now, then snatching up a dress and hurrying to the change room, closing the door really fast.

Natalie cleared her throat, then gave Gloria a careful kind of smile. 'I hope you don't take this the wrong way,' she said.

Gloria held her breath. Was there going to be another axe?

'You have what people in the trade call a fuller figure,' Natalie said, and lowered her voice. 'But you look comfortable in your body.'

Gloria was about to say she was a whole lot more comfortable now than she was a month ago. But she couldn't say that, could she? About the breakdown. Not to a stranger in a shop.

'I've had plus-size women coming into the shop,' Natalie said. 'They kept apologising for the way they look. But you seem to embrace your body. And you have a good eye for what suits you.'

Gloria felt herself blushing. Because the more compliments she got, the phonier she felt.

'I used to be bigger,' she said. 'I lost a lot of weight because I had a breakdown. I couldn't eat.'

'Oh, Gloria, I'm so—'

'It's alright, Natalie, honestly. I'm not telling you to get your sympathy. I'm just ... well, it's hard work, trying to lose weight. I didn't have to make any effort.'

Natalie's face brightened. 'Well, I admire you for being honest,' she said. 'And not to feel ashamed of what happened to you.' She leaned forward on the counter. 'Thank you,' she said. 'It's a rare thing that you've done.'

Gloria felt like choking up. She hadn't been fishing for compliments, but they were falling from the sky like manna from heaven. Isn't that what the priest used to say, before her mum found out he was robbing everyone blind.

Gloria signed for the dress. She didn't feel the need to rush out anymore.

'Thank *you*, Natalie,' she said. 'You've been really kind. And'— she looked around the shop, at the racks of clothes in all their colours and shapes and wanting to be noticed—'you've done a fabulous job here. The place is so inviting.'

She moved towards the door, just as the hunched-up woman emerged from the change room. Crept out, really. But at least she'd shown her face and she hadn't got stuck in the dress. In fact, it fitted her nicely.

'It suits you,' Gloria said. 'The A-line shape is flattering.'

The woman didn't look convinced.

'And the colour,' said Gloria. 'It suits your warm complexion.'

The woman gave a curt nod, turned, disappeared into the change room. Gloria turned to Natalie, a bit sheepish now, embarrassed.

'I'm sorry, I should have minded my own business,' she said.

'Not at all, Gloria, not at all. You said exactly the right thing.'

She took Gloria's arm and walked her to the door. She said

It's been lovely to meet you, as though she really meant it.

Gloria stepped onto the footpath, smoothed down her dress, waited for a break in the traffic. But then, in the heat of the day, and with everything that had happened—the dress, the shame, the machine that gobbled up money they didn't have— she started feeling a bit wobbly in the knees. Because Bernie wouldn't see her shining in her dress, and all *she* would see was his gloomy face. All she would hear was the silence. Her head was feeling heavy now, she needed to sit down. Weren't the pills meant to take away the axe? Or maybe she'd need to take more of them, or even go back to the clinic. A seat. She needed to find a seat. She must have overdone it: the walking, the hope, taking deep breaths now, spying a long wooden bench, trying to sit down and crash! Landing flat on her bum. She was ready to cry now, she really was, plonked on the footpath in a sad and sorry heap. Who did she think she was, dressed up all fancy and landing on her bum? And had she torn her lovely new dress? She checked front and back, in a flurry ... a hundred and fifty dollars ... had she ruined it, made a mess of things again? ... but no, thank goodness, there was no damage done.

She saw something out of the corner of her eye, looked up and saw a man walking towards her. Coming closer, bending down to her. A tall man with dark eyes, the darkest blue, lowering his head and saying *Are you alright? You took a bit of a tumble.*

She nodded.

'Let me help you,' he said, and held out his hand. He pulled her up, gently, and guided her onto the bench, sat down beside her.

'Are you hurt?' he said. 'Does it feel like anything's broken?'

She shook her head.

'Do you need a lift?'

She looked around and saw cars whizzing by, then a big noisy bus, and it was all feeling a bit too much again. But she steadied herself. She was safe. Nothing terrible had happened.

'A lift?' she said. 'I don't know.'

The man's eyes were worried. Was he thinking she was a daft old woman who shouldn't be let out on the street?

'Do you know where you live?' he said, quiet now.

'I don't want to go where I live.'

'Is there ... is there a problem?'

She took the deepest breath. In. Out. 'My husband,' she said. 'He ... we make each other so unhappy.'

The man said he was sorry. Which was nice of him to say.

'Would you like me to drive you somewhere else?' he said.

She had to stand. Walk. Put one foot in front of the other.

'Thank you,' she said. 'But I have to do this all by myself.'

She slowly rose from the bench.

'A few weeks ago,' she said, 'I went a bit mad for a while.'

She felt her cheeks grow hot. Why on earth had she told him that?

He stood up and patted her arm. 'We all go a bit mad sometimes,' he said.

'Gloria. My name is Gloria.'

'I'm pleased to meet you. I'm Hal. And your name? Gloria. It means a hymn.'

She wondered if he was religious, with the kind of religion that made a man ask a wobbly falling woman if she needed any help. She told him she only went to church at Christmas because the priest had turned out to be a rotten thief.

He laughed. 'That's the spirit,' he said. 'And that's a lovely dress.'

She told him it cost a fortune, and he said it was worth every cent.

Bernard

Where on earth had Gloria gone, brandishing her handbag like a weapon? Was she planning on spending money that they didn't have? But that didn't seem right. She wouldn't, surely. She was careful with money, and had never been one for *things*, had never been one of those women who expected diamonds or furs or whatever it was that women were supposed to yearn for.

He remembered once, in the early days, buying her a bunch of flowers. She'd lavished him with kisses and told him he was *so sweet, so thoughtful*.

She was still sleeping in Karl's old room. He'd offered to swap places but their bed was too lumpy, she'd said. *Their bed*.

But she didn't want him. It was as simple as that. Well, maybe another woman would. Not that he'd ever had another woman. He'd once dared to check the personal ads, years ago now, but had blanched at descriptions of busty women or versatile women or young Asian, slim. And now? Well, he knew he wasn't the answer to a young maiden's dreams, but at least he wasn't bald or hobbling in pain. He could tell he'd lost weight, as well: his trousers were looser, his shirts no longer strained at the stomach. Maybe he should step on the scales. The last time he'd checked, before Gloria went away, before his miserable life had slumped further into misery, the warning signs had been staring him in the face: diabetes, heart attack, stroke.

He made his way to the bathroom. Gloria must have been

cleaning: he could smell the sharp disinfectant, like a forest of pines, with gallons of chemicals mixed in. He stepped tentatively onto the scales. Well. Seven kilos. He wondered if there was a different set of scales that could measure other losses, the ones you couldn't see with the naked, pitiless eye. And besides, how could he take credit for the weight loss? He hadn't exercised any self-restraint, hadn't exercised at all. He should be pleased, he supposed, peering into the mirror. He looked thinner, yes, and sharper: his face had more definition. He could look out onto the world, definitively, certain that his life had been a waste. He'd sold thousands of items to repair run-down houses while his own house was standing in wretched disarray. He'd sold auto parts so that autos could clog up the city with pollution. He'd sold beds for people to make love in while his own had been loveless for years. And, finally, vacuum cleaners. What kind of legacy was that, for a lively, curious grandchild? Not that he'd seen Ella lately. Maybe he'd never see her again. Now that his services were no longer required.

The gym. He should go back to the gym, get back on that treadmill, even pump some iron. But then he remembered: he'd had to let his membership expire. Well, he could drive to the beach instead, jog along the shore, breathe in the briny air. Do something to shake off his torpor, if only for an hour. And who knew where Gloria had gone, or when she'd be back to give him another serve. Or give him nothing at all.

He grabbed a bottle of water from the fridge, picked up the car keys, opened the front door, and—there she was, walking up the driveway. Gloria. Wearing something ... what was she wearing? A purple sparkling dress, shining in the sun. What did she look like? She looked ... shapely. Lovely. And as she came closer, he could see something in her face. Determination? Some kind of conviction? She stopped dead in front of him.

'I bought a new dress,' she said.

Was she trying to provoke him?

'The woman in the shop said it was perfect.'

'Oh. Right.'

'And she thanked me for being honest. About my breakdown.'

He nodded.

'Then a man came.'

'A man?' Bernard felt his chest tighten.

'I went to sit on a bench but I fell over. A man stopped and asked if I needed any help.'

Bernard waited. Although he wasn't sure what he was waiting for.

'It's good for the spirits, isn't it?' she said.

'What is?'

'People being kind to you.'

Who *was* she? She wasn't the corrosive Gloria or the silent treatment Gloria, but the unexpectedly, mildly pleasant Gloria.

'I want us to be polite,' she said.

'Polite?'

'Yes. Speaking nicely. Remembering our manners.'

She sounded like a brochure for a Swiss finishing school.

She pursed her lips. 'Well?' she said.

'Well what?'

'Do you like my dress?'

He startled. 'It's nice,' he said, feebly. 'It ... it suits you.'

She gave him a warm smile, which startled him some more. Confound the woman! She'd been whipping his back for a week, and now this: the warmest, most winsome smile.

'I'm going to make some lunch,' she said. 'Would you like sandwiches?'

She walked inside. He was meant to follow, wasn't he? She'd offered him sandwiches. But he was wary. Waiting for her to pounce. Pleasantness was all well and good, but he wasn't really sure what was going on. Correction: he had no idea what was going on. Still, he was relieved to have some kind of truce, and grateful for her quiet movements as she set about making lunch. He couldn't help looking at her dress, which really *did* suit her. It wasn't idle flattery, and god knows he'd given her no flattery, idle or sincere, in the long, empty years of their marriage. As she reached up to the cupboard, her back towards him, he noticed how the dress clung to her bum. Then she swung round abruptly, and he noticed how the fabric clung to her breasts. He felt the beginning of an erection.

She asked him to set the table. Asked, not commanded, and he rummaged in a drawer for plates. She wondered aloud about a glass of wine, but then said she wanted to keep off the weight. Should he tell her she was slimmer? Well, she already knew that, didn't she? He didn't want to remind her that she used to be fatter, didn't want to upset the delicate balance they seemed to be creating, circling round each other, trying to be polite.

'You've lost weight, Bernie,' she said.

'I guess. I haven't been eating all that much.'

'While I was away?'

She didn't say *in the clinic*. Did she want to put all that behind her? Or pretend she'd never been there?

'And you must have been going to the gym,' she said.

'No, not really. Not at all.'

He'd been sitting on the sofa for listless hours instead of looking for a job or filling out a welfare form. He felt a weight pressing on his chest, but he would not, must not, falter. He must be courteous, open to her questions. It was so much better than her chilling glances or her lashings of contempt.

They sat down to eat. Gloria ate her salad sandwich in small, dainty bites. They were silent now, both of them. He wondered if he should ... start a conversation.

Gloria put down her sandwich. 'Have you been looking for work?' she said. Not nastily, not accusingly.

'I should have. But well, I can't see much point.'

She clasped her hands on the table. Decisive. 'Well, we can look together,' she said.

He felt his jaw drop.

'I might not be much help but—'

'It's good of you to offer.'

He felt that weight lifting from his chest.

'The lunch is … tasty,' he said, fumbling, always fumbling. 'And you look …' He petered out.

She tilted her head to the side. 'I look what?'

Why was this so difficult? He felt nineteen years old again. But finally, calling up that naïve, eager, clumsy young man who'd become a much older and even clumsier man, he managed to eke out the words: 'You look lovely.'

She laughed. 'And you look lovely, too,' she said. 'We could be in a before-and-after photo, the two of us.'

This was all feeling quite bizarre, he thought, like watching an old home video of people you vaguely knew but whose identity escaped you. And then something happened that surprised him even more, ambushed him, astonished him completely: Gloria leaned across the table and reached out her hand, placed it on top of his.

'I want you to see *me*,' she said. 'Not my dress.'

He flushed, told her he was sorry.

'I'm sorry, too,' she said, and withdrew her hand. 'But when someone doesn't see you, you try to make them hear you.' She was looking at him intently now, and he waited. 'I know I'm not smart, like you,' she said. 'But—'

'Gloria. Let me—'

'No. Let me finish. I want to explain.'

She was giving him the chance to take her seriously.

'I know I don't know so many things, all the things you know and read about, but that doesn't mean I'm stupid.'

'I never said you were.'

'You didn't have to.'

He looked down at his plate.

'Do you remember, Bernie ...'

He looked up to see her frowning.

'Do you remember our first date? You took me to see a play.'

'I do remember. You were all dressed up.'

'That's not what I'm saying. I'm talking about the play. Everyone was laughing but I didn't think it was funny.'

'It was written by Harold Pinter. He's a British playwright.'

Gloria shook her head. 'A playwright? Well, I think he got it wrong. The people in the play were so nasty to one another, so cruel. How can that be funny?'

He didn't want to lecture her about the Comedy of Menace. He didn't want to patronise, with his half-baked, useless knowledge. But she had asked him. She seemed to need to know.

'Sometimes people laugh when they're afraid,' he said.

'So what were they afraid of?'

'Some kind of threat. The feeling that life is treacherous, that you can't trust anyone.'

'What a terrible way to feel.'

'Indeed.'

She laughed. 'When you say *indeed* ...'

'Why is that funny?'

'You always sound like a professor.'

'Instead of a salesman who's been given the sack.'

She gave him a warning look, but then her face quickly softened.

'We'll get by,' she said. 'We can sit down together and work things out.'

He didn't want to speak, didn't want to break the spell of her kindness.

'You know ... I saw you once,' she said. 'I saw you through the window of the vacuum cleaner shop. You looked so sad. Like you didn't know why you were there.'

He suddenly couldn't eat.

'I never told you,' she said. 'I should have told you how sorry I was to see you like that. But you would have thrown it back at me, made one of your sharp comments.' She softened again. 'I should have taken better care of you,' she said. 'And I shouldn't talk so much.'

He didn't want her to stop, in this radiant, extraordinary moment. But he knew he had to speak, give her something in return.

'I should have taken care of *you*,' he said.

'But that's why you married me. You gave up your studies to look after me. I was grateful. I never told you that, either.'

'It was ... it was the least I could do.'

'It was a *lot* to do, Bernie. Even if you didn't show it.'

He was stunned. By her understanding. By what he'd never suspected she knew.

'And now you've paid for my time in the clinic,' she said. 'That must have cost a lot of money and you haven't once complained.'

'Karl paid,' he said. Ashamed. Always ashamed.

'So what?' Gloria fixed him with a look. 'Money isn't about caring. And I didn't let you visit me.'

'But how could I blame you? Who would want me as a visitor?'

'You're doing it again, Bernie. Feeling sorry for yourself.'

She said this gently but she was telling him the truth. He wanted to thank her, reach out to her, but what would she say, what would she do, if he took her in his arms?

'Isn't it funny?' she said. 'How you can meet a couple of strangers and ... well, it makes the world a brighter place.'

He wished she hadn't taken away her hand. He wished

he had the courage to tell her: I'm glad you've had a good morning, I'm glad you're feeling better, I'm glad we're sitting here together. But they continued to eat without saying a word. All he could hear was the raucous cawing of birds, and some car alarm wailing in the distance. Finally, Gloria rose from the table, gathered the plates, told him she was tired and was going to lie down.

'Are you feeling alright?' he asked.

She nodded.

'Thank you for lunch,' he said.

She nodded again, didn't smile, walked away. He wanted to call her back, but again the words wouldn't come. All he'd said was thank you. *Danke schön.* He could have said *Ich bin dir dankbar*: I am thankful to you, which was a touch more gracious. And wasn't there something more forceful, more fulsome? *Sehr aufmerksam*: that is very kind of you. When someone has done a kind deed, out of the goodness of her heart. *Sehr aufmerksam, Gloria.*

But none of it told the truth about his feelings. How she'd touched him with her kindness, her attention to his life. Their life.

Meg

She hadn't told Ella the whole truth and nothing but the truth. Because once she began to unpick the marital threads more honestly, the final, ugly stitch would be her child. The child her father hadn't welcomed with open arms. Maybe Ella would work that out for herself. Maybe she already had, because she seemed to understand that her father now saw her as a duty, instead of loving her own precious, particular self. But Meg wouldn't be the one to tell her that. It would be unfair, even cruel. Nor did she want to pin a shiny badge on her chest: World's Greatest Mother, formerly married to World's Most Indifferent Father. Maybe Ella would come to understand that her father's indifference was no reflection of her worth; that her mother's ferocious love had left no room for her father. She might begin to see her parents as messed-up individuals entirely separate from herself.

Maybe that's what it meant to be an adult.

Meg's heart was still warmed by that loving exchange, when her daughter had tried hard to understand. When she'd been *thinking of people things*. Meg didn't know what had prompted her daughter, had moved her to find some answers. Maybe Lola had told her a story about her own faithless father. Maybe Ella had promised not to tell. But Meg wouldn't prod any further. It was Ella's space, alone with her thoughts, trying to work out life for herself.

Hanna came for dinner, and she brought it with her, because she was all too familiar with Meg's cooking. The burning, the drying out, the glugging up, the falling flat, or putting in so much spice that one bite would have you calling out for water. Hanna placed a casserole dish on the table, lifted the lid.

'Chicken Surprise!' she said. 'And it's *meant* to be a surprise.'

Meg poured them both a glass of wine. She'd thought about mentioning Hal after Ella went off to her room, but what was there to tell, really? Three days now and he still hadn't called. Had he regretted what he'd told her, about wishing he'd had a child? About the women who hadn't wanted him to father their child? Had he been asking for her sympathy? Or was he telling her, without telling her, that he was ... what ... bad news?

At least Ella hadn't asked about their date. The more-than-a-casual fuck. Did I really say that, Meg thought.

Hanna folded herself into a chair, gave Ella a warm smile.

'So how are you, Ella, my love?' she said. 'Excited about going back to school?'

Ella shrugged.

'Sorry, that's a boring question,' Hanna said.

'It's OK. I like school because my teachers have all been friendly and fun. Except for Ms Morgan in year four, she always looked like she was going to cry, and then one day she did and she kept saying she was sorry and then the next day she left. But I have a cool teacher for next year, all the year sevens say that, but I know stuff will keep getting harder, 'specially the maths. I just don't get factors or brackets, or triangles with different sides.'

'That's a lot to not get,' Hanna said. 'But maybe your mum can help you, she's good at that kind of rubbish.'

Meg screwed up her face. 'I'm not sure that's a good idea,' she said. 'Not when the homework gets harder.'

Hanna gave Ella a wink. 'Your mum used to get help from her father,' she said. 'I believe he drove her crazy.'

'Hanna, come on.' Meg shook her head. 'He wasn't as bad as that.'

'Well, Meg, he *did* say you needed a new brain.'

Ella looked indignant. 'But that's so mean and nasty. Anyway, there's nothing wrong with your brain, Mum. You're really smart.'

'Well, thank you, sweetheart, I appreciate the support. And Hanna's being dramatic, as usual.' Meg leaned back, remembering. 'My father was ... well, irritating. He used to sit next to me and tap the desk with a pencil ... tap, tap, tap. So of course I couldn't concentrate.'

Hanna smiled. 'And Ella, guess what we used to call him? Jonah the Moaner. Or sometimes plain old Darth Vader.'

Ella looked delighted. 'And what did you call Grandma?'

'Grandma Georgina?' Hanna pursed her lips. 'Fart Face.'

Meg burst out laughing, and Hanna started laughing too. She knew they were behaving like puerile idiots (and they'd only just started on the wine), but it was impossible not to laugh, making Ella laugh as well. Until Hanna leaned forward, gave Ella an alert-teacher look:

'You too will learn this, my child,' she said.

'Learn what?'

'How being rude about horrible people in authority can make you feel a whole lot better. It makes you feel more powerful, even if it doesn't change a thing.'

Ella looked at her mother, unsure. 'Were you ever rude to your parents, Mum?' she said. 'I mean ... *really* rude.'

'No. I was a *good* girl. I just left home as quickly as I could.'

Hanna snorted. 'Didn't work for me,' she said. 'After I left home, my mother would call me every night to shriek about her ungrateful daughter leaving her to die all on her own. When that didn't work, she'd cry for hours on the phone like a puppy in pain.'

'Really?' Ella looked wide-eyed.

'That's why I'm crazy,' Hanna said. 'My parents come from Hungary and all Hungarians are crazy.'

'Hanna.' Meg shook her head. 'You're filling Ella's head with rubbish.'

'Sorry, Meg. And I'm sorry about Fart Face. Although I bet not half as sorry as you.'

'Well, the chicken is fantastic,' Ella said. 'Thank you, Hanna. I am eternally grateful.'

'Me too,' Meg said.

And grateful for Hanna's overblown stories, as well; for giving Ella a lesson in the value of being rude. This child her mother would never badger about homework.

She could still hear her father's pencil: Tap. Tap. Tap. Tap. Tap. Tap. She could still hear his exasperated sigh: *Margaret, you need a new brain.*

Ella

Pop had offered to teach her German. He said people didn't need a classroom to learn, and her German accent was promising. It might even be in her blood, he told her over dinner, and Ella was surprised. They were on to the pavlova, which was seriously delicious, and Nana said that when Ella was really little, she'd called it crunchy fairy floss. Ella didn't remember saying that and her mum called it childhood amnesia, which meant you couldn't remember anything much about the first few years of your life. Ella thought that wasn't fair, how other people knew more about you than you knew about yourself. It was a bit weird as well, because you were the person who couldn't remember being that person from a long time ago. It was also weird to have German in her blood, like Pop said. Ella knew he didn't mean it literally, she didn't have globs of German words floating in her veins, but it still didn't explain why he thought she sounded so ... well, German. And it might be confusing, too, if her mum was going to teach her French. What if she got the two languages mixed up? Still, Naomi would be surprised, and maybe a bit impressed. And Nana's dress was another surprise: a sparkling huggy kind of dress, like she'd been on one of those make-over shows.

Ella's mum leaned forward. 'You look fabulous in that dress, Gloria,' she said.

'I *feel* better too, Meg,' Nana said. 'Thanks to all of you for looking after me.'

Ella knew she hadn't done any looking after. Maybe she should do it now, ask Nana what she'd done in the clinic. A lot of sleeping, Nana said, and enjoying the food and having peace and quiet. Then she went on a bit about some doctor who kept *digging away* at her, asking all kinds of *ridiculous* questions about her family.

'Why were they ridiculous?' Ella said.

'Because my mum and dad were good people.' Nana shook her head. 'Oh, I know there are some terrible parents, but the doctor kept on at me, like I was hiding something awful. They loved me, my mum and dad, that's all anyone needs to know.' She cleared her throat. 'Bernie wasn't so lucky with his father, though,' she said.

'But I had a kind, lovely mother,' Pop said.

'Still, that doctor wasn't all silly,' Nana said. 'She said I should try talking. I don't mean ... not me just talking to myself, she meant talking with Bernie.'

Ella saw Pop's face go grey, like a potato before it got roasted.

'I lost my job,' he said, and looked down at the table.

'But it's not your fault,' Nana said. 'Everyone buys online these days.'

Pop still didn't look at her. 'But they kept on a young man,' he said.

'Who's not half the man you are, Bernie.'

Ella took a big bite of pavlova, watching Pop's sagging face.

'I'm so sorry, Bernie,' her mum said, quietly. 'It's not fair.'

Nana waved a hand in the air. 'We'll work it out,' she said. 'It's always a question of money in, money out.'

'And I'm not bringing any in,' Pop said.

Nana smiled like it hurt. 'But you don't need a lot of money if you don't lead a fancy life,' she said.

Ella heard what Nana was saying, but she was also thinking that if you had more money, you could do all kinds of amazing things. You could fly to Paris to check out the paintings and cathedrals. You could maybe learn to take great pictures if you had an amazing camera. Fern had just bought one that cost a whole heap of money, and she'd switched to taking pictures of noses, but Ella had said no way, you can take a photo of any other part of me but not my nose, PLEASE. Or maybe she could get a nose job.

She heard Pop asking if she had a favourite subject.

'I like my friends best,' she said.

Nana opened her mouth, went to speak, then closed it again. Ella wished she could take the greyness away. Maybe she could ask them a silly riddle, like Fern's: *How do you kiss a porcupine? Carefully*. Or maybe she could tell them about the poor people who couldn't read or write. But that was really sad. Or maybe she could tell Nana and Pop about Hal. That would cheer them up, wouldn't it, her mum meeting someone nice. But what if it didn't work out, like the last man? It might embarrass her mum. And anyway, maybe it was her mum's place to say. Ella sighed with all the complications, then let out a mighty yawn. Her mum gave her a look, said it must be time to go home. Ella remembered to say thank you for the dinner, but she wished there was a different way to say it. She wanted to say that the food was delicious but she wished all the talking could have been a bit more real. Not that it was all stuffy and strict like it was with Grandma Fart Face and Jonah the Moaner. It had just been a bit phony. But that would have taken a whole lot longer than saying *stop pretending to be nice*.

ΔΔΔ

Her mum did up her seatbelt. 'That was nice, wasn't it?' she said.

'The pavlova?'

'The evening. Nana seems much better. Quite chirpy, in fact. '

Ella wasn't sure about that. It had felt like Pop was all slumped over and Nana had kept trying to make him stand up straight.

'Still, it's sad that Pop has lost his job,' her mum said. 'And I guess it will be hard for him to find another one.'

'Why?'

'Because he must be close to sixty, maybe older. And it's harder for older people to get a new job.'

'Why?'

'Well, some employers think older people don't have enough energy, or they can't keep up with the new things to learn.'

'But Pop seems pretty smart. He knows a lot of stuff and he reads books.'

'You're right, Ella, but it's how things often are these days. It's called ageism. Not being fair to older people. Like sexism is not being fair to women.'

'And kid-ism is banning mobile phones.'

Her mum didn't bite.

'Anyway ...' Ella remembered Pop's grey face. 'Pop seemed a bit weird tonight. Like every time Nana said something, it was like he was shutting her out.'

Her mum nodded. 'I felt that too.'

'So why didn't you say?'

'Because—'

'Because you want me to think everything's always wonderful.'

Her mum smiled. 'Sometimes, Ella,' she said. 'Nothing much gets past you, does it? Maybe you can be a psychologist when you grow up. A counsellor.' She pulled back her shoulders. Another lecture coming up. 'You know, Ella ...' A quick glance. 'When Pop asked you what you liked at school ... You know you're doing just fine, don't you? Your teachers are always so pleased with your effort.'

Ella shrugged. '*Effort* is a bit lame. It sounds like ... I don't know ... I'm a plodding donkey.'

'Ella! You try hard, and that's what matters. And ... well, maybe I should have praised you more. Maybe—'

'But I'd hate you to be one of those mothers who carries on about their genius kids. Jeremy's mum tells everyone he's going to be a brain surgeon because only the best doctors get to operate on the brain, and Anika's mum was going to complain about Anika not getting the lead part. You should have heard her at pick-up time, about Anika having *a rare gift*. I'd die if you said anything like that about me.'

Her mum laughed.

'I take your point,' she said. 'But you know, Ella, it can take time to find your passion. Look at me. I moped away in office jobs for years till I decided to go back to study. Mind you, you don't need a qualification to be a speech pathologist in Australia.' She shook her head. 'It's a national disgrace, really.'

Ella leaned back in her seat, stretched out her legs.

'What do you call a doctor who fixes noses?' she said.

'I don't know the specific name. A plastic surgeon will fix a nose if there's a medical problem, a cosmetic surgeon if people are worried about their looks. If they're vain.'

'So, am I vain if I want my nose changed?'

Her mum cleared her throat. 'There's nothing wrong with your nose, Ella.'

'There's something wrong with your eyes, Mum.'

'Sweetheart, I know it's hard not to worry about the way you look. It's all rubbish, but we fall for it just the same. All those celebrity magazines and movies, with their images of impossibly beautiful women. It's called the tyranny of appearances. Girls and women have a tyrant in our heads that keeps telling us we're not pretty enough or thin enough or our skin has too many wrinkles. We have a centimetre of ... well, crap, in our otherwise sensible brains.'

'Do *you* worry about the way you look?'

Her mum kept her eyes on the road. 'Of course. I need to lose some weight and I'm getting wrinkles and ... well, never mind. No-one's perfect.'

Ella gave her mum a long, hard look. 'I think you're pretty,' she said. 'And Hal does too.'

Her mum laughed.

'I could tell,' Ella said. 'By the way he looked at you. Did you have a nice time on your date?'

'Sure. It was OK.'

'Just OK?'

'It was fine.'

'Will you be seeing him again?'

Her mum's hands went tight on the steering wheel.

'Probably,' she said, and looked in the mirror. 'I wish that idiot would get off my backside,' she said, and settled back in her seat. 'Let me ask you, Ella. Would you feel happier if you had a nose job?'

'I guess.'

'You see, that's the problem with cosmetic surgery. People have something done but they're still unhappy with the way they look, so they keep wanting more and more. It becomes an obsession.'

'Like Michael Jackson?'

'Exactly. And he ended up looking so unnatural, didn't he? Hideous.'

'But I'd still like a small, cute nose, Mum. There's a new girl in our class, Hela, and she has the cutest nose. Only she's not happy with her new baby brother cos he cries all the time and keeps her awake. His name is Olaf, which sounds like a cow sicking up on grass. Anyway, Hela's nose is so cute, and so is Lola's.'

Her mum sighed. 'It's what's inside you that counts, Ella. Your character.'

Ella felt another *blah blah blah* coming on, so she rushed in to save her mum the trouble.

'I can have a nose job when I turn eighteen,' she said. 'And a tattoo when I'm sixteen, without your permission.'

'Then you can wait till you're sixteen. Just don't get anything ugly, like snakes or skulls.'

'Definitely not. I'm going to get *I love Mum* tattooed on one arm.'

'Very funny.' Her mum shot her another smile.

It felt good to be driving with her mum, talking about silly stuff and big stuff. Even if my nose is way too big, she thought. Even if my stomach feels a bit yuk after two massive helpings of pavlova.

Gloria

At least the dinner last night had turned out alright. Tender meat. Chunky vegetables. And the pavlova? Well, you couldn't buy a better one in the Cheesecake Shop. Ella had eaten two huge helpings. Such a skinny girl, she could eat like a horse and still be skinny. Gloria remembered when she used to be like that, before she got her curves. She still had those curves, but Bernie didn't want them. Oh, he was talking to her now and trying not to make her feel stupid, but he didn't want her in *that* way. Maybe he'd lost the urge. Maybe he was so depressed about losing his job that the last thing he wanted was sex. He hadn't made a move to check Centrelink, either, at least as far as she knew, and two days on from the dinner, he still hadn't bothered phoning Ella, making a time to teach her German. Although why anyone would want to learn German was anyone's guess, unless you wanted to live in Germany. It wasn't useful like weeding the garden. She pulled hard at one of those stubborn weeds with prickles all down the stem. Damn prickles. *Fucking prickles*. There. She'd said it out loud.

She'd put her hand on his, but he hadn't made a move.

She pulled herself up from the ground, feeling a bit creaky, and looked across at Donna's house. The curtains were drawn, and Donna never closed her curtains. Had she found a man and smuggled him into her bed? Gloria couldn't see a strange car anywhere around, so maybe Donna had a system: a phone call when Lionel was away. Sneaky. Gloria had a mobile and she knew how to text but she didn't have a man to sneak up on her.

She brushed the dirt off her hands and made her way inside, needing a glass of water. She opened the door and saw Bernie sitting in his chair. His hair was completely grey and his body was thicker, but he was a still a handsome man. A handsome man reading a book, probably a detective one. She couldn't see the point of that, either, because if TV shows were anything to go by, the stories were always the same. There was a crime, a lot of clues and then you found out who did it in the end.

Still, he'd helped her clear the table after Meg and Ella left. He'd helped her do the dishes. He'd told her the meal was wonderful.

He looked up to see her standing in the doorway.

'What is it?' he said.

'What's what?'

'Why are you standing there?' Snappy again.

She felt a flame of anger rushing up her throat.

'I just want ...' She didn't know how to finish. She didn't even know what she'd started.

'Just want what?' His voice was all frosty, ice to her heat. This wasn't good, was it? Not good at all.

'I just want some water,' she said.

He sighed a big deep sigh.

'I don't know what to do,' he said.

He was still worrying about money.

'We've paid the mortgage,' Gloria said. She'd already told him a hundred times. 'You have money from your super that we might be able to get hold of. We don't buy things we don't need. We hardly ever use the car.'

Because we never go out, Bernie. We never have fun. We don't have fun *inside* the house, either.

'And when you're feeling better I'll go with you to Centrelink,' she said.

'When I'm feeling better!'

Was it going to go back to the way it was before? Till death do us part?

'You're sitting round the house like the end of the world is coming,' she said. 'I thought you were going to teach Ella some German but you haven't done a thing. I asked you to visit the neighbours with me but you turned up your nose like you always do.'

If he could snap at her, she could snap right back.

'I brought home some brochures,' she said, getting into her stride. 'Free courses at the Community Centre, pottery and tai chi. You didn't even look at them, just chucked them in the bin. I offered to teach you how to cook. I have eight cookbooks, Bernie. And you can read, can't you?'

He was staring into the distance now, not looking at her at all.

'You don't understand,' he said.

'Oh. So it's my fault again.' She folded her arms across her chest.

He turned to face her at last. 'It's no-one's fault,' he said. 'And I'm sorry. I just thought ...'

She didn't know where he was going.

'What are you thinking, Bernie?' she said. 'Tell me.'

He flushed. 'I thought ... you in that lovely dress ...'

Oh. She was beginning to see what he meant. Why hadn't she seen it before?

'I thought you wore it for me,' he said.

Now he was telling her. He was telling her his truest feelings.

'I didn't think you wanted me,' she said. Quiet now. Careful. Because.

'But I told you, Gloria. I told you were lovely.'

'But then you didn't say anything else.'

He looked down, then up into her eyes.

'Because I wasn't sure,' he said.

She walked towards him. Wanting to be closer. Needing to tell him too.

'It's alright,' she said. 'It's going to be alright.'

ΔΔΔ

She took his hand and led him to their bedroom. She stretched up, put her arms around his neck and kissed him. A soft, gentle kiss that flooded her with sweetness, and she heard him give a little moan. Then they fumbled at their clothes like a couple of awkward kids and dropped them on the floor, not looking at each other. She pulled him into bed, ready now, but their arms and legs kept getting in the way. It had been an awfully long time. Then he was kissing her and saying her name and she thought he would roll on top of her, but instead he just held her, held her close, kissing her softly, and it was good. It felt lovely. She stroked his back, his old, bent back, and could feel his hardness against her. She whispered for him to come inside her and he rolled on top of her and started moving, and then stopped. Waited. Waited for her, wanting to please her. You could tell a lot about a man by the way he waited, or didn't. It wasn't everything but it was something, and it was a whole lot more than she'd had in years.

'Are you alright?' he said, quietly.

'Never better.'

It didn't take long and it was over. Then they lay quietly, side by side, and didn't say a word.

ΔΔΔ

The next day Bernie found her sorting through some photos and he sat down beside her to look. Was he trying to make it up to her, for what had happened in bed? For what hadn't happened in bed. He didn't say and she didn't ask, so they just sat looking at the photos. She could hear his breathing, a bit ragged, a bit nervous, so she patted his hand and hoped he understood what she meant. That last night wasn't a disaster. That it was nice to be held, and to hold him.

She turned a page of the album, and there was Karl from all his glory days at school and university. Prizes and certificates held in front of him, and wearing a beaming, boastful smile.

Bernie cleared his throat. 'He looks very pleased with himself,' he said.

'Just what I was thinking.'

She turned another page: there was Karl on his wedding day, looking devilishly handsome in a dark, well-cut suit, his arm around Meg's waist. She was looking elegant in an emerald green velvet dress that almost touched the ground, and smiling at her new husband for all she was worth.

She heard Bernie sigh. 'Maybe I should have tried harder,' he said, quietly. 'To be closer to our son.'

'He wasn't close to me, either,' she said. 'Maybe some babies just pop out of the womb and decide they don't like their parents.'

'Or maybe he sensed that we were unhappy.'

She kept watching him closely. 'You might be right, Bernie, but ... maybe we were never good enough for him. I always felt he was ashamed of us.' She turned another page. 'Maybe he'll come to visit with his new bride.'

'Or maybe not.'

Would it make him feel better if she told him: I don't love our son. Would it give him the courage to say the same?

She turned another page and found what she'd been looking for: Ella, another child who had their blood running through their veins. Ella as a baby, Gloria holding her in her arms, tears in her eyes. Bernie holding her, looking all at sea. Ella the wobbly toddler, wearing a pair of blue dungarees that Gloria had made on her sewing machine. Ella eating a cake at her birthday party, Nana's rocket cake, for a child who wanted to travel into outer space. How old was she then? Six. And the slice of cake was so big that it almost covered her face. And now there was Ella in a green uniform, her first day of school, carrying a Superwoman backpack. Superwoman! Meg had started her daughter early.

'Look at that grin,' Gloria said. 'It's like she's going on a big adventure.' She gave Bernie a bit of nudge. 'Let's look at our wedding photos.'

There was a much younger Bernie, looking slightly dopey in a suit that was much too big for his skinny frame. And there she was, her arm threaded through his, wearing a loose white dress so the baby didn't show. Nineteen years old, he was, and she was seventeen. Babies, the pair of them, full of hopes and dreams. Well, *she'd* been full of them, anyway.

Bernie put an arm around her waist. She smiled, turned another page.

'Look, a telegram,' she said. She slipped it from the album, held it up to her. 'It's from my Uncle Ted.' She peered closely. 'I don't think you ever met him, did you? He lives somewhere in America. He ... oh Bernie, do you remember? My dad read it out at the reception. Listen to this. TO GLORIA AND BERNIE. MAY YOU FIND GREAT JOY AS HUSBAND AND WIFE. MAY YOUR LOVE ALWAYS BLOOM IN THE GARDEN OF LIFE.'

Bernie laughed. 'You're right, Gloria, I don't know your Uncle Ted, but I can tell he's a dab hand at poetry.'

He was making fun of her uncle. And even though she hadn't seen him for years and he might have been dead for all she knew, he'd taken the trouble to wish them a beautiful life.

'It's the thought that counts,' she said, stiffly.

Bernie removed his hand, shuffled about and told her he was

sorry. He took the telegram from her hand.

'Ella would love to see this,' he said. 'It's an ancient form of technology. We can tell her how long it used to take for people to send their messages across the world. You had to walk or drive to the post office, then write down your message, hand it over to—'

'I know, Bernie. I used to type them up, remember? When I worked in the post office.' The place where he'd first laid eyes on her.

'And now you can send a message in seconds,' he said.

'Still ...' She slipped the telegram back into the album. 'Just because the words are faster these days doesn't make them any better. And sometimes you need to say things, face to face.'

Bernie looked her in the eye.

'My old boss sent me an email,' he said. 'To tell me I wasn't wanted.'

She put her hand on his cheek, let it rest there. 'We'll work it out,' she said. 'And I'll come with you to Centrelink.'

'You are the kindest person, Gloria.'

'And you have nothing to be ashamed of.'

'But I'm ashamed I didn't ask you,' he said.

'About what?'

'About your time in the clinic.'

'I told you at dinner. When Meg and Ella were there.'

'But I didn't ask you before, Gloria. Just the two of us.'

She took his hand, held it gently. 'It was mostly feeling sad, really, very sad,' she said. 'Except for the voices. They were scary.'

'What did they say? Tell me. If you want to.'

Gloria took a deep breath. 'They said I was a very bad person who deserves to die.'

She saw him startle. Go pale.

'It's OK now,' she said, patting his hand. 'Those voices have gone. And I know that it's not true, what they said, I know that now. It was just my mind playing tricks on me.' She moved in closer, wanting to tell him more. Just wanting him now, because he'd asked her. Because she wanted to feel close.

'I wasn't very nice to you,' she said. 'I was horrible, wasn't I?'

'But I'd been horrible to you, Gloria. For many years. I'm so sorry.'

'Stop saying sorry, Bernie. We were both being horrible.'

'But I was horrible for a much longer time.'

She shook her head. 'Bernie. Stop it. Just stop it. We're trying, aren't we? Let's keep trying.'

He looked down at their hands, then up into her eyes. 'I can never say what I really want to say.'

'But actions speak louder than words,' she said. 'That's what my mum taught me.'

Bernie slowly, carefully, put an arm around her shoulder. 'I want to take you to bed,' he said. 'I want to try again. Will you let me try again?'

She felt a smile spread across her face. 'Any time,' she said.

Meg

She checked the time. Three forty-five. Another fifteen minutes and Ella should be home. Everything had happened in a rush, really: a chance meeting with Naomi at the mall, frantic hugs, Ella's breathless *It's SO great to see you!* Meg had no idea that her daughter was so besotted. She'd also had no idea where Naomi's mother was, or her father for that matter. But then the famous lawyer had miraculously appeared—Stephanie Rigg, looking glamorous in jeans and a white T-shirt—and in the blink of an eye, the girls were plotting to have a Boost Juice and *Can I catch the bus home with Naomi, please, please*, because Naomi's mother had an appointment somewhere else. *Please, please, pretty please, Naomi has a phone so I can call you if there's a problem and she knows the bus route and...*

Meg had in truth been deeply embarrassed by her daughter's dramatic pleading, and by the look of bemusement on Stephanie's immaculately made-up face. It was the look that told her: over-anxious mother, smother mother. So what could she possibly have said but *Yes, make sure you're home by four o'clock*. She didn't say be home by four or I'll be calling the police.

Ella's first word was *up*. She wanted to be picked up, be closer to the sky. Well, a bus ride wasn't exactly stratospheric, but it would be relatively safe. Ella would alight from the bus, wave goodbye to Naomi, walk one hundred metres to their home. It was settled.

Meg found herself feeling settled, too. Because the man hadn't shown his face for ... how long? She couldn't remember. Ella's concern about her father had wiped him off her mother's map. It was hard to believe that she, Meg Flynn, embarking on a new and challenging career, ready to change her life, had been thinking like a sixteen-year-old girl. When will he call me, why doesn't he call me, doesn't he find me attractive? Some women spent their entire lives posing these pointless, self-abasing questions. And besides, all the to-and-froing, his coming and going: he might well have a problem, but at least he could have called her. Even once. To tell her he had a problem.

He'd called her beautiful. He was just another smooth-talking liar.

She heard the doorbell ring. Why would Ella ring the doorbell? And no-one ever did except Australia Post or the occasional religious nutter. She headed for the door and opened it, just a chink.

'I lost your card,' he said.

She opened the door a fraction wider.

'So how did you find me?'

'I remembered your name. I checked online for your address.'

That was something, she supposed. If something was better than nothing.

'There were three M.R. Flynns,' he said. 'I phoned two, but they weren't you.'

'So why didn't you phone me next?'

He was frowning now, unsure. 'I kind of lost my nerve,' he said. 'I thought you might tell me to get lost.'

So she wouldn't tell him now? But he *did* look appealing. Hadn't that been part of the attraction with Karl? The way women gave him the eye, tried to chat him up. Was she really so superficial?

'You must have thought I'd forgotten,' he said, quietly. 'It's just that ...'

'Rachel?'

He nodded. 'I'm sorry for barging in on you,' he said.

'You *did* ring the doorbell.'

She found herself letting him in. She found herself offering him a coffee.

'No coffee, thanks,' he said. He was twitchy. Looking around, looking back at her. 'Well, maybe I do. You ... you make me nervous.'

Meg stood fixed to the spot. He'd told her he was out of practice, but this confession seemed so adolescent.

'I can't *make* you feel anything,' she said calmly. 'You told me that, remember?'

'True.'

Should she send him on his way, politely?

'Ella will be home any minute,' she said. Maybe that would speed up his departure.

He tugged at his collar. 'Would you like me to leave?' he said.

Hearing something in his voice—something unsteady, Meg couldn't really place it—she felt her hands clench.

'This is no good, is it?' she told him.

He said nothing.

'I mean ...' She wanted to be kind. He'd tried to find her, after all. He had a difficult experience to deal with. 'You must have a lot on your mind. Maybe you need to ... you know ... focus on that.'

And still he was silent.

'I'm not judging you,' she said. 'It's just that—'

The door flung open. Ella: eyes wide.

Meg felt the strain of her smile. 'You remember Hal, don't you?'

Hal waved, stupidly. Ella pointed through the window.

'Is that your white car out the front?' she said.

'Sure is.'

'It's cool.'

'It's a classic. A nineteen sixty-nine Chevy.'

'Chevrolet,' Meg said.

'Whatever,' Ella said. 'I like the fins at the side, they make the car look sleek like a shark. And I love the cool seats too.'

'The cover's houndstooth.'

'Does that make the car more special?'

Hal grinned. 'Those covers mean I never let anyone eat or drink in my car.'

Meg looked on, listened. Since when had Ella been so interested in cars? She moved towards her daughter, asked if she'd had a good time with her friend, but Ella was more intent on the visitor.

'Are you staying for dinner?' she said.

'I ... well ...'

Ella looked at her mother, then back to Hal, back to her mother. It was new to her, after all: a man in the house. A man with a sleek white car, who'd told her mother she was pretty.

'We could get takeaway,' Ella said.

Meg checked her watch. It was just after four, much too early for dinner. She was beginning to feel nervous again, wondering how to fill in the time. But then Ella rushed in, asked Hal if he liked playing Scrabble.

He grinned. 'I haven't played for years,' he said. 'But I was pretty good at it, I remember. I even won a competition at school.'

'Well, I hope you're a good loser,' Ella said.

△△△

They sat at the table, the box of Scrabble still unopened. Meg watched as Hal stirred his coffee, saw his slender fingers, the dark hairs on his arms. She watched him watching Ella, as she rattled off her stories about travelling on the bus. How an old lady sat fast asleep and snored really loudly, and how a bunch of feral boys were so noisy that the driver stopped the bus and told them off. How she and Naomi had played the little kids' game *I Spy*, and Naomi had insisted on *D for dinosaur* because she could see it in her head. Ella told Hal (not her mother) that she and Naomi both had a banana smoothie in the mall, and pretended they were called something else.

'I don't understand,' Hal said.

'Well, at Boost Juice you give your name when you order your drink, and they call it out when it's ready. Guess what we called ourselves.'

'Sleepy and Sneezy?'

'Ha ha. No. We were Ruby and Ernestina.'

'I see. And let me guess. You were Ernestina.'

'How did you know?'

'Because it's a mucking-around kind of name. Ruby is boring.'

'Exactly.' Ella looked pleased. Then, turning to her mother: 'What did *you* do while I was out, Mum?' Like the perfect hostess.

What *had* her mother done, indeed? A few stabs at a cryptic crossword. A few dirty dishes.

'Nothing worth mentioning,' she said.

Ella looked back at Hal. 'Mum's on a break from study,' she said. 'She's going to be a speech pathologist. It's a noble job.'

A noble job? Where on earth had Ella heard that?

'She's going to work with people who've lost their words,' she said. 'Or people with too many words.'

'People with brain damage,' said Meg.

'And babies, too,' Ella said, winding up like a circus spruiker. 'Mum's going to help babies who've had tubes down their throat so they have to learn to swallow. It's—'

'Thanks, Ella. I'm sure I'll win the Nobel Prize next year.'

'It *does* sound important,' Hal said.

'And Mum used to paint. She wanted to be a painter.'

Meg shook her head. 'I was sixteen years old,' she said.

Her daughter was grinning like a cat, one you wanted to nudge under the table.

'Scrabble time,' she said. 'And no, Mum, you're not allowed to play, I'm going to *demolish* Hal all by myself.'

Meg busied herself with washing up, sneakily intent on watching Hal. The way his hair curved at the back of his neck. His long legs. His face lighting up when Ella told a joke. He was looking, sounding, so much more relaxed.

Meg heard a whoop of triumph from her daughter. It seemed she'd used up all her letters in one go.

Hal looked at the tiles, looked up at Ella. 'What's a *cukadee*?' he said.

'It's a kind of bird,' she said, matter-of-fact.

'Have you ever seen one?'

'It has pink wings. And a big beak.'

'Well, *I've* never seen one.'

'Well, that doesn't mean it doesn't exist.'

Hal laughed. 'You're too clever by half.'

They prattled on. Ella had taken him over, won him over. And for a man who'd never had a child, he certainly knew how to talk to one.

It was heading for five o'clock. Meg joined them at the table, asked Hal if he'd like a drink. Wine? Beer?

He looked up. 'I'm not a drinker,' he said.

Oh hell. She'd been ... 'I'm sorry,' she said quietly.

'Oh, it's not about that,' he said. 'I'm allergic to alcohol.'

'Not about what?' Ella said.

Madam Busybody. Meg would have kicked her daughter under the table, if she'd been within range, but Hal seemed completely unfazed.

'My former wife,' he said. 'She has a problem with alcohol.'

'What kind of problem?'

'Ella. It's none of your business.'

Hal waved the words away, looked across the table, steadily, at Ella. 'It means she drank so much alcohol that she couldn't think straight anymore, couldn't look after herself. Some days she couldn't even get out of bed.'

Ella's face fell. 'That's so sad,' she said.

'It is, yes. But she's getting better. And she has professional people to help her. That's the most important thing.'

Ella was quiet. It was another one of those moments, Meg knew, when the world became more troubling for an innocent child. Like Meg's first year in high school, when she'd learned about the atom bombs and cried about the devastation. Her father had told her, sternly, that the bombs had been *necessary* to end the war.

'What sort of takeaway do you like?' Ella asked Hal.

'Anything and everything,' he said.

'Well, it's all bad for you,' Ella said. 'We learned about nutrition at school, and we did this debate about cooking classes, whether they should be compulsory.'

Meg knew about this debate, had kept hearing about it for weeks.

'My team said cooking means you're civilised,' Ella said. 'So like millions of years ago people used to eat food just to survive. You know, in the days of cavemen and cavewomen, when the men went off to hunt for meat and the women sat around and ... I don't know ... knitted with wool from a woolly mammoth. That was way before women got the vote and stuff.'

Hal laughed. 'So what does all that have to do with cooking?'

'Well, when people discovered fire they found out that cooked meat tasted much better than raw meat. So being civilised means enjoying stuff you don't need to survive. Like listening to cool music or playing Scrabble.'

'That's a great argument,' Hal said. 'I bet you won.'

'We came second. But there were only two teams in the final, which means we lost.'

She said this brightly. Unashamedly. Ella didn't care about winning or losing, except when it came to Scrabble. It was another thing Meg loved about her child.

'It wasn't my idea either,' Ella said. 'My friend Naomi told me. Anyway, if cooking means you're civilised, then Mum's a bit on the savage side.'

Hal looked across at the woman in question. 'You can't be that bad, surely?'

But before Meg could reply, explain her habitual overcooking, undercooking, her mother's carping criticisms, her wilting loss of confidence, Ella was off again.

'Do you have any children?' she asked Hal.

'No.'

'How old are you?'

'Ella. Don't be so nosey.'

'All good,' said Hal. 'I'm forty.'

She nodded, still studying his face. 'What do you do for work?'

'Ella. Will you stop grilling Hal?'

'It's fine, Meg, really.'

And it was. It was helpful.

'I'm a mechanic,' he said. 'An auto mechanic. I work on cars. SUVs. Pick-ups.'

'So is it your passion?'

He smiled, taken by surprise. 'I do love it, yes,' he said. 'I love diagnosing a problem, then working out how to fix it. Cars can have all sorts of problems, some of them really stubborn.'

'Like problems in science,' Ella said. 'Only I don't know how to fix them. Last year we had to do this project about playing sport on Mars, so we had to think about gravity and air pressure and stuff.'

Meg hadn't heard about this project. Had she been too busy with her own?

'Did you work in a group?' Hal asked.

'Yes, just as well. Two of the kids are amazing at science.'

'Then you've just found the solution to your problem. Always ask someone who might know the answer. It can save you a lot of time and trouble. And besides, Ella, no-one can be good at everything. I'm sure you're good at something.'

'Not really. Not super good. I'm not a genius or anything.'

'Well, I think you're pretty smart.'

Ella went bright red.

And now he seemed to have run out of puff, poor man, turning to Meg for relief.

'So you love cars,' she said.

He gave her a warm smile. 'And it's not just a mechanical thing,' he said. 'It's the design, the shape of them, even the smell of them.'

Would she have to cultivate an interest in the aesthetics of the machine? But looking at him now, and seeing his ease with Ella, she would have taken an interest in samurai sword collecting, if he'd been into samurai sword collecting.

She stood up, walked to the kitchen, wondered about dinner, but she could feel his presence behind her. She turned around to face him. If he'd been any closer, she would have seen her reflection in his dark blue eyes.

'I hope I didn't say the wrong thing,' he said quietly. 'About Rachel.'

'No, it's fine. You handled it well.'

'She's a smart cookie, your daughter,' he said. He looked back at Ella, turned back to Meg. 'So. Is her father around?'

'Her father?'

'I mean … is he involved?'

Meg felt herself stiffen. 'Not so loud, please.' She lowered her own voice. 'Her father lives in Sydney, but I don't like to talk about it when Ella's here.'

Hal mumbled an apology. Had she sounded too stern? Too much like her parents? Because he was looking sheepish now, chastised, and she suddenly needed some space, needed to gather her thoughts. Freshen up before dinner. *Back in a jiff*, she said. She heard herself sounding inane.

A brightly lit mirror wasn't what she needed right now, but she made herself look closely. He'd taken her by surprise, turning up at the door, and now she was seeing what he must have seen. Clear skin, a firm chin, good bone structure. A few wrinkles round the eyes. She wasn't in bad shape, all things considered, although she could have done with losing a few kilos. Oh, give over, Meg, you're no movie goddess but you're attractive enough. She ran a brush through her hair, fluffed it out, then waved at her reflection.

She closed the bathroom door, returned to the living room. Saw Ella and Hal sitting side by side, staring at Ella's laptop. Hal looked up and grinned.

'Ella's showing me her favourite band,' he said. 'The Black Eyed Peas.'

'Hal already loves them,' said Ella, bouncing in her seat. 'I told him they were great to dance to.'

They smiled at one another. Instant pals.

'I told Ella I wouldn't dance to anyone's music,' he said.

'But then you said you might change your mind.'

Meg jolted. What did this sound like? Flirtation?

'My problem is ...' Hal shrugged. 'I have two left feet.'

'What does that even mean?' Ella said.

And off he went, trying to explain, until Ella moved away, suddenly excited.

'Do you want to see my flamingos?' she said.

'Seriously? Are they your pets?'

'Don't be silly.' Ella laughed. 'They're my bookends, they're really cool.'

'Then lead the way,' he said.

Before Meg could protest, they rose from the table, Ella marching towards her room, Hal following, Meg bringing up the rear. Her daughter was taking over alright, pointing to her bookends, dragging down her book of poems, lamenting the absence of black bedroom walls. Hal talking now about his bedroom as a boy, and something else about pink feathers on flamingos.

The mother with the fluffed-up hair might just as well have been invisible.

Ella's eyes lit up.

'Can we go for a ride in Hal's car?' she said. Almost shouted.

'Sure!' Hal said.

He didn't wait for a mother's permission.

'Maybe some other time ... I'm ... not feeling well, actually.'

She hadn't known she was going to say that.

'I've come down with a pounding headache,' she said.

She rarely suffered from headaches.

'I think we'll have to forget dinner, too,' she said.

She thought Ella might protest, but she merely muttered something under her breath and turned away. Meg waited for Hal to move, but he seemed to be stranded, as though he'd forgotten how his legs worked. She waved at him to pass her and they somehow arrived in the living room, where he—finally—looked her in the eye.

'You must be feeling rotten,' he said. 'I'm sorry.'

'Me too. But it will pass.'

'So ... when you feel better ... how about I cook for you sometime? If you won't feel offended. About your cooking, I mean.'

She could think of nothing to say.

'How does next Monday sound?' he said. 'I'm taking a day off work and I do a great lasagne. I can bring the ingredients and ...'

She heard *eleven am* and *sous-chef*, so he must have meant what he said.

Two tense bodies standing apart, two pairs of eyes looking unsure. Then Ella sloped back into the room, stood on the spot, stabbing one foot into the floorboards.

'When can we go for that ride?' she said. Whined.

Hal turned to Meg, turned back to look at Ella. 'I'm coming back on Monday,' he said. 'Will you be here?'

Meg remembered his question: Is Ella's father around?

Ella's mouth turned down. 'Monday's no good,' she said. 'I'm going to my friend's house.'

'The one with the funny T-shirts?'

'No, the one who's a champion swimmer.'

'Then we'll do it another time, OK? Soon. I promise.'

He's trying too hard, Meg thought. He'd been trying too hard since Ella led him to her room and showed him those fucking flamingos. He thought her daughter was funny and smart. Promised to take her for a ride in his fancy white car. What game was he playing, now that he'd eased his way into their life? Offering compliments, dispensing advice, listening to Ella's every word. Meg felt a pounding in her head, the beginnings of a genuine headache, like a tom-tom sounding in her brain.

She opened the door and said goodbye. She didn't offer her

hand or a cheek to be kissed. She didn't say *See you soon* or *Looking forward to Monday.* He looked a little deflated, but she didn't really care, since she didn't care at all for insinuating men. Men who liked taking charge, when the father was no longer around.

Bernard

Did he feel more like a man after making love to his wife? After taking her to bed, returning her kisses, giving her satisfaction? Well, he didn't, not really, if being a man meant pumping away, shouting out his joy, finishing the deed by triumphantly beating his chest. The sex hadn't been wildly ecstatic. He hadn't been transported. What he remembered most was the calm. Sighing as he held Gloria in his arms, as she held him, as they breathed each other in.

It had surprised him, this feeling. The warmth of skin against skin.

He remembered reading somewhere that babies could die if no-one touched them. Well, he wasn't a baby, nor was he simply a man. He was a person who wanted Gloria's arms around him, and the softness of her smile when she looked into his eyes.

'Pop, are you OK?'

Ella, bringing him back. Because Gloria had given him this, too. Teach your grandchild German like you said you would. Don't make promises that you don't intend to keep. Not that he'd made a promise to Ella, but he understood what Gloria meant. Actions speak louder than words. Make an effort.

'So. Where were we, Ella?'

'*Der, die, das*,' she said. 'It's weird. Why is a street called female and a river called male? And why is it *das Mädchen*, when a girl is a female?'

Bernard loosened the collar of his shirt. It was so damn hot in here. But they were saving on air con. Gloria had tried to put a brave face on things, talked about ways to save money. No more spending on empty calories, all the cakes and biscuits they'd been devouring for years. No need to buy new clothes, either, she could take in the seams on her sewing machine. And they wouldn't splash out on a wedding present. Why should they, when they'd never even met the bride-to-be, might never meet the bride-to-be, once she became their daughter according to law. Still, even as Gloria spruiked her austerity plan, she must have known they needed money coming in.

Ella's face was glowing, but she hadn't said a word about the heat. Maybe children didn't feel the heat. She was wearing a bright green shirt and a spotted yellow skirt. He supposed this was the latest fashion.

'I'll tell you what,' he said. 'How about we skip these dreary old nouns and learn some useful expressions? Let's start with the basics. *Please. Thank you.*'

'But Pop, that's boring.'

He winced. 'OK. How about ... let me think ... how about *Thank you for baking me this delicious hippopotamus?*'

Ella laughed. 'You're being ridiculous,' she said. 'Anyway, I'd much rather thank someone for letting me join in a gigantic cream-cake fight.'

'A cream-cake fight?' What a treasure she was.

'I saw it on some really old movie,' she said. 'Me and Mum watched it last night. Hundreds of people were shoving heaps of cream cakes into other people's faces and having so much fun. I'd love to do that one day.'

There were far less worthy ambitions, he supposed.

'Let's think of German for a *cream-cake fight,*' he said. 'One of those compound nouns, you know, lots of words strung together. How about ...' He flipped back to his childhood.

'*Sahnetorte* is a cream cake, and *Kämfpen* means fight. So maybe a *Sahnetortekämpfen*? Does that sound like fun?'

'Definitely. So maybe I can have a Sahne ...whatever ... for my birthday.'

She started looking round the room. Was she wishing her Nana was here? But her Nana had kissed her hello and goodbye, kissed her goodbye again, because she'd promised to go with Wendy to puppy preschool. Puppy preschool, Bernard thought: was there no end to the folly of the pampered and the privileged? Still, Ella had looked rather wistful, as if the prospect of a tail-wagging canine seemed a much better option than learning German with her Pop.

She suddenly sprang from the sofa, waving a hand.

'Your house is a bit gloomy,' she said.

'Gloomy?'

'It needs more light.'

'Well, let's turn one on.'

She started pacing round the room, staring at walls, up at the ceiling, back to the walls. Why on earth was she doing that?

She turned to look at him. 'Natural light, Pop,' she said, slowly, as though he'd damaged his brain. 'Look. You could rip up this old brown carpet and put in some light-coloured floorboards.' She pointed to the ceiling. 'Maybe a skylight.' She pointed towards the kitchen. 'And you could take out that dark benchtop and—'

'Ella. Stop. That would cost a lot of money. And ... well, I don't have a job, remember?'

It was hard, he knew, but sometimes a child had to face the cruel facts of life.

'I'm sorry, I forgot,' she said.

She sat down next to him. She was almost level with his eyes. She was going to be tall, like her father. Like Gloria.

'Does it make you feel sad?' she said.

'No. Just a bit … well, useless, really.' He smiled. 'I didn't like my job, anyway. Selling vacuum cleaners. It was unbelievably boring.'

She looked at him, earnestly. 'I've got no idea what I want to do,' she said. 'Did you, when you were growing up? Because … well, you probably didn't plan on selling vacuum cleaners.'

'I once wanted to be an architect, but it didn't work out.'

'What happened?'

What could he tell the child about his dismal truth?

'I didn't have the passion, I guess. But maybe I passed it on to you, Ella, the way you were leaping about the house, thinking about making changes.'

'It was something I saw on TV, a program about places needing natural light. Like houses and offices, old people's homes. It can stop people feeling depressed.'

'That sounds educational.'

'It was. There's a lot of crap on TV but there are some really good programs where you don't have to watch all the crappy ads. Me and Mum watched the show about light after we watched the cream-cake movie.'

Bernard wondered if Meg spent her life watching TV with her daughter. She was a good-looking woman, Meg. He remembered Karl bringing her home and thinking *Mein Got, she is lovely*.

He saw Ella staring at him again.

'Do you know about war?' she said. 'Did you ever fight in one?'

She was leaping from one subject to another.

'No, I've never fought in a war,' he said. 'Why do you ask?'

'Well, my friend Naomi, she's from Canada, she told us the Canadians helped Americans who didn't want to be soldiers.'

'That was the Vietnam War. Vietnam is in Asia.'

'So what were people fighting about?'

How could he explain capitalist versus communist ideology? The industrial-military complex? And he certainly wouldn't tell her about the American president who'd called his penis Jumbo, had whipped it out when reporters kept asking him: *Why is America at war with Vietnam?*

'Pop?'

'Oh, sorry. I was just thinking.'

What right did he have to give her *those* cruel facts of life?

'Wars have been going on for centuries,' he said, 'and they're usually about money, land or hatred. Sometimes all three.'

Ella looked pensive. 'I get the money part,' she said. 'Lots of people are greedy. Just walking round the supermarket with Mum, you see trolleys loaded up with huge packets of chips and mountains of chocolate and boxes of Diet Coke. Not that I don't like chips or chocolate, but Diet Coke doesn't even taste good, it's so full of artificial stuff.'

Bernard had to smile at this roundabout chatter. She was sounding more and more like Gloria. It was quite disarming, really.

'I get the land part,' she said, 'because the land might have gold or oil or just more room for people to live in. But I don't get why people hate each other. I mean, I know people have fights. Like last year at school, Charlize called Avril *a big fat turd*. The teacher made her apologise and promise not to say anything like that, ever again. But that's not really hating each other, is it? I mean, so much that people want to kill other people.'

'Ah. Well.' He paused. How to explain this one? Conflicting ideologies again? Religious mania? Fear of difference?

'Sometimes people hate other people who look different from them,' he said. 'Say, when their skin is a different colour, or their noses have a different shape.'

He was quoting Joseph Conrad, more or less. *Heart of*

Darkness: another lost book returned to him.

'Noses?' said Ella. 'Like big noses you wish were smaller?'

'Not exactly. I mean that people from different races have different shaped noses. So, for example, some white people hate black people, and they justify ... they tell themselves it's because they hate the much bigger, flatter noses of black people.'

Conrad had put it so much better.

'I have a big nose,' Ella said. 'But I'm not black.'

Bernard tried not to smile. He didn't want to condescend. 'You have a beautiful nose,' he said. 'It's called an aquiline nose, and beautiful women throughout history have had a nose shaped just like yours.'

'Really?'

'Really. I'll show you some pictures if you like. But first ...' He eased his aching bones up from the sofa. 'I'm going to make us some afternoon tea. *Schönes Enklekind.*'

'What does that mean?'

'It means *lovely grandchild.*' He smiled down at curly-haired Ella. 'I tell a lie,' he said. 'It means there's an elephant swimming in my soup.'

She laughed. 'You must have been a really fun dad,' she said.

ΔΔΔ

After a strong coffee for him and a glass of milk for Ella, not to mention sharing the Tim Tams she'd snuck into her bag, it was time to take his sneaky grandchild home. Virginia Woolf's elegant nose had to wait for another day, but he wouldn't speak of her anguished madness, her terrible suicide. This too, he remembered, from the days when reading had been a revelation.

As they settled into the car, Ella turned to him with a serious face.

'I don't want to call you Pop anymore,' she said. 'It's the name a little kid would give you.'

'OK. Fair enough.'

'You tell me about important stuff,' she said. 'And you listen to me. And you're not like my other grandpa, who stomps with his feet *and* his voice. He's a pain.'

Should he remind her about respecting one's elders? But what the hell, he thought, the child was entitled to her opinions. Besides, he couldn't help feeling pleased. That she liked him. That he wasn't stomping his way through her life.

'Why not call me Bernard?' he said.

Ella shook her head. 'It wouldn't feel right. You're my grandfather.'

He had an idea, from his other language. Isn't that what he'd called it, so many weeks ago, when he'd first taken care of Ella?

'What about Opa?' he said. 'It's German for grandfather. It's a friendly word.'

Ella sounded it out, twice. 'You're right,' she said. 'Opa.' She stared through the window, still thinking hard. 'I'll have to find another name for Nana, too,' she said. 'It's only fair. Maybe Nana G. No, that's too much like a rapper. I'll have to think about it some more.'

She settled back in her seat, as if ready to travel with her thoughts. Bernard started the car, set to release the handbrake, when she turned to him with that serious face again.

'Why didn't you fight in a war?' she said.

'Well ... I could have fought in the Vietnam War, but I chose to protest instead. I marched in the street, along with thousands of other people, because we believed the war was wrong.'

'Was it about money? Land? Hate?'

'All of those things. I'll tell you all about it someday. I promise.'

She looked at him, quizzically. 'Did you have to go to prison? Because you didn't want to fight?'

He shook his head. 'I was lucky.'

'So what happened when you marched in the street?'

'Not much, really. A lot of people stood on the footpaths, staring at all the marchers as if we'd gone completely mad. I remember how one man spat at us.'

Ella gasped.

'They thought we were cowards,' Bernard told her. 'But we were just ordinary people who thought war was a terrible thing. We knew that thousands of people on both sides would die. And they did. Or they lost their arms or legs. Lost their minds.'

Ella held his gaze. 'So, not like a cream-cake fight,' she said.

ΔΔΔ

Centrelink. Gloria had kindly offered to go with him, but he didn't want her witnessing his ritual humiliation: taking a ticket and taking a seat, then an interview with some acned youth who was lucky to have a job in these days of retrenchments, voluntary redundancies and trickle-down economics, in which the rich merrily pissed on the not-rich.

He heard the front door slam, looked up from his computer. Gloria was home, and judging by the look of excitement on her face—eyes wide, cheeks aflame—he braced himself for a barrage of canine stories. But he smiled, despite himself. It was good to see her happy. Happy? She was flapping her hands and bowling right up to him, saying his name several times over.

'I've been offered a job!' she said. She plumped herself down next to him, clutched his hands. 'I can't believe it, Bernie. I was hopping into Wendy's car and my phone rang and you wouldn't believe who it was, it was Natalie and she wants me to—'

'Gloria, Gloria. Slow down, please.'

She took a big, deep breath. 'OK, then. Here's the story.'

It seemed that Natalie, who'd sold Gloria the purple shimmering dress, had come up with *a brilliant idea*. Gloria as her assistant, the perfect person to deal with women embarrassed about buying clothes. Larger women. Because, according to Natalie, Gloria was *a whole lot of things that are good.*

'Like what?' said Bernard, and then heard how that sounded.

'She said I was sensitive to other people's feelings. And diplomatic. And ... oh, never mind; she was just showering me with compliments, Bernie, I didn't recognise myself.'

'So how did she know this?' Bernard said, and flinched. 'I don't mean that you're not like that ... I just mean—'

'I know what you mean, Bernie, just don't keep interrupting. Please.'

Off she galloped, with a story about a customer who'd bought a dress on Gloria's advice ... another story about Gloria being honest with Natalie ... another story about Gloria praising the shop without being phony. And he'd never guess how Natalie tracked her down ... something to do with a Trudy ... *you know Trudy, her dog died last year* ... it seemed that Trudy with the deceased dog had walked into Natalie's shop, looking to buy a dress, because her neighbour, Gloria, had bought one there and it was *positively divine.*

'Now, that was just amazing, Bernie. Trudy, who's never worn a sparkling dress in her life. But even more amazing, she and Natalie got to talking about the neighbour and it was me, wasn't it? And then the next thing you know, Natalie has my phone number and she's calling me and ... two days a week, Bernie. Two days a week, working in *Natalie's Place.*'

Bernard said nothing.

'So ... what do you think?'

Still he said nothing.

'It's only two days,' she said, slowly. 'We'll still have lots of time together.'

Did she think he would resent her absence? Fall into a deep, dark well of self-pity?

'I think I can manage without you,' he said.

She narrowed her eyes. 'You're being sarcastic,' she said.

'Oh no, no, not at all.' Would he ever get this right? 'I just meant ... of course, two days is nothing, nothing at all.'

That didn't sound right, either. As though her job was of no account.

'I meant ... I can handle two days without you,' he said.

She eyed him carefully. 'You still sound a bit ... you're not sure, are you?' She moved in a little closer. 'You know, people do things differently these days,' she said. 'If that's what you're thinking.'

She was thinking of him and his pride.

'And we need the money,' she said.

He nodded.

'And you know, Bernie, you can be useful while I'm working in the shop.'

'Useful?'

'You can clean the house. And the bathroom showerhead needs replacing. The kitchen sink needs unclogging. You could even learn to cook dinner.'

'Really?'

'It's good to be useful, isn't it?' she said. 'Otherwise ... well, what's the point of anything?'

He was tempted to call her *profound* but feared he would sound sarcastic again.

'I'm an excellent vacuum cleaner,' he said. 'Doing it, I mean. I'm not a machine.'

Gloria smiled with what looked like relief. Had she seen him as a tyrant, a bully like his father?

'It's OK, then?' she said.

'You don't need my permission.'

'But I want you to feel happy about it. We're in this together, aren't we?'

He drew her to him. 'Yes, we are,' he said. 'And Natalie certainly approves of you. She knows you'll be good for business. And she knows you're a decent human being.'

Gloria squeezed him. Almost squeezed the life out of him.

'You're also our *deus ex machina*,' he said. 'A god out of the machine.'

She drew away from him. 'What on earth does that mean?'

'It comes from ancient Greek theatre. They used machinery to lower the gods onto the stage, to sort out the characters' problems. So a god out of a machine means an unexpected and welcome solution. Saving the day.'

Gloria shook her head. 'It's Natalie who's the ... whatever you called it,' she said. 'But in any case, I don't want another play. I'm too busy dealing with life.'

Bernard had to smile. His wife wasn't the least bit intellectual, but then who was he to judge? He'd read worthy fiction in his youth that he'd never once returned to. He read detective fiction in middle age because he liked to guess the outcome. He read a monthly magazine that rarely challenged his views. What filled his head these days was much more difficult, he knew: the need to listen, to strive to be less cynical, to stop feeling superior to his unschooled wife. It was hard work, this self-help business, and people made a lot of money selling it. The small changes, the life changes. He'd even seen a title called *Braving your Inner Wilderness*, although he wasn't quite sure what the metaphor proposed. Did it mean grappling with the beast within, confronting your secret, dangerous desires? Or was the wilderness the desert of your unfeeling heart? But what did such questions matter, when the flesh-and-blood answer was standing right in front of him.

'You're looking far away,' Gloria said.

'Well, I'm seeing you in the shop,' he said, 'and feeling so proud of you.'

She beamed.

'And I'm thinking of how much we've changed,' he said.

'Have we?' Gloria smiled. 'Maybe we just got lost, then found our way back again.'

Meg

She'd felt lost for two whole days, mulling things over, changing her mind, changing it back again. Wondering if she'd been hypersensitive, even a touch irrational, about Hal. Maybe he hadn't been trying to muscle in, take over. He'd told her, after all, that he wished he'd had a child. Maybe he didn't have a family he was close to. Or maybe he just liked Ella; it might be as simple as that.

Still, he could have paid her mother more attention.

And now who was being a child?

It didn't help that Ella kept nagging her. *When can I go for that drive? He was a lot of fun. He talked to me about school, Mum, but not in a boring way. He has a cool car. He likes playing Scrabble.*

Meg tried to shrug off her resentment, let it run off her shoulders in the shower. She blow-dried her hair, put on a loose, sleeveless dress, checked her watch. Hal would be here in half an hour, and she could feel those long-forgotten flutters in her chest. She went in search of her novel, but when she sat down and tried to read, the sentences kept floating in front of her. She checked her watch again. Ten fifteen. She didn't have his number. Why hadn't he given her his number? Was it strange that he hadn't? She hadn't thought of that before. Another sentence floated in front of her: *Madeleine stubbed her toe on the porch.* Why hadn't he called to say that he was running late? It would have been polite. Or had he lost his phone again? Had he lost her number? But he knew where she lived, so it would be alright, wouldn't it? He would remember her street, remember her house with the white picket fence.

Was she a woman from the fifties, waiting for a man?

She put down her book, walked to the sink, wished there were some dishes to wash.

She checked her watch. Ten twenty.

Maybe she could put on some washing.

Maybe she should call her parents, since they never called her, never asked about her life, their granddaughter's life. But why should she call them, when she'd only get an earful from her mother about *your father*, how he'd dragged her all the way to Melbourne for a job he hated and the plumbing was deafening and had Meg found a man yet because ... Maybe she could phone a friend, make a date for coffee sometime. But Hanna would be working and didn't like being interrupted. So would Laura and Ruth, old workmates still slaving away in the ATO. And there was no point texting the students who'd helped her with statistics, Hayley and Madison were twenty years old, said they hated kids and spent most of their time on their phones. The only other mature-aged student had looked Meg up and down in a disapproving way, as if her dress was too tight or her hair too blonde. What about Audrey, then? She'd be working, too. The whole world was either working or disapproving or talking on their phones, but Meg needed to *do* something.

Maybe she could go to a movie, and too bad if he bothered turning up when she was miles away, munching on popcorn. She checked the sessions online, but most of it was rom-com or action rubbish. Then she saw *Bright Star*, about the doomed love of John Keats, the tubercular poet. But remembering the sad, cramped room in Rome where Keats had languished on his deathbed, Meg knew she didn't want to see a movie about doomed love and dying. She picked up her novel again. Struggled through a page, put it down again.

Ten forty. Maybe something terrible had happened. She hadn't thought of that before. A car accident. A heart attack, although he didn't look the type. Or maybe, right now, his former wife was pleading with him to stay, her eyes stricken, her hands clutching his. He was trying to help her, wasn't he, to make up for past neglect. He was a good man, or at least a man who'd changed for the better. Or maybe ... Rachel had died.

The doorbell.

She opened the door. He was wearing a crisp white shirt and a pair of jeans, and holding a bunch of flowers. Purple lisianthus. How did he know they were her favourite?

'I'm so sorry I'm late,' he said.

Really late, she thought. He looked embarrassed, knotted up.

'These are my apology flowers,' he said, and handed them over.

Meg looked down at the flowers, then up into his eyes.

'Can I ... can we talk?' he said.

She stood on the doorstep, unable to move.

'It would help if you let me come in,' he said quietly.

Did she want to help? Or talk? Did she? But she found herself standing aside. She saw that his hands were clenched. Should she give him back the flowers, give him something to do with those anxious hands?

'Look, Meg ... this is ... it's difficult,' he said.

'Rachel?'

He looked away. 'It's ... it's more than that.'

He couldn't seem to look her in the eye.

'Things are tricky,' he said. 'I think it's better if we call it quits.'

He gave her a tight, forced smile.

'So you're not going to talk after all,' she said.

'I ... look ...'

He started scratching the side of his neck. She wanted to wrench away his hand, tell him to stop.

'It doesn't matter,' he said, and lowered his hand, lowered his eyes. 'I mean it does, but ... well ...'

She took a deep breath. Did she really want to buy into what seemed to be a mess?

'I've had ... I mean, it's been great,' he said.

'Great?'

'Spending time with you. And Ella. It's been ... it's been great to talk to her. She's a special kind of girl.'

'Special?'

Meg heard herself echoing his words. She couldn't find her own.

'She's unspoiled,' he said.

Unspoiled?

'You've raised a great child,' he said. His shoulders were sagging and his face was grim. 'Say goodbye to her from me,' he said. 'It's better for her too.'

'Better?'

He cleared his throat.

'If I don't come back.'

Then he turned around and headed for the door, opened it, disappeared. Meg heard an engine starting up, then a roaring down the street, as if he couldn't get away fast enough. She heard the humming of the fridge, and then a buzzing in her ears, felt a sudden hammering in her chest. She had to sit down. She had to think. Try to make sense of what he'd said. *A lot more than that ... tricky ... better if we call it quits ...* It didn't matter, and then it did. And what had he called Ella? *Special. Unspoiled.* That it was better for her if he didn't come back. What was he saying? What did he mean? He couldn't mean ... surely. That he liked little girls? That he was—she could hardly even think the word—a paedophile. But she hadn't found him creepy, had she? Ella hadn't found him creepy. She would have said. She knew about stranger danger from her mother, from school. She knew to listen to her body for signs of unease. But then ... he'd asked Ella how old she was. Was it the first time they met? The second? Puffing her up, telling her she was smart, laughing at her jokes, offering to dance with her. Offering to cook a meal at her house, hoping to see Ella. Asking where her father was.

A picture flashed into her head: a hand on her thigh, moving up her thigh. She was eight years old and frozen, her mouth clamped shut, but then jumping up, pushing past knees and rushing out of the cinema, sobbing with fear, her mother rushing after her. By the time they returned with the manager, the nasty, horrible man had disappeared.

Just like Hal.

Those stories on the news ... teachers, cops, ordinary husbands and fathers, caught with child pornography. Stories about men who flew to foreign lands to pay for ravaged children. Who fucked them over, passed them on to other men.

She shook her head.

This is madness, she said to the wall.

Witches had green eyes, he'd told her. They burned witches at the stake.

She must drive out the forces of suspicion.

She had to ring Hanna.

'Are you OK, Meg?'

Hanna must have heard the edge in her voice.

'I'm fine. I just ... wanted to say hello. I'm sorry for interrupting.'

'Well, you saved me from screaming at a client, actually.' Hanna sighed. 'Look, I'm sorry I can't talk, Meg, I have to dash out to see another client. He wants his place to look like a display home, and *he* looks like a suntanned Ken doll.'

'I'm sorry for bothering you, Hanna.'

Silence.

'Are you really OK, Meg? You sound a bit—'

'I'm fine, fine. Really.'

And she was. Better, anyway, for hearing Hanna's voice. They promised to catch up soon.

Meg heard a noise, turned to see the front door swing open. Ella, all gangly legs and skinny arms, striding into the room.

'Lola's been called up for extra training,' she said. 'Her mum just dropped me off.'

'Oh, that's a shame.'

'She felt really bad but it's OK. Now I can have that ride in Hal's car.' She looked around the room. 'Where is he? Where's his car?'

Meg cleared her throat. 'He's ... well, he's been and gone, Ella.'

'Gone?

Is he going away somewhere?'

'I mean we won't be seeing him again.'

Ella frowned. 'But why? What happened?'

'We ... we had an argument, sweetheart. We knew it wasn't going to work out.'

'What kind of argument?'

Meg walked towards her, put a hand on her arm. 'Nothing serious,' she said. 'But we agreed to go our separate ways.'

'But you liked each other, didn't you?'

'Sure. But sometimes liking isn't enough, is it? We're just ... you know ... different.'

Keep steady, Meg, for your own sake, as well as your daughter's.

'I thought he was great,' Ella said, staunchly.

As if her mother could have tried a little harder.

'And he thought *you* were great, too,' she said.

Maybe a little too much.

Stop it, Meg. Just stop.

'He was so nice, Mum. Why couldn't you—'

'Ella. It wasn't my fault, OK?' She took a deep breath, wishing that could be the end of the story, but she knew she had to say more. Try to keep it light. 'Just in case ... if you see Hal around and he offers you a ride in his car ... just say no. OK? I don't want him thinking we can start again. Go out on dates.'

Ella was staring at her, her face furrowed.

'Anyway, how about getting something to eat?' Meg said. 'We could have pancakes at the mall. We haven't been there for months.'

It was the least she could do for her daughter. *A smart little cookie*, he'd called her. Eating girls up: the honeys, the cupcakes, the sugars.

She could see disappointment smudging Ella's face.

'Go and wash up,' Meg said. 'And run a brush through your hair, OK?'

Wash up. Brush your hair. Be normal.

And then, as she watched Ella walk away, as she tried to forget Hal's halting, cryptic words, something else returned to her. A man who'd sat Meg on his lap when she was a little girl. A man who'd bounced her and pressed her close and she'd felt something hard in his pants against her bottom. It had made her feel funny, the hardness, and she'd squirmed, wriggled off his lap. She was five or six years old and had never told a soul. He hadn't come around after that, and her mother had wondered why. *So interesting to talk to*, she'd said. *Such a charming, clever man.*

Ella

Hal thought she was clever. He'd laughed at her joke about the woolly mammoth, and he'd made her feel a bit sad, too, about the woman who drank too much and maybe he'd been madly in love with her and that made it even sadder. But he loved working with cars, and he wasn't like Tyson's dad who drove up to school one day in a hot red sports car and hooted and waved, letting all the kids know what a cool guy he was. And Hal hadn't minded when she cheated at Scrabble, because she *had* kind of cheated, making up a word and pretending it was real. But he didn't get all huffy and mad. He didn't care about winning. And he'd kept looking at her mum when her mum wasn't looking, like he couldn't take his eyes off her. But not in a creepy way. Not like her father and the girls in their bikinis.

Why would it matter if she took a ride in his car? Just because her mum didn't want to have fun ...

Ella took a sad bite of cereal. She didn't like Nutri-Grain, anyway. It tasted like cardboard. Not that she knew what cardboard tasted like, because you'd have to be really stupid to try it. Or starving.

Maybe she could phone Lola—on her mum's phone—and ask to play with her new kitten. Smudge, he was called, because of the marks around his big yellow eyes. Or maybe Fern would let her take pictures with her new camera. They could go to the beach and *capture the dance of the waves*. That's what Fern called it, sounding all poetical. It would be good to have some fun before they all went back to school, in those daggy lace-up shoes and that daggy black skirt that some girls hated, they said it made them look fat. And what about—she heard her mum's phone ringing on the kitchen bench and went to take a peek. Maybe it was Hal, wanting to come back. But her mum beat her to it, picking up the phone, listening, nodding, saying *Just a moment, please.*

'Naomi's mother's inviting you to a movie,' she said. 'You and Lola and Fern. Do you—'

'Yes. Yes.'

It was Naomi! And the gang! Ella was ready to pounce into the day. She heard her mum making arrangements. Arrangements!

'One o'clock this afternoon,' she said. 'Naomi's mother will go with you. Does that sound OK?'

'Sure. Yes. Yes.'

'The movie's called *Bright Star*,' her mum said. 'It's rated twelve years and over, but I've already checked it out. It's not scary.'

OTT again.

'It's a movie about a poet,' her mum said. 'I'd quite like to see it myself.'

A poet? No wonder it wasn't scary. But would her mum want to come with them? No, she had to buy groceries, she said, there wasn't a thing to eat in the house. Ella was glad her mum had to buy groceries, not because she didn't like her mum, but because … well, just because. She was going to see a movie with her three best friends. They could be an all-girl band, except that none of them could sing. The music teacher had told them that last term: *You sound appalling, ladies, like the mating call of a stomach pump.*

ΔΔΔ

Finally. Naomi's place. Naomi's bedroom. But Fern and Lola weren't coming after all. Fern had fallen off her bike and her mum was worried about concussion, and Lola had some family thing she had to go to. Naomi said *family thing* like she'd just swallowed milk way past its use-by date.

'I wanted the gang to get together,' she said. 'It's too bad.'

But then she smiled at Ella, said it was great to see her, saying it for real, and so Ella said it was great to see her, too. She looked around the room, but there were no posters of monsters with demonic eyes. There weren't any posters at all. The room was bare: just a bed, a desk and a wardrobe, and all of it painted white. Like everything was disappearing.

'Do you like my new look?' Naomi said. 'It's called minimalism.'

Ella nodded. She figured it must mean keeping things to a minimum. But what could she tell Naomi? To sort of pass the time. The apples. She'd seen a picture of the painting, she said, and weren't the apples amazing, and—it was a bit weird— Naomi patted her on the head, like she was a puppy that had learned a new trick. Then Naomi started looking round the room, looking up at the ceiling, with that bored, what's-next kind of look on her face. Ella was beginning to wish Fern hadn't fallen off her bike and Lola didn't have a family thing. And she wished Naomi hadn't patted her on the head.

'So what shall we talk about?' Naomi said.

Maybe, Ella thought, I can tell her about learning German. But that would mean saying that *der*, *die* and *das* was way too hard because it didn't make any sense. She wouldn't tell Naomi Lola's secret, either, because a promise was a promise, and anyway, Lola thought Naomi was a show-off.

Maybe Lola didn't have a family thing.

She saw Naomi look up the ceiling again. What now, Ella thought. What could she say that was interesting?

'I like your dress,' she said. 'It's a beautiful blue.'

'It's called teal,' Naomi said. 'And I love the stitching round the collar.'

Does she like my dress, too? Ella thought. With its swirly kind of pleats.

How long until they went to the movies?

And then she remembered. Her mum. Hal.

'My mum met this guy,' she said, trying to sound casual. 'He's really nice. He's smart and funny and he has a really cool car.'

'Is he good looking?'

'I guess so. Sure. But ... well, he and mum had a fight and now he's gone.'

'That's too bad. Did your mum like him a lot?'

'Well, he sure liked *her*. He kept giving her *looks,* if you know what I mean.'

Naomi nodded.

'And he liked *me* a lot,' Ella said. 'I've met him a couple of times now, and he listened to me properly and laughed at all my jokes before Mum gave him the flick.'

Naomi narrowed her eyes. 'So what did they have a fight about?' she said.

'Mum didn't really say. Just that they were different. But she said if he came back, not to go for a ride in his car. Like I wasn't allowed to have any fun.'

Just then Naomi's mum poked her head into the room and said it was time to go. She was wearing long dangly earrings and a whole lot of eyeliner without looking trashy. She wasn't a nosy kind of mother, either, always bugging you with questions about what you were doing or going to do or had been doing since the day you were born. And she'd said to call her Stephanie, only Ella didn't feel right with that.

Naomi kept giving her smiles in the back seat of the car, but every so often her face would turn sort of dark. It started bothering Ella a bit, that look, but she didn't want to say. Then the car pulled up at the cinema and everything started happening without her: Naomi's mum rushing them inside, handing over some money, saying she'd pick them up in two hours from this spot where they were standing. OK? Then she just took off in a hurry. Just like that. Ella felt a bit twitchy, but Naomi was all calm and cool, looking around, checking her phone, like she was used to her mum leaving her. Maybe she even went to the movies by herself. Ella told herself it would be OK, that she'd been here heaps of times. She knew how much the choc bombs cost, and how her mum always said she'd have to take out a second mortgage to afford one. And Ella knew that when she walked into the dark tunnel of the cinema, just before she saw the screen, it was like moving into a different space where lights were brighter and people were bigger and laughs were louder and she'd always loved it, like being in a different world where anything could happen.

Naomi nudged her in the side.

'I don't want to watch this *Star* thing,' she said.

'What?'

'I looked up reviews online and they said teens would find it boring.'

'But we're not teens, Naomi.'

'Well, near enough.'

'And we have two hours to wait.'

'Ella.' Naomi gave her a cross teacher-look. 'Nothing bad's gunna happen. OK?'

Did Naomi think she was a baby? Well, maybe she was, just a bit.

'I've been thinking,' Naomi said. 'Ever since you told me.'

'Told you what?'

'About the guy your mum had a fight with.'

'But—why?'

'I think something's not right.'

'What do you—'

'It's like this, Ella.' Naomi drew closer, lowered her head. 'I think he might be creepy.'

'Creepy?'

'You know ... with kids.'

Ella jolted. She stared at Naomi, who was looking back at her. Like she was daring her to disagree.

'But he didn't make me feel creepy, not a bit,' she said. 'He was just being friendly and nice.'

Naomi shook her head. 'But here's the thing, Ella. Men like that are devious. You, know, sneaky. They make you feel special but they take the longer view.'

'The longer view?'

'They take their time, lure you into thinking that you're friends. They trick the parents as well.'

Ella didn't know what to think, except that Naomi was being a bit weird.

'And your mum being a single mum and all,' Naomi said. 'She's an easy target.'

This is *really* weird, Ella thought. She wanted Naomi to stop.

'Ella. I think your mum knows. That he's creepy.'

'So why didn't she warn me, then?' Ella shot back.

Naomi sighed. 'Think about it. If he's not coming back, your mum wouldn't tell you what was really going on. She wouldn't want to scare you for no reason.'

Ella took this in. Was that what her mum had been up to? Like not telling her the truth about her father? Thinking she couldn't handle it.

But Hal couldn't be like that, could he?

'I don't think he's creepy,' she said.

Naomi moved in even closer. Ella could smell mint on her breath.

'Are you really sure, Ella? This is important, you know.'

'I'm really sure. You know how they say to listen to your body? How if someone makes you feel weird and makes you want to run away, then you know they're nasty. They want to hurt you. But my body didn't say that. No way.'

Naomi was nodding now. 'Our bodies tell us the truth,' she said.

'Do you believe me, then?'

'I do. You have such conviction.' She moved away, gave Ella one of her dazzling smiles. 'Let's go track him down,' she said.

'*Track him down*?'

'So you can do the right thing.'

'What do you mean?'

'You can defend his character.'

'I ... I don't get it.'

'Look, Ella.' Naomi was sounding put out, like Ella was a bit of a *dummkopf*. 'What's the worst thing that can happen to you?'

Ella bit her lip. 'I don't know. Maybe ... I'd get really sick and die. Or my mum would die.'

'Sure. But how would you like it if other people thought really bad things about you that weren't true? Wouldn't you like to clear your name? Let the whole world know the truth?'

'Yes. But—'

'And then your mum would know the truth, wouldn't she? Maybe they could get back together. He sounded really nice.'

'But—'

'Look, Ella. We can do it together.'

It was like being on some crazy merry-go-round that kept getting faster and faster.

'I don't know where he lives,' Ella said. 'I don't know his phone number. It's ... you'll never find him, Naomi.'

'OK, let me think.' Naomi put her hand to her forehead,

like she was pressing on her brain. 'What does this guy do for work?'

'He ... he fixes cars.'

'A mechanic,' Naomi said, all dramatic, like she'd just solved the world's biggest mystery.

'So what do—'

'Shh. I'm still thinking.' She screwed up her face. 'I'm the detective. What should I do?'

Ella had no idea.

'Does he work in a car place, Ella? Like ... you know ... a garage?'

'I don't know.'

'What's his name?

'Hal.'

Naomi licked her lips. 'Right. Give me ten minutes. If I haven't found him in ten minutes, we'll ... I don't know, do something boring. Have a choc bomb or something.'

Ella was beginning to think that eating a choc bomb might be the most exciting thing in the world. She was beginning to think that Naomi was just the tiniest bit crazy. She watched her whip out her phone and walk to the door. She watched her talking on her phone in the distance; it was like watching TV on silent and you had no idea what was going on. Ella waited. She waited some more. And then Naomi was waving at her, flapping her hand like a mad thing. Ella figured she'd have to go and join her.

'I've tracked him down!' Naomi said, waving her phone in her hand.

'How?'

'I found a garage called Hal's Auto Repairs.'

'But how do you know it's *my* Hal? My mum's Hal?'

'Well, it wasn't a man who answered, and I don't know what your Hal sounds like, anyway. But it's not far from here. It'll be easy to find on Maps.'

'But what if it turns out to be the wrong Hal?'

'So what? It'll still be an adventure.'

Everything was happening so fast again: Naomi telling her she was wrong, then telling her she was right, hatching a plan, finding clues, sounding so sure of herself. It was the right thing to do, wasn't it? Defend Hal's character? Tell her mum the truth? And so what if it turned out to be the wrong Hal? They wouldn't have to say a thing. But if it was the right Hal, they could tell him it was all a big mistake and maybe, just maybe, he and her mum could start all over again. She'd seen the way he looked at her. She'd seen what her mum couldn't see.

'You're right,' she said. 'Let's go.'

∆∆∆

Ella didn't say a word as they walked along the footpath. She was hot and didn't have any water, and was beginning to wish she were back in the cinema, where at least it would be cool and she could buy some water and still have enough for a choc bomb. But she had to see this through. Do the right thing. Didn't her mum say it was your character that mattered?

Naomi checked her phone again. 'Nearly there,' she said.

They turned a corner and: there it was. *Hal's Auto Repairs* in big red letters, with cars and trolleys and petrol pumps and a massive truck with gigantic wheels. Naomi grabbed Ella's arm.

'Hold on,' she said. 'This could be amazing.'

Then Ella saw it: a shiny white car, with big fins, gleaming in the sun. Hal's car. It had to be. She felt a stab of triumph in her chest. She leaned in close to her friend.

'That's his car,' she whispered, as though someone else might hear.

'It's way cool,' Naomi said, not bothering to lower her voice. 'OK, let's act casual.'

'There *he* is,' Ella whispered again.

She saw him in the distance, looking at some car, wiping his hands on a rag. Then he turned to talk to someone, nodding away, turned back to the car. He must have been trying to work out a problem. But then everything changed in a flash, because seeing his hands and his talking and thinking, Ella saw something else, something new: that she didn't know him at all. That he had nothing to do with her or Naomi or even her mum. He only belonged to himself. But before she could whisper stop, no, I don't want to do this, Naomi was pulling her along and Hal was turning and he'd seen them. He stopped dead. Then he started walking, walking towards them, getting closer and closer. It was way too late to turn back.

He looked Ella straight in the eye, his face all puzzled. 'Ella,' he said. 'What are you doing here?'

She felt her heart knocking in her chest.

'We went to see a movie,' Naomi said, loud and clear. 'But we knew it would be really boring.'

Ella wanted to hit her now, with her boring this and boring that. Hal was still looking straight at her. Confused.

'Does your mother know you're here?' he said.

'Ella wants to know,' Naomi said.

Hal looked at her like she was a creature from outer space, then turned to look at Ella.

'What do you want to know?' he said.

Ella felt her legs shaking. 'I don't know,' she said.

Naomi blurted out: 'We're here to defend you against a baseless accusation. Ella's mum thinks you're a paedo.'

Oh My God. Hal's face turned as hard as a rock. Then he took a big deep breath, turned to face Ella, boring into her with his eyes.

'You're joking, right?'

And still she couldn't speak. And still he was staring, making her feel so small and trembly all over and his face was all hard and dark.

'You're joking,' he said again. 'What's going on?'

Ella couldn't speak, staring into Hal's hard face, and she couldn't ask Naomi for help, she couldn't ask for anything when he was staring like that, like he was about to explode right in front of her.

'Where are you two meant to be?' he said.

'My mum's picking us up at the movies,' Naomi said.

'Then go back and wait for her.'

Ella tried to speak, she *had* to speak, but some terrible lump was blocking up her throat.

'Just get out of here,' he said, looking from one to the other. 'Don't let me see you here again. I don't want to see you anywhere.'

He turned and stomped away. Big angry steps, one foot after the other.

Naomi reached out her hand.

'Hey, I'm sorry,' she said. 'I kind of messed up, didn't I?'

Ella felt herself being pulled along the footpath, heard Naomi saying *Don't cry, Ella, please don't cry.* But how could she stop crying when she'd been a mean, stupid person, a dumb tagalong person who'd turned Hal into stone, then made him spit his words at her and for the first time in her life she knew she'd done something horribly cruel. Underneath Hal's cold angry face and his cold angry words she felt like she'd stabbed him in the heart. Even though she hadn't said that ugly word. Naomi had said it. But Ella hadn't said no. No. It isn't right, Naomi.

She felt a pair of arms around her, heard Naomi saying something about a car and how they could have had a fabulous ride.

Gloria

She'd ended up taking the car after all. She'd planned on taking the bus to save money, but after waiting half an hour for a bus that never came and getting more and more worried about being late, she really didn't have much choice. Which meant wasting money on petrol. But it also meant saving on wine, because she didn't drink and drive. No-one should drink and drive because they'd end up dead or even worse, make other people dead, you saw it all the time on the news, idiots who wouldn't know their bum from their elbow, like her dad used to say. Besides, she'd seen the price of a glass of wine in the restaurant and nearly died. Fourteen whole dollars, and not even halfway to the top! She'd insisted on paying for the meal as well, when she'd phoned Meg to ask her to lunch. *A celebration*, she'd said, and to thank Meg for being so kind. But sitting in this restaurant, some fancy place in Leederville that Donna had recommended, Gloria could have kicked herself for not checking the prices first. Twenty-five dollars for a Caesar salad, do you mind. The cheapest thing on the menu, and it was just a mountain of soggy lettuce with a few measly bits of bacon hidden in the depths. The waiter was snooty, the place was packed, and the car park was costing a packet. Plus she'd noticed that Meg had picked the cheapest red on the menu, and was drinking it sip by tiny sip. Which was really kind of her, but also a bit embarrassing.

Oh, lighten up, Gloria! So what if the meal would set her back a bit? She was earning two hundred and fifty dollars for two days a week, more than twenty dollars an hour. And so what if the waiter was snooty? She didn't have to see him again, and who'd want to work in a crowded restaurant, anyway, poor man, run off his feet, probably earning a pittance, and maybe with two kiddies and another one on the way. It was time to start telling her story, she thought, but where could she possibly start? With being so nervous, she told Meg, she was jumping out of her skin on her first day at work, but Natalie was so encouraging, and the first day was just for training. Natalie wouldn't have dreamed of throwing Gloria into the deep end, she said, how could she even think that? Instead, she'd shown Gloria the stock and how to use the machine for the credit cards, how to re-order.

'I thought it would be hard,' Gloria said. 'I had that moment of panic and thought, can I really do this? But then I remembered what Bernie had told me, how I used to work in a post office and knew exactly what I was doing. Plus I'd charmed the socks off him, hadn't I, so I'd charm the socks off the customers. He's so proud of me, Meg, I can't tell you, boosting me up. I thought he'd be a bit edgy about it, him not having a job and all, but it's just rotten bad luck. And now we've had a stroke of *good* luck. We've had a machine out of the sky.'

'Machine?'

'Something about the Greeks, but ... never mind. Anyway, Natalie and I went through the different racks and I could see the point of arranging clothes by size, but I was already thinking that colour is the key, it's what women notice first. But it was my first day and it was a learning day, and I didn't want to upset the apple cart. Not that Natalie seems like a woman who'd get upset with a bit of advice. Still, I don't want to be pushy, and I have to try not to rabbit on.'

She saw Meg grinning, and Gloria shook her head.

'I'm rabbiting on, aren't I? she said.

'Keep going,' Meg said.

'Well, over lunch, Natalie offered me some of her sushi, which I didn't much care for, but it would have been rude to say that. Besides, she doesn't eat meat or even fish because she thinks it's wrong to kill animals just so people can eat them. She said other things as well, about people and animals, and when she started talking about her two poodles and how Mitzi and Mop were her children, my ears really pricked up. She couldn't have children, she told me. Just like that, all sad in her eyes. Then she asked me if I had any children and I told her Karl lived in Sydney and no, I didn't mind, because he left me a long time ago.'

Would Meg flinch at this part of the story? No, she didn't.

'Then Natalie had a suggestion, and I panicked again, thinking I'd done something wrong. But she wanted me to take a couple of outfits from the shop, for free, which is just as well because her clothes are so pricey but of course I'd never say that, although a big sale every now and then would be a good idea. I might say that further down the track. Anyway ... where was I ... the point of wearing nice dresses from the shop is so customers will admire them and maybe ask where I bought them and then maybe they'd buy them for themselves. And all that time, Natalie was being tactful, you know. Sensitive. She wasn't saying you don't look the greatest, Gloria, in that green striped dress. So I said I'd happily pick two outfits, thanks very much, and hoped it would be good for business. But then I also told her she was being very kind. She turned bright red, and I was thinking, maybe she doesn't get many compliments and maybe I'll find that out as well.' Gloria took a breath, smiled. 'So that's my story,' she said. 'And I'm glad you're here to celebrate.'

Meg smiled too. A real smile, full of teeth. '*I'm* proud of you, too, Gloria. I know you'll be a big success.'

Gloria pushed some lettuce round her plate, decided to give

it a miss. Meg suddenly reached her hand across the table.

'There's something I want to tell you, too,' she said.

Heavens! Was she pregnant? But there wasn't even a man, was there? And how old was Meg? Forty. She was forty.

'I want to apologise,' she said, looking Gloria straight in the eye. 'For all the years I've neglected you. Kept Ella away from you.'

Well. Gloria was stunned. You could have lifted her off the floor.

'You spent so much time looking after her. Caring for her. I didn't ... well, I didn't appreciate it at the time.'

Gloria waited. She was guessing there was more.

'I used you. And I'm sorry.'

She put her hand over Meg's. Two hands together.

'It's OK, Meg, honestly.' Looking into her lovely dark green eyes. 'I'm seeing Ella now. I'm seeing you right now. And you've been so good to me.'

Meg smiled, awkwardly.

Gloria knew there must be something else. She might not be the sharpest knife in the drawer, but a person didn't say such a big, important thing without something lurking in the shadows.

'Why are telling me this now?' she said.

Meg squirmed in her chair.

'I've been a bit worried about Ella. And it made me think of you. Value you. Because you kept her safe.'

'Safe?'

Meg bit her lip. 'I mean ... I could trust you. And I took it for granted. I shouldn't have.'

Well, there was something going on that Meg sure wasn't saying.

'Has something bad happened to Ella?'

Meg shook her head. 'No, no. I ... well, I thought there might be ... I don't know ... some danger.'

Gloria sat back. '*Danger*?'

'No, no, it's OK, honestly, it's fine. I shouldn't have worried you, there's nothing to worry about. I really wanted to say ... what matters is how much you cared for Ella. And that I didn't mean to hurt you by taking her away.'

Gloria wished she'd ordered a glass of wine.

'I *was* hurt,' she said. 'I'd be lying if I said I wasn't. Look, I know I rabbit on and—'

'You're the best grandmother a child could have. And I'm glad you're my moth ... my ex-mother-in-law.'

'And I'm glad you're my ex-daughter-in-law.' Gloria laughed. 'It's a mouthful, isn't it?'

If she had a glass of wine, she would offer Meg a toast.

'Thank you for telling me,' she said. 'It means a lot.'

They smiled at one another, a bit shy, really, and looked away. Gloria was feeling teary now and she didn't want to cry, not in this crowded place, anyway. The last thing she wanted was everyone staring at her, blubbering like a fool. But still it was biting away at her, what Meg had said about the danger.

'Are you sure Ella's OK?' she said. 'Can I help in any way?'

'It was just some mean stuff on kids' phones. Some bullying going on. Which is why I won't let Ella have a phone until she's older. I ... I'm sorry, Gloria, I didn't mean ... you wanted to buy her one and ...'

Gloria patted Meg's hand. 'It's OK, Meg. You're her mother, not me. And I wish you'd stop saying sorry now, OK? I've spent too much time feeling sorry, saying sorry. What's the point? Say it once and then get on with it, is what I think.'

Meg took a sip of wine, put the glass on the table.

'So how are you, Gloria?' she said. 'I mean, you and Bernie? It sounds like things are better.'

'Well, a lot better than we were before. I mean ...' Where was this taking her? Where did she want to take Meg? 'We're trying,' she said. 'To be nice to each other. Listen to each other, you know. *Really* listen.'

Meg took another sip of wine. Relaxed now.

'For better or worse,' Gloria said. 'And I know which one I like better.'

'I'm really pleased for you. You've both been through a tough time.'

'And ... well, we're getting on well in bed.' Gloria smiled, remembering. 'If you really want to know.'

Meg laughed. 'And even if I don't.'

She had a lovely laugh. Kind of throaty.

'And what about you, Meg?'

Meg raised an eyebrow. 'Sex, you mean? Well ...' She set down her glass. 'What can I say? I'd be right at home in a convent. I'd be the head nun.'

She was making a joke but it wasn't funny. Gloria knew how awful that felt. The loneliness. The aching for touch. Because a man could put himself in and out, get all hot and heavy, but it was the touching and holding that mattered most of all. Telling each other you were there.

'You won't let on to Bernie, will you?' she said. 'He's a bit shy about things like that.'

'Oh no. Of course not. I wouldn't dream of it.'

Gloria looked at Meg's face. She didn't look so hard, like she used to. Or maybe she looked just the same but Gloria was seeing her differently. Or maybe it was the wine Meg was drinking. But whatever it was, it was good to feel closer. She liked it. She liked it a lot. But she wouldn't ask Meg about Karl, she'd never ask her again. Just get on with it, she'd said.

'Would you like a man in your life?' she said.

Which was sort of asking about Karl.

Meg shook her head. 'I thought there might be someone but I made a mistake. I ... well, it doesn't matter. It's over.'

Gloria wondered if she should give Meg a pep talk, tell her to bounce right back. She was a good-looking woman, with cheekbones to die for, a nice curvy figure, and those lovely, dark green eyes. Bedroom eyes, they were called. And she was a good person, too. Kind. They didn't come around every minute of the day.

Meg looked down at her plate, then looked up, her face tight.

'The man told me he had a problem,' she said. 'But he didn't wait around to tell me what it was.'

'Do you feel better off without him?'

Meg shrugged. 'It's only been a few days,' she said. 'But yes, I do. It's ... well, it's easier.'

Gloria leaned forward. 'If *easy* is what you're looking for,' she said.

Meg looked away, then looked back at her and smiled.

'That salad was rubbish, wasn't it?' she said. 'Twenty-five dollars for a mountain of lettuce.'

Gloria laughed.

'Let's have dessert,' Meg said. 'There's an ice-cream place around the corner, and it's all homemade. The pistachio is the absolute best.'

Gloria leaned forward in her chair. 'You deserve a nice man,' she said. 'Because it's not just the sex, is it?'

Meg nodded, but she didn't say another word.

Meg

She hadn't meant to say so much, or mention danger, or tell a lie about cyberbullying. It was thoughtless. And not fair on Gloria, either, although she seemed to be reassured. So why did I tumble out all that stuff, Meg thought, when I'd planned not to give too much away. Well, Gloria didn't judge her, for one thing. She could ask a personal question without sounding like a snoop. She didn't tell you how to live your life.

She's not like my mother, Meg thought.

She'd been hurt, Gloria said, but she hadn't torn her hair with self-pity. It had been enough for her to speak her truth and then to let it go. And she was having good sex, it seemed. She was heading for sixty and having good sex. Would that I should live to see it myself, Meg thought. She could joke about it now, if only to herself, because four days had gone by and the man hadn't returned.

Was he, after all, a paedophile with a conscience?

So what if he had a conscience?

Ella had been gone for a couple of hours, on an outing with Hanna to buy a new pair of shoes. Not school shoes but classy ones. Stylish. Anything she liked. Meg had been on the point of objecting—*Not anything, Hanna, just within reason*—but Ella had been ecstatic. And she deserved a touch of joy in her life, after the Hal debacle.

Ella had been thrilled by the Keats movie, too (*amazing*, but she couldn't remember the details). She was even keen to go back to school and work hard to improve her maths. Naomi was going to help her, apparently. Meg was delighted by this new motivation and pleased to chat with Stephanie when she'd dropped Ella home. Even if the famous lawyer made going to Paris sound like shopping at the corner store. Had Meg been to Paris? *Just the once, I'm afraid.* Had Meg seen the McCubbin exhibition at the art gallery? *Last Impressions? No, I haven't, I'm afraid.* But at least Meg could talk about the radical change in McCubbin's style after 1907 ... *Influence of Turner, Constable and Monet ... brighter colours ... more adventurous use of a palette knife.* Stephanie had looked impressed.

Standing at the front door, looking at her garden (she still hadn't re-potted those plants), Meg told herself she must see that exhibition. She also had to clean out the junk mail stuffed in her letterbox. She didn't wave to Mrs Ryan from two doors down the street. The old bat who'd stood gawping at the removal van, then hobbled over in the afternoon to hand Meg a stinging commandment: *A wife has to keep a marriage together ... look what's happening to the world because wives don't do their duty.* Meg had wanted to call her moralising old bag, but she'd managed to keep her mouth shut. She looked forward to seeing the funeral car pulling up at the old bag's door.

You're a horrible person, Meg.

She opened the letterbox, pulled out a wad of leaflets. Dog washing, lawn mowing, discounts at a local nail salon. Well, she didn't own a dog, had wood chips instead of lawn, and thought those witch-like plastic talons coated with chemicals were probably carcinogenic. Did Perth have more nail salons per capita than any other city in the world? Staffed by tiny Asian women wearing flimsy masks to protect them from the toxic fumes. It was a form of madness, really, this desire for long, plastic nails. Meg looked down the street again and saw that it was empty. Mrs 1950s Moral Custodian must have shuffled back inside. Not a car in sight, either. No sign of white fins, a man in blue jeans. The neighbourhood was quiet, almost desolate, like a set for a movie after the cast and crew had left.

She made her way inside. It was time for a cuppa; too early for a glass of wine. She put her hands on her hips, surveying her paintwork. She'd turned out to be a dab hand at house-painting, at least. No annoying patches, no blurry lines. Maybe she could paint the ensuite before she went back to uni. Or maybe she could read that chapter on aphasia. Or sort through those Hanna-and-Meg photos. The fluffy-haired young women who'd made Ella laugh. Meg smiled to herself, remembering how they'd met, Hanna nudging her in a lecture hall, whispering *This dude is sending me to sleep, do you wanna go for a coffee?* Or she could finally sort through some Karl photos, the ones she'd shoved into a drawer so she didn't have to look at that handsome, smarmy face.

The doorbell.

It couldn't be, could it? It might be. She stepped carefully to the window. Oh no. Yes. It was him. Heading for her door. But now he was walking back to his car, stepping inside his car. But he wasn't driving on. What was he waiting for? *Who* was he waiting for? And now he was getting out of the car again, looking around. Was he ... stalking her? Stalking her daughter? Should she call the police?

The doorbell rang again.

Whatever this was, she could deal with it. She had to.

She opened the door and went to speak, but something in his face made her stop. He was glaring at her. Rigid. Angry.

'We need to talk,' he said. 'About your daughter.'

'My ... daughter.' Meg felt the panic rising.

'Is she here?'

'No, but—'

Before she could finish, he'd barged right past her. By the time she turned around, he was sitting on the sofa. Sitting tall. He looked hostile. Ready to strike.

'So. Talk,' she said.

'Are you going to keep standing? This might take a while.'

She sat down slowly, never taking her eyes off him.

'I want an explanation,' he said.

'For what?'

'Do you know what your daughter was doing last Saturday? Early afternoon?'

'Of course I do. She was seeing a movie with a friend.'

'Well, she and that friend were at my garage. Did she tell you that?'

'I have no idea what you're talking about.'

'Well, let me enlighten you. Your daughter's friend told me that *you* thought I was a paedophile. A paedo, as she so charmingly put it.'

Meg sat up. 'Naomi. Her name is Naomi.'

'I don't give a damn what she's called. I mean, did you really say that? About me.'

'No, no, of course not. I mean ... I didn't say ...'

'But you *think* that, don't you?' he said. 'I can see it on your face.'

'I ... well ...'

He leaned forward, compelling her to look at him.

'Tell me,' he said. 'What makes you think I might be into little girls?' He leaned back again, folded his arms. 'I'm waiting.'

Meg felt her hands trembling. 'It was the day you ... played Scrabble ... with Ella.' She could barely say her daughter's name.

'And?'

'Well, you paid her so much attention. Made her feel special. That kind of thing.'

Why was she being so tentative, so timid?

'Seriously? That's it? I paid her some attention?'

'Well … no …' She pulled herself up. 'You asked about Ella's father. Whether he was still around. And before that, the first time, you asked Ella how old she was, and … it was all starting to feel a bit … creepy.'

'Creepy!' His eyes were boring into her. 'Oh, I get it now, I get it. You're one of those mothers who won't let their kids out of their sight in case some monster molests them. Who won't let their kids—'

'What would you know about that?' she snapped. 'You don't have any children.'

'And being a mother always makes you right?' He threw his hands in the air. 'She's a kid, for Christ's sake. What kind of man do—'

'You told me you were calling it quits.'

'Well, you've got one thing right, at least.'

'Because you said you had a problem. You said it was better if you didn't see Ella.'

He stood up abruptly, looking down on her. 'That's the worst thing anyone's ever called me,' he said. 'The worst. But you know what, I feel sorry for you. It must be terrible living inside your head, feeling suspicious of every man you meet just because he's a man.'

She sprang to her feet. 'Try checking the news,' she said, livid now. 'You'll read all about sickening fucking men every single day. Men who rape women, beat them, murder them. Men who watch child pornography, who lure girls—look, just go. Leave or I'll call the police. I'll—'

She stopped. He was standing in the middle of the room, looking … What did he look like? Ashen. Defeated.

'I want to tell you the truth,' he said.

'What … what do you mean?'

'I … the truth is … I was a patient in the clinic,' he said, flatly.

'I'm an alcoholic. I don't have an alcoholic wife. I've never had any kind of wife.'

'Oh.'

She saw a reel of moments blurring together, coming into focus.

'So ... that's why you ...' She stopped, started again. 'That's why told you me all those lies?'

'Yes.'

'And ... why you kept running away?'

'Yes.'

She saw that his hands were twitching again, as though he was holding an invisible hat.

'I'm a recovering alcoholic,' he said. 'I'm a liar. But I'm not a paedophile. Can you give me that much, at least?'

She could find nothing to say.

'I didn't mean to deceive you,' he said, quietly now. 'I thought I could come into your life but I didn't ... I don't ... have the right.'

His tone was matter-of-fact. She could hear no shred of self-pity.

'I ... Hal ...'

'You don't need to say anything. And I'm sorry for giving you such a hard time.'

He turned away, and before she could call him back he'd opened the door and was gone. She heard the engine reving but she couldn't move, couldn't think, everything rushing through her mind, the pretending, the lies, the mask and the shame. About getting things wrong and feeling afraid, so many feelings that she couldn't even name.

But her instinct told her to believe him.

She felt a sudden urge to weep.

ΔΔΔ

An hour had passed and she was waiting at the window. Would he come back? No. Would he storm into the house again and demand an apology? No. He was done. It was over. There was nothing left to do but wait for Ella to come home. Meg could still hear that ambush of his devastating words, and then his sad-eyed explanation. His shame. How could she have got it so wrong? Failed to pick up the clues? Meeting him twice at the clinic, his reluctance to meet for coffee, his running away and coming back, then running away again. *I'm allergic to alcohol ... better to call it quits ... I had no right...* And as for Ella ... Hanna's car was pulling up, and Meg watched her daughter climb out, give a goodbye wave. So Hanna wasn't coming inside. That was something to be grateful for, because speaking with Ella simply couldn't wait. Because she didn't want Hanna to be a witness to her folly.

The door opened, and there was her knock-kneed, dark-haired daughter.

'Hanna said to say hi,' she said. 'She was in a hurry and ...'

But Meg wasn't listening. She'd become a pair of eyes watching her secret child. And she knew, in the looking, that she would need to take this carefully.

'Come and sit with me,' she said.

Ella's face paled.

Meg beckoned to her, patted a space beside her on the sofa. Ella walked over, put down her parcel, slowly, carefully, as though it were precious cargo. She sat, looked up at her mother. Waited.

'Hal's just been to see me,' Meg said.

Ella's face fell.

'He told me you'd been to his garage. He told me what was said. Now I want to hear your side of the story.'

Ella burst into tears. Meg put an arm around her.

'I'm not going to get angry with you,' she said. 'I just want you to tell me what happened.'

'I don't know,' Ella mumbled, between gulps of air.

'But you were there, sweetheart.'

'I ... I think I got lost.'

'Lost?'

'It all happened so fast and I didn't know what to do.'

'OK, start from the beginning. Take your time.'

'I told Naomi,' she said. 'We were sitting in her room and I told her ... I told her how much I liked ... Hal. And how he thought I was clever and funny and all that.'

'Why did you tell her that?'

'Because ...' Ella sniffed. 'I was showing off.'

Meg wouldn't judge. Not now. Not yet.

'So what happened next?' she said.

'I don't know.' Ella swallowed hard. 'I think ... Naomi said that Hal might be creepy ... he was trying to make me feel special. Then she said you wouldn't tell me he was creepy because he wasn't coming back. And then ... and then ...' She swallowed again. 'I said he wasn't like that and Naomi said ...'

Meg was trying hard to follow this sudden stream of words.

'Slow down, slow down,' she said.

Ella gulped. Sniffed. 'I didn't think he was ... you know ... I never even used that word. Ever. And Naomi believed me. She said we should go and find him and ... we ... we did.'

Ella's eyes were wet with tears.

'OK, sweetheart. So you did that after the movie?'

'We didn't see it. Naomi's mum left us there and—'

'She *what*?'

'Don't get mad, Mum, please don't get mad.'

'I'm not mad at *you*, Ella. I just ... OK ... keep going.'

Ella swallowed hard. 'Naomi said the movie would be boring,' she said. 'And then she came up with this idea. To go and find Hal and tell him. That I didn't think he was ... you know ...'

'But why? I don't understand.'

'It just all happened and I thought it would be OK to tell him, I thought ... I thought he was a good person and I wanted you to know that ... and, well, I thought you could sort things out with him. Just be more happy.'

'Oh, Ella.' Meg felt on the verge of tears herself. She drew her daughter close, hugged her gently. 'It's not your job to make me happy.'

'But Mum, I didn't say anything in the end, I just couldn't. Naomi told him but it was my stupid fault. I shouldn't have just tagged along, I should have ...'

She burst into tears again.

'I'm a horrible person,' she sobbed. 'I was just showing off and I should have stopped her and he was so hurt and I lied to you and ...'

Meg stroked her daughter's curly hair. 'You're not a horrible person,' she said. 'Horrible people don't care if they've done something wrong. And they don't try to understand why they did it.' She drew away, smiled at her trembling child. 'You made a mistake, Ella, but I made one too, being suspicious of Hal. And mistakes can sometimes be undone.'

'How?'

'I'll work it out. But you know I'll have to talk to Naomi's mother, don't you? I won't get angry. I just need to talk to her about our different rules.'

Take note, Ella. Your mother's not going to get angry with another mother who dumped two young girls at the movies. So much for being a famous fucking lawyer.

'Do you remember where Hal works?' she said.

Ella looked startled. 'Oh no, please don't. I can't—'

'I'm not going to make you see him. I'm not going to see him either. I just want to phone him and apologise. For both of us.' She patted Ella's cheek. 'Do you feel better now?'

Ella nodded, sniffed again.

Meg kissed the top of her daughter's head.

Had Hal been right, after all? That she saw every man as guilty until he proved his innocence?

She remembered one of Hanna's stories. How she'd been out late at night in a deserted street, heading for her car, and seen a man walking towards her. She'd felt her heart begin to race, her nerve ends on high alert, until the man put his arms up in the air and shouted, shouted in the silent, empty street: *I'm not going to hurt you. I'm going to walk straight past you and I'm not going to hurt you.* She'd caught a glimpse, she'd said, of a good guy: a man who understood a woman's fear. Who might even have felt ashamed of being a man.

Bernard

What kind of man have you become? Bernard still had his father's words in his head, after nearly forty years. *A traitor. A rotten coward.* Not the young idealist who'd opposed the Vietnam War, who'd been prepared to go to jail for the sake of truth and justice. Not that truth and justice had won out in the end. The allies had stopped bombing citizens, raping women, mutilating children with Agent Orange, because it was costing too many dollars to wage an unwinnable war.

But still, he'd shown his face in the streets, hadn't he? Displayed some kind of courage.

He closed his magazine. It would be his final edition. If Gloria was earning the money, he had a duty not to waste it. And *waste it* was right, given the story he'd just finished reading. A man with large ears and a very small brain, ranting about numbers: *More than 4,000 asylum seekers in the last three years, Australia has lost control of its borders.* They were just numbers to the ghastly man, a chance to score some points against the government. Abbott was his name, and Bishop was his deputy. It sounded like a clerical conspiracy, and no doubt a pathway to hell.

He snapped out of it. Gloria was in the garden, pulling out more weeds. It was the least he could do to help her.

He went in search of sunscreen, recalling the Slip Slop Slap campaign and the skyrocketing rates of melanoma. Australia had the worst rates in the world, apparently. We were right up there, he thought, top of the heap: rates of skin cancer, and more carbon emissions per capita than any other country in the world. He was getting fed up with the prime minister, too. A lot of bluster and not enough substance, even if he could speak Mandarin. Bernard liked his deputy, though, a redhead who sounded like a fishmonger's wife but whose speeches made a lot of sense. She had some conviction, too, as far as he could tell, and kept hammering the importance of education. Well, good luck with that, Madam. Good luck with educating the deluded masses. Still, she seemed decent. Fair. She would make a good prime minister. But was Australia ready for a female prime minister? Was Australia ready for anything except the next season of football or cricket?

He refused to be reduced to watching sport on TV. He would never sink so low.

He slapped on the sunscreen—mostly slopped it—covering his face and arms. The garden was waiting. *We must cultivate our garden.* Voltaire. The man who might disagree with what you said but would defend to the death your right to say it. What a fool, Bernard thought, what a Gallic ignoramus. Why should bigots have the automatic right to spew out their hatred and lies?

Maybe he should have stood for parliament. Bernard Newman: the candidate who wants to gag every nutcase in the nation.

Or maybe he'd just pull out some weeds.

He heard a phone ringing. The landline. Because he'd given up his mobile to save money. He made his way to the phone ... probably one of those overseas call centres trying to sell you a timeshare in the Bahamas or a condo on Mars. Still, the poor bastards had to earn a living somehow. He picked up the phone, poised to hang up, but it was Donna's voice, trilling down the line. Was Gloria OK, she said, tried calling her mobile, was everything ... Bernard rushed in to reassure.

'She has her mobile outside,' he said. 'In the back garden. She's ... well, weeding. Maybe her hands are dirty.'

Which made him feel even more useless. But it was Donna's turn to rush in, inviting Gloria to dinner. And then, to his surprise, indeed to his consternation: 'Why don't you come too, Bernie?'

'Well ...'

'Lionel won't be there,' Donna said, and laughed. 'He's on another business trip.'

More like a woman-trip, Bernard thought. But of course he would never say that. Cultivate your garden. Mind your own business.

'He's *such* a bad liar,' Donna said. 'And the last time I did the washing, there was some gaudy orange lipstick on his shirt. Ever so hideous.'

Bernard swallowed hard. 'I'm sorry, Donna,' he said. What else could he say?

'You knew, didn't you?'

'Knew what?'

'That Lionel was having affairs.'

Bernard felt deeply embarrassed; morally compromised; jammed up in his throat.

'I could tell by the way he looked at you,' Donna said. 'At Christmas dinner, and last year's Christmas dinner. The nudge nudge wink wink look he gave you. Ever so obvious, really.'

Should he have denounced Lionel at the dinner table? Whispered to Donna in private? Painted blatant accusations on the side of a bus?

'I'm not having a go at you, Bernie,' Donna said. 'It wasn't your place to say anything. I know it must be ever so hard, not knowing what to do with a secret. It's just ... well, do you know what really hurt me?'

Bernard had no idea.

'He didn't give me a choice. I don't buy the argument that what people don't know won't hurt them. Everyone deserves to know what's going on in a marriage, and then they can decide for themselves what to do. Don't you agree?'

Bernard nodded. Then realised that Donna couldn't see him nodding.

'It's more dignified that way, isn't it?' he said.

'That's the perfect way of putting it. I've been turning a blind eye for some time, but now ... well, it's a question of your self-respect, isn't it?'

'Yes. It is. Absolutely.'

'And besides,' Donna said, 'I'm having a bit of fun myself at the moment. I'm going to tell Lionel when he gets back.'

'Oh. Right. Well ... good for you.'

'I knew you'd understand, Bernie, you're a clever man. And thanks so much for listening, it's ever so good of you. And what's more, Gloria told me you're keeping the house as neat as a pin.'

'Did she? Well ... a man has to do something.'

What else did she and Gloria discuss, in their womanly *tête-a-têtes*?

'And you're twice the man that Lionel is,' Donna said. 'You know that, don't you? He might have a flash job but he's got nothing else worth having. Not like you. Gloria tells me that you're so proud of her, and that you tell her so. It's ever so important, isn't it, to tell people things like that. And you're lovely with your grandchild. Gloria told me that as well.'

Bernard blushed, relieved that Donna couldn't see him.

'Well then. Are you coming to dinner, Bernie? Gloria says you need to get out of the house a bit.'

'Oh. She did. OK. Well ...'

He heard Donna's peals of laughter.

'It's alright, Bernie, don't worry. Gloria doesn't gossip about you. She's ever so protective of you, you know. She would never reduce you to gossip. She respects you too much for that.'

At some point the call must have ended and Bernard put down the phone in a daze. He could barely remember the details of that astonishing conversation, but he remembered Donna's sincerity. Her honesty. Her taking things apart, then giving them some thought, before putting them together again. Nor could he forget—how could he ever forget—her unexpected, remarkable coda: that his wife was ever so protective of him; that she would never reduce him to gossip. That she respected the man who'd dismissed her for so many terrible years.

Maybe that's what he'd have chiselled on his tombstone: *Here lies a man who learned to be surprised.*

Meg

In the first year of her studies, Meg had learned a great deal about speech. How the mouth and tongue were shaped to produce certain sounds; how and why speech became impaired, diminished or nonsensical; and how the damage might be healed. She was learning to watch and to listen, to help people feel more in control of their lives. To feel less alone. But now she knew that she hadn't watched Hal carefully enough. She hadn't known how to read the tenseness of his face, the clenching of his hands, the way he'd sometimes turned away from her. Nor had she listened carefully to his halting, slanted words, and to the spaces in between.

She checked to see if Ella was still asleep, then closed her bedroom door. She googled *Hal's Auto Repairs*, pressed *return*. That was the easy part. A few typed words and there it was: a phone number. The address was there as well, but that would have been the difficult part: the face-to-face encounter. She knew she was being a coward but it was the best she could do, and saying sorry into a machine was surely better than heartless silence.

Eight am. His garage would be open, wouldn't it? Didn't garages open at the break of dawn?

She wondered if she would look back and remember the time and place of her call. She wondered why she was thinking this.

She sat on her bed and pressed the numbers. A receptionist's voice: middle-aged, by the sound of her, and pleasant. Meg asked to speak to Hal. She hoped she wouldn't be asked for her name in case he refused to talk to her. She wasn't. She waited. What if he was too busy? He might be lying under a car, trying to fix a problem. Isn't that what a mechanic did? You would only be able to see his legs. Or would he be staring up at a car perched on a hoist, or whatever they were called. She had an image of him wiping his hands on a rag; a close up of those hands, as though he were in a movie.

But he was real. He had given her his truth. She owed him an apology.

'Hal speaking.' In a cheery voice.

'It's Meg.'

'Oh.' He cleared his throat. 'Hello. I mean … what can I do for you?'

Good question.

'I want to apologise,' she said. 'You apologised to me, and I—'

'It's fine,' he said, breezily. 'No harm done.'

Silence.

'Ella wants to apologise too,' Meg said. 'She feels really bad about—'

'It's OK, it's OK,' he cut in again. 'She's just a kid. And … well … I'm really sorry I flew off the handle. I've been thinking a lot about … our conversation. And I don't blame you for being suspicious. Men as a species are pretty awful.' He laughed, nervously. 'I had an awful specimen in just now. A pitbull. Or a rottweiler.'

Silence again. Meg felt a stupid urge to bark.

'You're not,' she said. 'A pitbull, I mean. Or any of those nasty breeds. I just didn't know what was going on with you. I didn't really think … you were … well, I just didn't think, full stop.'

Another silence.

'I'm sorry,' she said again.

'OK, sure, glad to get it settled. And now—'

'I'd like to ...' She didn't know what she would like, holding a machine in her hand, sending her useless words.

'I need to get back to work,' he said. Briskly now, hurried. 'But thanks for calling. I ... appreciate it.'

She could almost touch his shame. And she didn't want him feeling like that. She didn't want him thinking she was judging him. She didn't want to not see him again.

'I'd like to ask you a favour,' she said.

'A favour?'

'Will you take me for a spin in your car?'

Nothing.

'Is that what it's called? A spin?'

Silence. Had he hung up on her?

And then: 'Are you sure?'

She knew this was the last chance to change her mind, or the first chance to meet him honestly.

'I'm sure.'

The silence seemed to last for hours. She was beginning to wish she'd driven to his garage, looked him in the eye and said: I'm here. You're here. What shall we do next? Tell me. You need to tell me.

'Are you *really* sure?' he said.

'Are you warning me about your bad driving?'

He laughed. She'd never been so relieved to hear a man laugh.

ΔΔΔ

Meg had a checklist because she believed in being organised. She believed in the value of clear thinking.

One. She sat Ella down and told her that Hal understood, that all was forgiven, that she didn't need to worry anymore. Ella gave her a hug, said she was feeling much better and Naomi was SO sorry and they would learn from their mistakes. Meg insisted she would do the same. Then Ella gave her another hug and thanked her for being such a wonderful mother and she would really like to go to Paris with her but it could wait until her mother found a job that she loved. It was a long, breathless stream of repentant, hopeful words that made her mother feel a bit teary.

Two. Meg phoned Naomi's mother. She didn't exactly accuse the woman of lying but made a point of saying that *taking* two young girls to the cinema didn't mean driving them there and leaving them to fend for themselves. She heard the quaver in Stephanie's apology, and then the apprehension: *They went where?* That's right, hanging around in a garage, talking to a mechanic. But no harm done, Meg reassured her, beginning to feel a little smug. Then she hit the target, insisted on parental supervision should the girls ever go out again. The famous lawyer was profuse in her agreement. So how could Meg not feel vindicated? She had to stop herself from saying: M.R. Flynn for the prosecution has just wiped the floor with the defence.

Stephanie invited her for dinner. *Let's get to know each other*, she said.

Three. Meg asked Gloria to babysit for the day. It was another attempt to make amends, as well as stealing some time and space with Hal. Gloria was overjoyed, knew that Bernie would be too, they were planning to go to the aquarium and would it be OK to take Ella because they'd never been there and it was good for Bernie to get out of the house now and then, he needed to be more adventurous, and they could have lunch and afternoon tea but there weren't any whales, which was a pity. It was one of Gloria's long, looping sentences, straight from the heart to the mouth. And of course it was OK, Meg told her. It sounded wonderful.

Now the time had finally arrived. Meg didn't tell Ella to keep safe. She didn't issue Gloria with a long list of instructions about the need for vigilance. Ella was excited because she'd never been to the aquarium but Fern had told her all about the sharks and stingrays and heaps of colourful fish and how you walked in a long tunnel with water all around you so it felt like you were in another world. So this, too, was childhood, Meg thought: living for pleasure, living for the moment, with your conscience parked behind a building. You could always find it later and take it for a spin.

She gave her daughter a kiss, wished her a fine time, and told her to watch out for the sharks.

'Very funny, Mum.'

'Let's get cracking,' said Gloria, and put an arm around Ella's shoulder. 'Bernie's packed us lunch. He's even baked an apple strudel from his mother's old recipe.' She gave Meg a nod. 'We'll be back around three o'clock, if that's OK.'

She was wearing shorts. She had great legs: shapely.

Meg took out her purse but Gloria shook her head.

'Not on your life,' she said. 'I'm earning money now, and we're saving on food today with Bernie's lunch. And this morning we made a decision. We're giving up wine and beer during the week. So much better for your health.'

'But I know how much the—'

'It's our treat, Meg. And we all have to have a bit of fun now and then, otherwise … well, life's not worth living, is it?'

Gloria and her clichés. Still, if you were going to use them, why not make them happy ones? A cheap goal, Hanna called happiness, but she loved her work, despite her complaints. She loved her friends, her house, and having fun with James. She loved the family she'd made for herself: her dear friend Meg, and her dear friend's only child.

Gloria tilted her head to the side, like a curious bird.

'You're looking really pretty, Meg. That blue dress suits you.

Are you doing something special today?'

'I'm not sure yet.' Meg hoped she didn't sound mysterious. She'd had enough of mysteries and muddles. 'I'll see you around three,' she said. 'Have a great time.'

It was nine o'clock in the morning. Hal would arrive in an hour.

Meg had no idea where they were heading.

ΔΔΔ

She opened the door. Hal looked on edge, and his dark hair was damp, as though he'd just stepped out of the shower. She felt instantly befuddled, all at sea, mumbled that she'd get her bag, be back in a minute.

'I'd rather talk first,' he said. 'If that's alright.'

Of course it was alright. Is that what she'd managed to say? Inviting him inside, offering tea or coffee, hurrying to the kitchen, and—

'Please sit down,' he said. 'You're making me, no, you're not making me ...'

He was already seated, his hands clenched on his lap. And seeing the tension in those hands, in his jaw, she had a glimpse of what this meeting might be costing him. She sat down on the opposite sofa.

'I wrote a list,' he said. 'I wrote a list of what I wanted to say and ... and now I don't know where to start.'

'Start wherever you like. And take as long as you like.'

He scratched his head. 'Well, maybe I'll start with ... I want to apologise for getting so worked up. So angry.'

'But you've already done that.'

'Then let me explain,' he said. 'I need to explain.' He was sounding urgent, now that he'd started. 'I'm not an angry person, Meg. Even when I was drunk, I was never aggressive. I was always a happy-go-lucky drunk, you know the kind of guy who has hundreds of friends and laughs a lot. The joking drunk.'

He kept hammering the word *drunk*, as if wanting to punish himself.

'I told myself to stay calm,' he said. 'That it was crazy for you to be thinking that about me, that the kids must have been mucking around. But as soon as you opened the door, as soon as I saw you ... you had suspicion all over your face. And I lost it.'

'But you had every right to be angry.'

He waved her words away.

'Maybe I wouldn't have cared if it was someone else,' he said. 'I might even have laughed it off. But it was you ... and, well, it mattered, what you thought of me.'

'Then I need to explain something, too,' she said. 'It was Ella's friend who planted the idea in her head. About you. But she must have picked up my suspicion. I ... well, I let some crazy things run through my head. My only excuse, no, my only explanation, is that I wanted to protect my daughter.'

He didn't flinch. 'It can't be easy, bringing up a kid on your own, especially a girl. My thirteen-year-old niece wants to party, wear make-up, and she and my sister have terrible fights.'

'Ella is actually pretty easy,' Meg said. 'It's me who makes things difficult.'

'I do like your daughter,' he said. 'And I get how much she means to you. That's why ... well, maybe I went over the top because I wanted to impress you. Pathetic, isn't it?'

'It's what people do,' Meg said. 'And we don't always know that we're doing it.'

'You're a very reasonable person,' he said.

She had to smile. 'Sometimes,' she said. 'I'm sorry I didn't trust—'

'I can see now why you felt that,' he cut in. 'Like when I asked you where Ella's father was. See, I had a relationship with a single mother some years back, and her ex punched my lights out, just because he could.'

'Well, you can be certain that Karl—my ex—wouldn't do that.'

'He's not a macho kind of guy?'

'Well, it's more that I don't matter to him. And he doesn't matter to me. But he's not a monster. We just didn't work out.'

She couldn't be more reasonable than that.

She saw Hal shuffle in his seat, as if preparing for something else. Maybe something tougher.

'I want you to know about my problem,' he said.

He was taking this, her, seriously. And she knew she was already in deep.

'I've been an alcoholic for maybe ten years,' he said. 'I haven't had a drink in three months. And so far, anyway, it's been pretty easy.'

'Easy?'

'Well, just headaches, nausea, chronic insomnia. A high fever.'

She sat up. 'That's *easy*?'

'Well, some people get the DTs. Delirium Tremens. It's life-threatening. People die. So I was lucky, and I could afford a good clinic to help me get through the worst. And keep me away from my boozy friends.'

'So ... what made you start drinking heavily?'

He gave her a wry smile. 'You can say *alcoholic*,' he said. 'The professionals call me a person with an alcohol addiction, but I prefer the more ruthless term.'

'OK. So what made you become an alcoholic?'

He cleared his throat, as if preparing to deliver a speech. Maybe he'd rehearsed what he was about to say, a scrap of paper in his hand, thinking: this is who I am. This is who I'm trying not to be.

'I just like ... liked ... getting high on booze,' he said. 'My dopamine levels said thanks a heap, this feels wonderful, but they fucked up the chemicals in my brain. Then my brain kept asking for more to give me back the high. But I'm not blaming the chemicals. It was *my* hand that poured the booze, *my* mouth that opened wide.'

'So you weren't ... you know ... troubled? Depressed?'

'It's a bit of myth, about alcoholics,' he said. 'We're not all damaged or broken. In fact, my life has been easy, which makes me feel even more ashamed. And I have wealthy parents who bought me a garage.'

'To do work that you love,' she insisted.

He nodded. 'Machines are easy too,' he said. 'They never argue back.' He gave her a tiny smile. 'I like that you argue back.'

She wanted so badly to touch him. Not to offer her pity, even her sympathy, but simply to say that she liked him. That she was glad he was here.

'That's your story, then?' she said. 'No trauma? No drama?'

'Yep. It's all a bit boring. You won't find me on one of those TV shows that slather on the suffering to boost the ratings.'

He sat back. Had his talking come to an end? He was a good talker. Reflective. Rational. Honest. But she wanted, needed, to know more.

'But didn't anyone notice?' she said. 'About your drinking. Didn't anyone try to help?'

'I'm what's called a high-functioning alcoholic. It sounds like some sort of praise but it's really a curse because you can hide your addiction for years. From yourself as well as from others.'

'So you went to work?'

'Yep. Paid my bills and taxes.' He shrugged. 'We Aussies love our booze, don't we? Most of my friends can't go a day without it. Sometimes I think a beer can should be our national emblem.'

Meg saw herself resisting a second glass of wine, or watching the clock for an *appropriate* hour. She saw Hanna's wine glasses almost filled to the top. Remembered Hanna's joke about drinking at breakfast if she didn't watch out.

'What made you stop?' she said.

'Well. Not a good story. I started having trouble waking up, then I started having blackouts. Going out with friends, and then one day at work. It was scary. Losing time, losing myself, coming to and seeing strange faces, strange walls. And feeling ... humiliated.'

She heard the weight of that final word.

'And now you're trying to recover,' she said.

'The counsellor in the clinic didn't have much truck with *trying*. You either do it or you don't, he said.'

'That sounds ... well, very harsh.'

'He also told a woman in the group, who said she was doing just fine, that her feet were planted firmly in mid-air. That's harsh, too, but she was in the clinic for her third time. The counsellor told her, told all of us, to get real, *be* real.'

He folded his hands in his lap, as if willing himself to relax.

'Are you still in the clinic?' she asked.

'I left a week ago,' he said. 'They were good to me, kept an eye on me. You remember that time we met for coffee? The first time? When my phone rang and I took off in a hurry?'

Meg nodded.

'It was the clinic checking up on me,' Hal said. 'Making sure I was OK. But now it's up to me. And ... well ...' He looked down at the floor, then up again. 'They say the first three months are the easiest.'

She understood what he wasn't telling her.

'I have to stay away from my boozy mates,' he said. 'From pubs. Wine bars. Liquor stores. The lot.'

'But ... you must have other friends to support you?' she said.

'Well, that's another thing about being sober,' he said. 'You find out who your real friends are, not the ones who want to feel noble about helping you. My friends in Dunsborough, they're the best ones, because they know how hard it can be. They've been on the wagon for fifteen years.'

Meg took this in. The causes, the symptoms, the struggle. Trying to imagine how it felt like to be Hal. But how could she? She was a white-bread, well-bred woman who no longer drank herself blind, no longer partied, had never once blacked out. Who had control of her comfortable life.

'So what do you feel like now?' she said. 'Being sober, I mean.'

'Being sober? I feel lighter. And I think more clearly. It's like—how can I describe it? Maybe it's not really thinking. It's more like my instincts are sharper. Like the first time I met you.'

He smiled, shyly.

'Listening to you talk,' he said. 'When you told me about your friend in the clinic, you weren't telling me how good you were. And then, after that, talking about your daughter. Your studies. Everything ... *you* ... sounded real.'

She knew this was the moment when she could thank him: for trusting her with his story, for finding the courage to confess. She could say that she admired him for confronting his problem, and refusing to feel sorry for himself. She could say all that, sincerely, and then send him on his way. Or she could choose to let him stay, begin to let him into her ordinary life. She was, as he'd told her all those bungled weeks ago, the one who was calling the shots. Did she have courage, too? To step into something unknown and possibly unwise? But since when had wisdom been her strongest suit? Pressing Karl to have a baby when he wasn't ready, might never have been ready; giving Gloria a wide berth; losing her grip on reality because she smothered her daughter with care.

She saw him sigh, heavily. 'I guess it's time for me to leave,' he said.

What might Ella say, if her mother chose to let him stay?

Maybe *Great, Mum, now you can be more happy*. And Hanna would be pleased, wouldn't she, that her friend had finally stopped drooping. But what about her studies? He would need to understand that she would have to knuckle down, that the coming year would be even harder, that—she made herself stop listening to the voices in her head. She wasn't asking him to marry her.

She stood and walked across the space between them and it felt remarkably easy. She sat down beside him but didn't touch him, in case he really *did* want to leave.

'Meg,' he said. He didn't take his eyes from her face. 'It's good to meet you at last.'

'And you. Hal.' She smiled into his eyes. 'Is that your real name?'

'Promise you won't laugh?'

'Promise.'

'Hector.'

She laughed.

And because she knew that he was waiting, she took his hand, felt the welcome warmth of his skin.

'Shall we go for that spin?' she said.

Gloria

Bernie was driving so slowly, practically crawling, it was taking forever to get home. He was making a point, wasn't he, because she'd asked him not to speed. Just once or twice. But then he went through an orange light and she shrieked, just a bit, and he said, *Gloria, have I ever had an accident, have I ever smashed the car and left you mangled on the road?* Then he said sorry and she said sorry, put his hand on his leg and made him jump a bit. They laughed together. Then he started giving Ella more words in German, things they saw on the drive. There was *das Auto*, which meant a car, and there were a lot of them whizzing by. A lot of *das Haus*, as well. Not so many of *der Baum*, though, which meant a tree, because people chopped them down to make way for roads, he said. And did Ella know that the Christmas tree originally came from Germany? Then just like that, he started singing a song in German about a Christmas tree, which made Gloria smile and pat his leg again.

She felt a tap on her shoulder.

'Nana, can I borrow your phone?' Ella said. 'Please. I want to message Mum.'

Gloria passed Ella the phone with a smile, watched her tapping away. But she was taking a long time, a really long time, until she finally handed back the phone.

'You can read it if you like,' she said. 'And read it out loud, so Opa can hear it too.'

Gloria took a deep breath. She could see that she'd need it.

'We saw massive stingrays that glided in a scary kind of way but with a smile on there face and dazzling coral and a spoooky shipwreck and clownfish of so many colours. We saw the cutest seahorse and sleek and beautiful sharks but everyone hates them which isn't fair. Then Opa ate three slices of cake and Nana told him off and they do shark sleepovers for ten years and over so I'm old enough to go and did you have a good day too?'

Bernie laughed. Gloria heard a message coming through. She wondered if Meg had enjoyed herself, too, in her lovely blue dress. She looked down at her phone and—what was going on here?

'Read it, Nana. Please.'

Gloria cleared her throat. 'It's not from your mum,' she said. 'But it's for you. It says ... it says Hi Ella, it's Hal. I borrowed your mum for the day. I hope that's OK with you.'

Ella gasped. Gloria turned to face her.

'Who on earth is Hal?' she said.

Ella went bright red. 'I think it's Mum's new boyfriend,' she said. 'He's really really nice. He's funny and smart and he doesn't talk to me like I'm a little kid and he likes my mum a lot.'

'Well, I never,' Gloria said. 'That's ... well, it's fantastic.' She turned to look at Bernie.

'That *is* good news,' he said.

Gloria smiled at Ella. 'Do you want to reply?' she said.

'You do it, Nana. My fingers are tired. Just write: That's fine with me really fine and I hope you're having fun and I hope you have lots of other fun days with my mum.'

Gloria sent the message as best she could, then settled back into her seat. She looked through the window at the bright blue sky.

'I am so pleased for Meg,' she said. 'A nice man in her life.

Hal.' And then she remembered. The man who'd come to help her. The man with dark blue eyes. 'I met a Hal a little while ago,' she said. 'He was really kind to me. Wouldn't it be funny if it was him?' She turned to look at Bernie. 'You know, the world would be so much better if people helped each other more, instead of dropping bombs all over the place.'

Bernie laughed. 'Gloria for prime minister,' he said.

'You're making fun of me. Don't.'

'I wasn't, Gloria, honestly. But you have to admit that you won't solve the world's problems just by helping people out.'

'And how are *you* solving the world's problems, Bernie?'

'But it's not about me.'

'But it is. It's about everyone. All of us.'

Ella poked her head between them. 'Remember the seahorse,' she said. 'And the clownfish and the shipwreck and the sharks. Everything. It was all beautiful.'

She tapped Bernie on the shoulder.

'Slow down, Opa,' she said. 'You're driving much too close to that car.'

Acknowledgements

My heartfelt thanks to Fremantle Press for accepting my second novel; I'm grateful for their continuing support. Special thanks to my editor Georgia Richter, for her sympathetic understanding of my intentions, her thoughtful attentiveness to every sentence, and her calm, patient manner. Many thanks, too, to Claire Miller and Chloe Walton at the Press for their enthusiasm and hard work in promoting my work. And huge thanks to Nada Backovic for designing the vibrant and inventive cover.

My use in the novel of the word 'madness' does not refer to the severe mental illnesses from which people suffer. Rather, I use the concept to refer to a range of not uncommon psychological phenomena: anxiety, depression, self-aggrandisement, and the harbouring of unfounded suspicions by more-or-less rational people. I have also used 'madness' in a colloquial sense, to describe normalised events that strike me as ludicrously unnecessary, such as the use of leaf blowers and the desire for long, fake fingernails. (Lovers of leaf blowers and long, fake fingernails should feel free to disagree with my opinion.)

The opening chapter (Bernard) is a re-working of my short story 'Working it Out', from my third short story collection *Feet to the Stars*. I've always considered my stories complete or self-contained, but somehow Bernard, the only character among the many I have created, began asking me to give him another chance. He offered me the challenge of making an unlikeable character capable of change. Since I began work on this novel, the original story 'Working it Out' has, coincidentally, been chosen for inclusion in an anthology of short stories about ageing: *A Lasting Conversation* (Susan Ogle and Melanie Joosten, eds. Brandl & Schlesinger, NSW, 2020).

The reference in the novel's penultimate chapter to a counselling session, in which the counsellor refers to a self-deluded alcoholic as having her 'feet planted firmly in mid-air', is taken from the poet John Berryman's semi-autobiographical novel *Recovery* (Farrar, Straus and Giroux, 1973).

Thank you, wholeheartedly, to Gail Jones and Josephine Wilson, two of Australia's most gifted novelists, for their generous responses to *Everyday Madness*.

Readers of early drafts of *Everyday Madness* offered helpful criticisms and suggestions. Thank you to my friends Kristina Bratich and Linda Martin for their patient reading of an earlier draft; and for reading a later draft twice, huge thanks to two fine writers as well as friends: Carmel McDonald-Grahame and Josephine Taylor. I also thank Bonnie Goldsmith for her feedback on the voice of the character of Ella in the earlier sections of the novel. It's a long time since I've been eleven-going-on-twelve, so I'm grateful for young Bonnie's response.

Thanks to my son Harry Midalia, a practising speech pathologist, for checking my references to the profession.

My greatest debt is, as always, to my husband, Dan Midalia, for giving me the reflective time and hard-grind time required to write a novel. I couldn't have done it without him.

This book is dedicated to my kind, intelligent and literary women friends in our spirited book club, which continues to flourish after three decades: Pam Bagworth, Victoria Burrows, Lucy Dougan, Lekkie Hopkins, Carmel McDonald-Grahame, Sherry Saggers and Jane Southwell. The book is also for Gail Jones, with thanks for even more years of precious friendship and writerly support.